LADY FEROCITY

A Series of Senseless Complications
Book One

Kate Archer

DRAGONBLADE PUBLISHING, INC.

Dearest Reader;

Thank you for your support of a small press. At Dragonblade Publishing, we strive to bring you the highest quality Historical Romance from some of the best authors in the business. Without your support, there is no 'us', so we sincerely hope you adore these stories and find some new favorite authors along the way.

Happy Reading!

CEO, Dragonblade Publishing

Additional Dragonblade books by Author Kate Archer

A Series of Senseless Complications
Lady Ferocity (Book 1)

A Very Fine Muddle
Romance Me, Viscount (Book 1)
Be Daring, Duke (Book 2)
Stand With Me, Earl (Book 3)
Sweep Me Up, Baron (Book 4)
Write for Me, Marquess (Book 5)
Convince Me, Viscount (Book 6)

A Series of Worthy Young Ladies
The Meddler (Book 1)
The Sprinter (Book 2)
The Undaunted (Book 3)
The Champion (Book 4)
The Jilter (Book 5)
The Regal (Book 6)

The Dukes' Pact Series
The Viscount's Sinful Bargain (Book 1)
The Marquess' Daring Wager (Book 2)
The Lord's Desperate Pledge (Book 3)
The Baron's Dangerous Contract (Book 4)
The Peer's Roguish Word (Book 5)
The Earl's Iron Warrant (Book 6)

PROLOGUE

ROLAND NICOLET, THE Duke of Pelham, had reached a comfortable middle age blissfully unaware that most of his opinions were unusual, not quite correct, downright wrong, or otherwise wide of the mark. By no means was this an uncommon circumstance, as very rarely is a duke told he is mistaken on any matter. His elevated title left him to solely rely upon his own instincts.

Like others of his station, his estimation of his own discernment shone far more brilliant than it ought to have done.

The duke found it an exceedingly comfortable way of going on—rather like drifting pleasantly down a river with nary a ripple or current going against him.

This fine state of affairs might have gone on agreeably forever, had not his sister, Lady Penelope Marchfield, arrived to his estate in the Yorkshire Dales to see about his eldest daughter's launch into society.

There would be quite a few of those launchings in the next years as there were seven of those feminine offspring haunting his halls. The duke's poor wife had been ever hopeful of a son, but after the fifth girl, the duke had very sensibly given up the ghost.

His duchess had also been rather hopeful of the various temperaments these daughters would bring into the world, gamely naming them after virtues that would please.

That had been a pipe dream too. None of them remotely

resembled their name and the last of them had been so lacking in courtesy as to send the duchess to her grave as a final rebuke to her optimistic naivete.

Final score in the baby-making games: zero runs and seven daughterly wickets.

Still, the duke had carried on bravely in the face of all seven of these dreadful setbacks. He did not explicitly tell any of his daughters that she was a dreadful setback, at least not when he was sober, but they got the idea well enough.

He happened to love them in his own original fashion, though he could not for the life of him figure out why. He certainly did not let on that he harbored any paternal feelings, lest that army of daughters take more advantage of him than they already did.

Now finally, he was poised to begin launching these seven daughters out the door and into the world. One by one, they'd be catapulted out of his house and into somebody else's house through the time-honored tradition of marriage.

The duke had not known he would need assistance in unloading his daughters, until his sister, Lady Marchfield, had written and explained it all to him. According to her, no man could be expected to do a credible job of it. As the duke had to do it seven times, Lady Marchfield declared that he was on the verge of drowning in the societal seas.

The duke had replied to his deranged sister in a long and strongly worded letter. He was firmly in command of the family ship and there would be no drownings on societal seas whatsoever. There would not even be the faintest luffing of a sail. His ship would sail easily from ballroom to ballroom, heaving daughters over the side with abandon, as he expertly manned the helm.

That remarkable piece of writing was now stuffed in a desk drawer, as it had not had a moment to exit the house before Lady Marchfield stormed into it.

As a further shock to his sensibilities, the lady had not liked what she'd discovered when she arrived. The duke was to understand that all manner of things were wrong and must change. All manner of people were wrong and must change. Most incredible of all, *he* was wrong and must change.

Every time he thought she must surely have come to the end of her *wrongs and must changes*, there was more.

His pleasant drifting down the river with no ripples on the water had come to an abrupt halt—his ship had run aground on the banks of Lady Marchfield's sensibilities.

CHAPTER ONE

A Remote Estate in the Yorkshire Dales, 1801

FELICITY NICOLET, ELDEST daughter of the duke, pressed her finger over her lips at the six sisters trailing behind her. They had tiptoed down the stairs to listen at the drawing room doors.

Through the gap between the two doors, she could see Lady Marchfield pacing while her father lounged with his feet up.

"Lady Marching Orders is giving Papa another what-for," she whispered to Grace.

Grace whispered the message to the twins—Patience and Serenity—who passed the message to Verity, who in turn told Winsome, who finally informed Valor.

Not a one of them was surprised, except perhaps Valor, who was generally surprised by everything. Their Aunt Penelope, known to the wider world as Lady Marchfield, had been giving out her complaints and orders since she'd set foot in the house.

The very first evening she'd arrived, the lady had been shocked that the girls all dined with their father. It was her opinion that Winsome and Valor should have their dinner in the nursery. As there was no nurse in the nursery, there was something faintly ridiculous about the idea.

Then, Lady Marchfield had been shocked when they'd all stayed on at table to keep the duke company while he sipped his port. Further, she'd been shocked at the modes of conversation that took place between them during that pleasant hour.

The duke would tell his daughters that he could not wait to see the backs of them. He'd outline his plan to foist every one of them onto the nearest foolish gentleman and, once gone, they'd better not even return home for Christmas.

They would loudly accuse him of being a terrible liar. Grace would launch a roll at his head, which was perfectly safe, as she was exceedingly clumsy and that item never came anywhere near him. She occasionally hit a footman, though they did not mind, as they'd made it a bit of a game to lay bets on who would be struck down.

All of the duke's daughters enjoyed these encounters exceedingly. Well, except for Valor, who had just turned seven and was of a skittish and worry-prone temperament. She took everything to heart and could not seem to recall that they'd had the very same nonsensical conversation the evening before.

Valor would not go to sleep until she was assured once more that they would all come back for Christmas, even if they had to break the doors down. Patience would invariably tell Valor that they might break the doors down just for fun, though Valor never seemed particularly cheered by that idea.

Since that first night, Lady Marchfield insisted that all ladies must retire to the drawing room after dinner, while all gentlemen might stay at table with a glass of port. That was how things were done and it was high time the duke's daughters learned it.

Their poor papa was left to get drunk quite alone.

"Roland," Lady Marchfield went on, pacing the drawing room, "I very much fear that Felicity is not ready to go to Town. She has no polish, her playing is dreadful and really, the things she says… it would almost be better if she did not speak at all."

"The house in Grosvenor Square has been opened and the dust shook out of it so we will go. Surely, some young fop will take her off my hands. Then, it's just six to go—my dream is within reach!"

"Once again, you've drunk too much port."

"Which is why I shouldn't be left alone with the bottle!"

"I very much fear you do not know what you face in London. You have been too isolated here, the girls have grown up like heathens. Why do they have their own fowling pieces? Why do they ride those Dales ponies as if they were on a military campaign? Why did I find a decanter of Canary in Felicity's bedchamber?"

Felicity, whose nickname was *Ferocity* for very good reason, began to get very hot. Everybody knew she liked a half-glass of Canary before bed.

"Heathens, smeathens," the duke said dismissively. "They have guns to shoot with, the horses in this part of the world like to get going and not dawdle around, and everybody knows Felicity likes a half-glass of Canary before bed. They've all got dowries and none of them look like a monster, that ought to do it."

"For heaven's sake. May I enquire what you intend to do with the youngers while we are in Town? You cannot possibly leave them alone with Mrs. Right, they run roughshod over the woman."

"I'd never leave them with the housekeeper, that poor lady can barely stand the sight of them."

Felicity slapped a hand over her mouth. Her father was an inveterate liar, usually for his own amusement. They were all very fond of Mrs. Right, and she them.

"They'll all come with us, of course," the duke said.

"To Town? All of them?" Lady Marchfield asked with incredulity.

"To Town or Timbuktu, one or the other, I leave it to you to select the destination. With that collection of girls, who really cares where we end up?"

"Do not be ridiculous," Lady Marchfield said. "Now, I must also insist you hire a butler. It will not do to have the footmen trying to manage everything."

"They manage nothing. Mrs. Right is the general in the servants' hall."

"Mrs. Right, affronting creature that she is, cannot answer your door in London, though she makes so bold to do so here. Fortunately, you live in the middle of nowhere, and few people are aware of the aberration."

"Is there something *wrong* with the Grosvenor Square doors? Do they not open properly? Do they stick? Will Mrs. Right have difficulty getting them open? I'll have them repaired!"

"Really, Roland!" Lady Marchfield cried.

Felicity hopped up, as did the line of sisters behind her. They stole up the stairs and then down the corridor to Felicity's room.

All of them knew by now that when Lady Marchfield cried, "Really, Roland!" she'd reached the end of her tether and would retire to her room to regroup.

They had closed the door to Felicity's room and stayed quiet as Lady Marchfield huffed down the corridor and slammed her door behind her. Grace rang the bell to the servant's hall, using the code for tea and biscuits. Two quick pulls for tea, a pause, then three quick pulls for the biscuits.

Mrs. Right, so recently impugned by Lady Marchfield, would manage to get it all up the back stairs without being caught out by the dragon.

They did not wait long, as that good lady had known perfectly well that they would ring for tea and biscuits. They'd already had a very weak tea in the drawing room, but Lady Marchfield did not feel that young people should be eating biscuits so late in the day. Fortunately, Mrs. Right was not one little bit frightened of their recently arrived houseguest.

As the housekeeper set up the tray, Valor said, "Our poor dear Mrs. Right, we must be parted from you as our father says we're all to go to London." Valor paused, looking thoughtfully at the stuffed rabbit she dragged everywhere. "Who will check my room before I go to bed? Who will get rid of… you know."

Mrs. Right, a sturdy and comfortable-looking woman, said, "Nightmares?"

Valor nodded sadly. Their youngest sister was prone to them, and then thinking about them afterward.

"What makes you think I'm not going?" Mrs. Right asked.

"Are you going?" Patience asked.

"Does the sun rise in the east?" Mrs. Right said with a chuckle.

"Does it?" Valor asked, apparently never noticing which direction the sun rose.

"It does, Valor," Verity said. "Always, unless there is a cosmic disturbance and then it might not."

"Liar," Winsome said to Verity.

"Stop with all these clues!" Valor said. "Mrs. Right, are you really going?"

"Of course I am, you dear little mite. I would hardly leave you to face your nightmares alone."

Valor whispered into her stuffed rabbit's well-worn ear, apparently alerting her to the idea that Mrs. Right would be on the scene if they experienced any nightmares in Town. The rabbit, going by the name of Mrs. Wendover, stared into the distance with her black and dead button eyes. Of all the nightmares Valor had, Felicity sometimes wondered how Mrs. Wendover never featured in them. There was something inherently unsettling about that rabbit.

However, she could not give much thought to Mrs. Wendover now. The important thing was that Mrs. Right would go with them to London! Felicity did not really think her father would get his way in that, though she supposed she should have. Mrs. Right had been all but running the duke's life since the butler left.

Always unhappy and beleaguered, Mr. Herring had some sort of breakdown of the mind one spring morning. He'd left in a house-shaking fury, shouting about how he would not tolerate the "duke's tomfoolery, the disordered workings of the house, and the most wretched housekeeper in England." That had been over five years prior.

"Does Lady Marchfield know you're going?" Felicity asked

with interest. The two women, as far as she could see, were like oil and water.

"I doubt it," Mrs. Right said, "but she'll find out soon enough. The duke will drop it on her when it suits him. Of course, it only makes sense that I go. Wasn't I there in those early years when His Grace and the duchess used to go to Town for the season? Who else knows that house better than me?"

This bit of information was particularly interesting to Felicity. She had thought the only people who knew anything about London were her father and her aunt. The duke could not be trusted to tell her anything rational and Lady Marchfield only ever talked about manners and rules.

"You know what it's really like!" Serenity said. "You must tell us, as we do not have the first clue about it."

Mrs. Right poured herself a cup of tea, as she always did bring an extra cup just in case she was needed. Winsome jumped up from the nearest chair and the housekeeper settled comfortably in it.

"The stories I could tell," Mrs. Right murmured.

She was immediately beset by pleadings and cajolings, which was rather a tradition. Mrs. Right liked a fuss to be made before she would spill a story.

"They're different creatures, the *ton* that haunt London. Never in my life did I see so much prettiness on the outside and rottenness on the inside. Why, I remember a dinner at Pelham House where the Countess of Gentian said, 'One hears the most alarming things these days.'"

Mrs. Right sipped her tea and nodded. It was abundantly clear that she'd never heard what the alarming thing was. Felicity was at a complete loss as to why that question was emblematic of rottenness on the inside.

Verity had nodded at Mrs. Right knowingly, though she was in the habit of pretending to know things she certainly did not.

Winsome's brows knit. Valor had seemed to have lost track of the conversation now that the question of nightmares had been settled and put her attention on the tray of almond biscuits.

Grace shifted in her chair and promptly slid off of it, which was very usual and so could not be pinned on Mrs. Right's opaque storytelling.

Serenity whispered to Patience. Patience nodded and asked, "What does it mean? What alarming thing?"

"Who knows? A sentence like that is a prelude," Mrs. Right said. "Any lady who says that is *really* saying—'I have terrible gossip to share but don't want you to think I enjoy gossip so you better pull it out of me and then we will happily destroy another lady's reputation.'"

"It never is," Felicity said.

"It *always* is," Mrs. Right said, nodding vigorously.

"What else?" Felicity asked. "What else do you know about London?"

"The gentlemen are feckless and the ladies are fan-waving furies," Mrs. Right said, looking supremely satisfied to have condemned the whole town in one fell swoop.

It sounded to Felicity as if they ventured into a regular viper's pit. "But why should Papa wish to go there if he already knows what it's like?" she asked.

Mrs. Right set her cup down. "He's as mad as a spring hare, isn't he?"

"But what about our aunt?" Grace asked, having settled herself upright once more. "Why does *she* want to go?"

Mrs. Right sniffed into the air and said, "I reckon she's one of 'em. I reckon she hears alarming things she's determined to repeat all the day long when she's in Town. She was a sour thing when she was young and she's a sour thing now. London suits her.

MR. PERCY STRATTON, eldest son of Viscount Denderby, was just now trapped in a conference with his mother and father. He was generally skilled at slipping in and out of the house unseen, but they had been lying in wait.

The dreaded conversation he'd known was coming had arrived. His father was determined that he marry. He was only twenty-four! Three of his friends had been roped into it so far. They did not seem to be having as much fun as they once had and what was left of his set had taken note—avoid the state for at least one more season.

"Now, I do have some requirements," the viscount said. "As you are second generation and your grandfather was not a viscount all his life—"

"Stop reminding us all," his wife said. "Nobody else will be able to forget it if we cannot."

Percy's grandfather had built a shipping concern that had done some small and some large favors for the crown. He had been rewarded with the title and an estate in Kent.

"I warn you!" the viscount said in a raised voice.

Percy could not imagine who the warning was for, as his mother only looked bored.

"As I said," the viscount continued, "I have requirements. One, the lady must be decently titled. Do not present us with a Miss So-and-So, daughter of some lowly baronet or, God forbid, the daughter of a tight-lipped cleric. I don't care if he's a bishop! Two, choose one with a hefty dowry—the estate could use an infusion. Three, pick a comely girl, I cannot abide ugly offspring."

The viscountess snorted. "You cannot abide ugly offspring— I've seen the portrait of you as a young child. It still gives me the shivers."

As the viscount was brows-knit and attempting to think up some sort of retort that was not the usual "I warn you," Percy was thinking as fast as he could for a way round this ghastly situation. Then it came to him.

"I quite agree with you, Father," he said smoothly.

"Do you really?" his mother asked, with a look of surprise.

"Of course he does, it's only good sense," the viscount said, looking far more sanguine than he had been.

"The only wrinkle, if it *is* a wrinkle," Percy said smoothly, "is that ladies coming with the lofty qualities *we* seek are not falling out of the trees. It may take some time. Naturally."

The viscount's brows drew even closer together and met at the top of his nose. Percy thought he may have chosen the wrong gambit.

"You've got the season," the viscount said. "That's it. Come summer, if there is not a bride on your arm, I'll cut off your funds and throw you out and you can live penniless until I kick off." The viscount pounded his chest. "Unfortunately for you, I am not planning to kick off any time soon!"

"Well that was dramatic," the viscountess said. "You'll probably want to ease up on the port if you're planning on hanging about long-term."

"I warn you!" the viscount shouted, his face getting very red.

Percy thought if there were one thing that would kill off his father, it would be his mother. Port would play a very secondary role. As for himself, he had no intention of marrying this season. However, he must placate his father. He must appear as if he were desperately trying.

How hard could that be? After all, there was no end of ways a courtship could *seem* to be going well and then suddenly take a disastrous turn.

Close calls, jilts, bad timing, bad luck, childhood sweethearts reappearing, diagnosis of the consumption, whispers of questionable parentage, dashing suitors sweeping in at the last moment, rumors of madness in the family line—and *those* debacles were only what he could think of off the top of his head, there must be hundreds more.

Any or all of those unfortunate circumstances must be his own to avoid a penniless summer trapped in Kent, living in a tent on his parents' bowling lawn.

Mr. Percy Stratton must appear to be the most doomed and

hapless suitor that had ever set foot in London, ending the season as a bachelor through no fault of his own.

TRANSPORTING ONE DUKE, seven daughters, one countess, a bevy of servants, and the piles of trunks associated with them from Yorkshire to London turned out to be not as straightforward as Felicity had imagined.

The proprietors of the various inns that this lumbering convoy descended upon learned an important lesson from the experience. Down to a man, they had hoped and dreamed that such an elevated personage as a duke might turn up someday.

It was a thing they might boast of—they could casually mention it to friends, nonchalantly recall conversations with that illustrious person, and they might even put up a plaque documenting the date of the rarified visit. Further, a duke's rich friends might begin to stop there.

With prestige would come guests with deeper pockets. There was even the possibility of the prince himself coming. Their fortunes would be suddenly and gloriously on the rise.

Sadly, the sun had set rather rapidly on those happy imaginings, making way for hideously dark nights.

The inns in which the duke sought his repose were turned upside down—maids quit en masse, cooks tossed pots, waiters balled up their fists, grooms threw saddles, and innkeepers' wives glared accusingly.

Lady Marchfield was never satisfied with the rooms, making the typical operation one of moving three times before going back to the original.

The duke appeared to despise his daughters and was forever vowing to unload them on the next passing stranger. The daughters themselves seemed to find this threat amusing. In response to it, one of those confounded offspring liked to throw rolls in the vague direction of her father, though those floury missiles never came anywhere near him and far too often broke a bottle on a shelf.

There was a diabolical housekeeper who insisted on examining the food stores and throwing out anything she considered not up to snuff. Which was most things.

The duke's valet might be the only sensible person traveling with them, but what good was he? He said nothing and just backed away and disappeared whenever things seemed to be going in a bad direction.

The duke's footmen seemed to think they were young lords on a grand tour of the continent, drinking to excess and vomiting in the yard.

Ordering dinner was an excruciating process in which the duke demanded everything that was not to be had. At times, he ordered things that could never be had. Why did he find it so amusing to demand he must have roasted brocabbage pie, which was advertised as a Yorkshire staple? And why was he so amused after a ten-minute discussion on what it was, only to inform the waiter that he'd made it up?

The entire operation was so much confusion that, at three different inns, one of the party had been left behind and had to be retrieved hours later. That one was all three times the youngest who would set to wailing, though why she had been hiding in a linen closet when the carriages departed, she could not say.

One innkeeper after the next learned that they had been entirely stupid to wish for a duke resting his head anywhere near their inn. Mr. Kendall had been particularly affected. He'd gone so far as to inform Lady Marchfield that he was selling up and closing down so she would not think to ever bring her dreadful circus back to darken his doors. He privately vowed that if she did, he really would sell.

Finally, after ploughing a swath of destruction across half of England, this ill-omened caravan limped its way into Town.

Fortunately, the *ton* could not know of the nervous exhaustion and broken dreams the party had left in their wake. Society was all keen interest concerning the duke's arrival.

Though the duke was odd by anybody's standards, he was after all a duke. Word had spread like a wave, dousing every hostess with the news that the Duke of Pelham and Lady Marchfield had brought the duke's eldest daughter for her season.

The effects of the information on these matrons were varied. Some were delighted and determined that the duke and his daughter would attend their entertainments. Others prayed the eldest daughter was no better looking than a hound, as they had their own daughter to worry about. Others were wary, as if the duke were the last wolf in England—they'd heard him described as wildly unpredictable. Others remembered him from twenty years ago and went round looking as if they required a vinaigrette. Still others wondered if he would host a ball, and whether they would make the list.

Naturally, all this went on without the duke having the first idea of it. The result was a pile of invitations waiting at the house on Grosvenor Square for his perusal.

As the duke had not been to London in years, hardly remembered who anybody was, and never had very good judgment in selecting acquaintances to begin, Lady Marchfield confiscated them.

Since her aunt would dictate which invitations would be accepted, Felicity was certain they would only accept the driest and dreariest of occasions.

Mrs. Right took charge as soon as they entered the house, though there were dark hints from Lady Marchfield that a butler would soon be hired and it would be all up for the housekeeper.

Felicity did not see how it could be so—their last butler had never dared cross Mrs. Right. He'd mentioned her specifically when he'd had his mental unraveling and stormed out of the house.

Lady Marchfield was determined to stay the night and see them settled. On the morrow, she would return to her own house on Bedford Square, where it was presumed her lord was desperately missing his upright lady.

At least, it was hoped that somebody presumed Lord Marchfield was pining for his wife, though the duke was not to number amongst them. The last he said on the subject was: "You can tell Marchfield he can thank me in a heartfelt manner for affording him this break from his bride which was, I am certain, badly needed."

Lady Marchfield had sniffed over the sentiment as the sisters backed out of the drawing room and raced up the stairs without so much as a by your leave. Their aunt called after them that they ought to walk like ladies and that running was unseemly, but she could not slow any of them down.

Felicity thought that was indicative of how little her aunt knew her nieces. It had been all too predictable that there would be a war over who would sleep where. There were plenty of bedchambers, and plenty to spare. But one does not have six sisters without the occasional battle for an advantage.

Felicity took the last bedroom in the east wing, as she knew her father would be in the west and he snored like thunder, talked in his sleep, and sometimes shouted in his sleep. Grace would have taken the one next to Felicity, but Serenity tripped her in the hall.

Serenity was to see the fates circle back around when Patience knocked her out of the way. Verity told everyone there were cakes in the drawing room, which there certainly was not, but that at least got Winsome out of the way.

By the time Lady Marchfield got to the top of the landing, Patience and Serenity were rolling on the floor of the corridor, Verity had locked herself in her preferred room, and Valor had given up and stood in a corner weeping.

Felicity really did not know what else her aunt had been expecting.

The rest of the night might have gone somewhat smoother, had her father not recalled that he had a fully stocked wine cellar.

After the duke had made his way through two bottles of claret and brought a third into the drawing room, Lady Marchfield ordered everybody to bed.

All in all, it could have been worse.

CHAPTER TWO

PERCY HAD CALLED a conference of his friends in a private room of White's. As he had considered his plan to appear the keen but hapless suitor, he'd realized that he could not do it alone. This plan would take whatever sort of army he could throw together. At the moment, he was down to two friends who had not yet been yoked into matrimony. They would comprise his army.

He was calling his plan *Operation Sadly Hopeless*.

Lord Magnon appeared skeptical. "So the idea is that you pretend to woo a lady who wants nothing to do with you."

"Exactly," Percy said.

"Stratton," Wiles said, "where do you propose finding this lady who will be agreeable to refusing to consider a proposal?"

Percy rubbed his chin. That was indeed turning out to be the problem.

"He doesn't know," Magnon said.

"I do not know *yet*," Percy said. "It will have to be a very particular lady. As it has turned out so far, I've got two refusals."

"You've gone round asking ladies?" Wiles asked.

"Of course I've asked," Percy said. "I'll get nowhere if I do not ask." He paused, thinking of how to explain how the idea had gone over. Or not gone over, as the case was. "Well, as it happens, Miss Sprig claimed she was mortally offended—seemed a bit of an overreaction really. It's her third season, why not at least *look* as if something is in the works?"

"She did not view it that way," Magnon said.

"She did not. And then there was Lady Jane—she's a cousin, you'd think she'd help a relation out."

"But she declined too?" Wiles asked.

"She said I was an idiot."

"That about sizes the whole thing up," Magnon said.

Percy poured a second round of brandy and raised his glass in the air. "I will not be chained!"

"We'll all be chained eventually, one way or another," Wiles pointed out.

"Then revised—I will not be chained this season!"

Magnon sighed. "What is it you want us to do?"

"Buy your tickets for Almack's," Percy said. "There is no place in the wide world where so many naïve ladies gather. There is bound to be somebody there who will happily have nothing to do with me, while I pretend to be smitten. I'll find a lady who disdains a new-minted title or has aspirations to become a duchess or just doesn't like the look of me. There must be a hundred ladies who would refuse to wed me."

"Probably even more," Wiles pointed out.

"Again, what is it you want *us* to do?" Magnon said.

"Keep your eyes open and make inquiries," Percy said, a little concerned over how slow Magnon was to catch on. "Dance, ask questions, find me the right lady."

"This is doomed," Wiles said.

"It can't be doomed," Percy said. "It's the only idea I've got."

"You could always find a lady you like and wed her," Magnon said.

"I will not be chained!"

"So you said," Wiles said. "As for me, I believe I will take the sensible route and look about for a lady I like. I've got to marry at some point so I might as well find somebody I like."

Percy sighed. Of course they'd all have to marry at some point. He just did not see why that point needed to be this minute.

"In other news," Magnon said, "my mother waxed on about the Duke of Pelham returning to Town to launch a daughter. I interrupted her with the strong recommendation that she does not attempt to engineer a match between myself and that duke's daughter."

"As you had every right," Percy said.

"Perhaps the right, but there was no point in it. As it happens, I was too precipitous in crossing her. There is, in fact, nothing to cross. She was telling me of that gentleman's arrival to warn me off. She says that when she last saw the duke, he was vulgar, drunk, and had set a lady's curtains on fire. He was as unpredictable as a cornered badger. She does not expect an improvement and would not care to be related by marriage to him."

"Good fun, though," Wiles said, "to see what he's like now. With any luck, he'll have half the hostesses in Town fanning themselves. After all, what is one to do with a deranged duke? One wishes to know a duke, and yet not know a deranged person."

"A deranged duke?" Percy said softly. "Would not a deranged duke have a deranged daughter?"

"Who's to say?" Wiles said.

"I bet he does," Percy said. "I cannot know too much until I clap eyes on the lady, but a deranged daughter might be just the thing for my plan. Think of this—every lady who comes to Town comes for one thing only, a husband. It would follow that a *deranged* daughter would come for… not a husband. And then, she is a duke's daughter, one might suppose a lowly mister destined to be a viscount would be quite under her deranged shoe."

"Your feats of logic continue to astound," Magnon said.

"More like feats of fantasy," Wiles said.

"I will not be chained!" Percy said.

Really, it was the phrase that kept his spirits up. He had to keep his spirits up. Nobody ever won a war against their father if their spirits flagged. He would not be chained. Not this season, anyway.

Fingers crossed that the duke's deranged daughter would see fit to help him out.

MRS. AGNES RIGHT had been housekeeper for the duke for nineteen years. Other servants had come and gone, most notably a butler whose mind collapsed on one glorious spring day. All along, Mrs. Right had gone on steady.

There were some who could not hold up against the duke's eccentricities, but she was well-used to his bizarre habits and they did not ruffle her feathers one bit. In truth, she was fond of the old soldier.

As for his girls, well, it felt as if they were her own children, they were all that close. She had been there to run to at all hours and she had guarded their futures carefully.

Mrs. Right had made certain that her girls had every tutor they would require and shielded those tutors from the more uncomfortable aspects of the duke. It was essential that her girls learn to dance well, and draw middling, and she taught them embroidery herself. They'd had a French tutor until they were at least conversant. The music tutor had not fared as well, and Mrs. Right had quietly closed the pianoforte and no longer bothered to have it tuned. They'd even had a governess for a very short period of time, though that lady had decamped one early morning, leaving behind a note that only said: GOODBYE.

People had come, people had gone. Just now things were very comfortable. There was the duke's valet, who was no trouble to anybody as he was a private person who did not stick his nose in. The two footmen were clever enough to know their lives were made easier without a butler. The cook was left to his own domain and managed his own staff. The housemaids were a good sort of girls who made sure to do just enough. The stables were its own world entirely and run under the stablemaster. None of these people had need of a butler, and all of these people were satisfied with Mrs. Right taking on the mantle.

The duke's girls were satisfied with her too. All along, it was Mrs. Right who was the girls' constant presence to rely upon. She'd always felt that she must be the protector of these seven young ladies.

She felt particularly protective at this moment, now that Felicity was to be shown round the viper's pit some liked to call London. The poor girl was to be led forward by one of the preeminent vipers—Lady Marchfield.

That unpleasant lady had been in the house on Grosvenor Square all the day long, sniffing round, inspecting every corner, and threatening to hire a butler.

Let her go ahead and hire a butler. Mrs. Right would drive him out as fast as he came in. The last one, Mr. Herring, had fled the house over five years ago. Everyone presumed it had been the duke's fault, but the truth was Mr. Herring could not cope with the various salvos she'd fired in his direction.

Mrs. Right snorted as she remembered sitting at the servants' table and making an announcement. "I would very much appreciate it, Mr. Herring, if you would stop making eyes at me or brushing up against me in the corridors. Make no mistake, my bedchamber door will remain firmly and forever locked."

What was a butler to say to that? He denied it vehemently, but it predictably sent the gossip in the house into a frenzy. Mrs. Right had helped the talk along by pretending at being the modest and injured party. She'd touched her cheeks with rouge to appear always blushing and she got into the habit of clutching her shawl tightly round her, as if to ward off impertinences.

Then of course she had been free with switching the dinner menus around. The duke was in the habit of leaving a note on his desk in the morning regarding what he wanted for his dinner. Mrs. Right had assiduously collected a pile of them and switched them with abandon. After Mr. Herring had gone in and read the old note she'd placed there, she would tiptoe back in and return the original. The duke wished for beef and got a ham instead. Day after day.

The duke was very particular about his dinners and went mad each time they were not what he wished for. He fell into the habit of asking Mr. Herring if he were going senile.

That had been the beginning of Mr. Herring's mental collapse. After that, it had only taken a few light pushes to send that butler plummeting off the cliffs of insanity. The final shove was slipping a copy of *Fanny Hill* into his rooms for a maid to find, firmly painting him as a rake of the highest ill-repute. That was particularly hilarious, as Mrs. Right was certain Mr. Herring could not seduce a post.

She sometimes wondered where he was now.

Yes, Lady Marchfield, bring in any butler you like. However, be prepared for the consequences.

She quick-knocked on Felicity's door and strode in. Mrs. Right was everything to the girls, including lady's maid, which was another thing Lady Marchfield was intent on changing.

Her dear girl was in front of the looking glass, having made significant headway on her hair. A marvelous dress of dark blue silk lay on the bed.

If Lady Marchfield had done anything helpful at all, it was to arrange a wardrobe for her niece. She'd had it all composed ahead of time and then a modiste turned up with six assistants to take in the dresses to fit.

"My girl, you look very well."

Felicity smiled into the glass. "I hope that is true, Mrs. Right, but I cannot be sure—you have always praised all of us to high heaven."

"And why should I not?"

She really meant it too. Felicity had piles of rich brown hair, streaked with the color of late honey due to her habit of leaving her bonnet behind all summer. Her large brown eyes were as soft as a doe's. Her delicate features belied her nickname—Ferocity. One first looking at her must conclude she was a modest and careful young lady. One who crossed her would find out otherwise. She was entirely perfect.

"I cannot imagine what this evening will be like," Felicity said.

"Aye, I heard the whole palaver about it between your father and Lady Marching Orders," Mrs. Right said.

They were to attend Almack's and it had been an anxious two days for Lady Marchfield, waiting for the vouchers. At one moment she was certain they would come, and then the next she was despairing of it. It all seemed to hinge on whether the patronesses would have any recollection of the duke. Lady Marchfield was praying that they would not. If they did, she said, all was lost—nobody who'd ever met her brother ever went out of their way to do so again.

The duke, on the other hand, could not at first recall anything about Almack's. When the vouchers arrived, he was reminded of several sojourns there and claimed he would not go. Why should a duke put up with that gaggle of clucking hens?

Lady Marchfield explained that it was absolutely essential to Felicity's success. The duke had considered that information and then said, "Well, if it will get her out of my house and into some young fool's house, then I suppose I'll have to put up with it."

"This is my first real venture out in Town and I am determined to enjoy it," Felicity said. "After all, who knows who I will meet there?"

Mrs. Right put the finishing touches on Felicity's hair. "Aye, it's both happy and sad for me. You're set to take your rightful place in society, I can't be against it. But then, you'll wed some fella and when will we ever see you?"

"Oh I imagine I could talk my husband round to visiting often," Felicity said.

"We are rather remote—the Dales are not for everyone, alas," Mrs. Right said.

"I am beginning to think, considering what I've heard my aunt say, that Papa is not for everyone either."

"No, he certainly is not," Mrs. Right said.

"Any gentleman wishing to approach me must express a regard for my father."

"Quite right," the housekeeper said. "If a gentleman cannot even be counted upon to pretend at a regard for a girl's father, what is he even worth?"

"Do you suppose he'd have to pretend?" Felicity asked.

"Probably. Young gentlemen can be surprisingly persnickety and not likely to take a joke. They get their backs up, you see. It's the youth in them—trying to be manly and ever on the watch for any perceived slight."

"Hmmm. Papa does like to sling round a slight or two. But really, if other people knew him as we do… if even my aunt understood him as we do. He really is a dear, if one digs down deep enough. Very deep, naturally."

"Very, very deep," Mrs. Right said.

The door burst open, and six sisters piled through it.

Predictably, Grace did not make it far. Fortunately, she fell on the bed and was very clever at lending the operation a certain panache, as if it were done on purpose. Mrs. Right had high hopes the girl would become better acquainted with her feet before her own season.

Patience and Serenity pushed at each other, each wishing to be first. Verity examined her sister's dress knowingly and said, "Exactly how I pictured it."

Winsome stared at Verity with her usual suspicious mien. Verity was forever claiming to know things and Winsome was forever arguing that she did not.

Valor yawned, as she really ought to be abed.

"I do hope you dance with all sorts of handsome gentlemen, Felicity," Grace said.

"And you will tell us all about it over breakfast," Patience said. "We ought to get up very early, there is no reason to lie around in bed. Or you could even wake us up when you come in."

Serenity dabbed at a tear in her eye. Mrs. Right could not imagine what set her off, but the girl was easily touched. She had wept over more sunsets than could be counted.

"Just be careful, Felicity," Winsome said. "Do not be taken in by a rogue."

"Are there rogues at Almack's?" Valor asked, twisting her hands together. "What are rogues?"

"Nothing you need concern yourself over at your young age, I'm sure," Mrs. Right said. "It's the vipers, the feckless gentlemen, and the fan-waving furies a person's got to look out for."

"Oh yes," Valor said, "I remember you saying that, Mrs. Right. Be careful of them, Felicity—do not let any of them sneak up on you!"

"I will be on my guard," Felicity said.

"I forgot to say," Grace said, "our aunt is toe-tapping in the drawing room and Papa just poured himself a second glass of brandy."

"Gracious, we'd better get you dressed, girl," Mrs. Right said. "It would not be well to send your father to Almack's after he's gone a bit under the table."

At that idea, Felicity jumped from her seat and was quickly buttoned into her ballgown.

PERCY GAZED ROUND Almack's ballroom. So far, *Operation Sadly Hopeless* was humming along at a good tick. There had been the question hanging in the air of whether his family would receive vouchers. As much as his mother would like to forget it, they were only a second-generation title, and his father was only a viscount.

However, the viscountess was the daughter of an earl and

had long been acquainted with the Countess of Westmoreland—they squeezed in that way.

His father had been pleased to see his son put his name down on a number of lady's cards. Though, the viscount would be less pleased if he understood his son was on the hunt for a key player in the theater troupe primed to perform in *Operation Sadly Hopeless*. Percy was keeping an eye out for the deranged daughter of a deranged duke as being one of the more promising candidates.

"I say, Father, I've heard the Duke of Pelham brings his eldest daughter to Town this year."

"Pelham?" his father said. "I'd hoped he'd got himself lost on the moors and was dead by now. I do not suppose I am alone in that wish either."

Percy nodded knowingly. "Because he's deranged?"

"The man is a danger to society."

"Who cares?" the viscountess said. "He's a duke—she'll have a pile of a dowry."

The viscount seemed to consider this. "True, true," he said. "In any case, if you brought her home you would not be bringing *him* home. As long as she's nothing like him!"

"That's very good sense," Percy said, knowing his father was particularly fond of hearing about his good sense.

His mother practically snorted at the idea. His father whispered heatedly, "I warn you!"

"In any case," Percy said, "do you see him?"

The viscount scanned the ballroom. "There he is, the unpleasant fellow. Probably still laughing about setting fire to Lady Vanderwake's curtains. I suppose the young lady standing by him is the daughter. And there is Lady Marchfield, the duke's sister, just turned to speak to Lady Westmoreland."

Percy had no idea how Lady Vanderwake's curtains had gone up in flames, nor did he much care. He followed his father's eyes and his gaze landed on an older gentleman with the sort of generous middle that advertised a friendliness with port. A stunner of a lady stood by his side.

She was positively cracking. What a pile of hair, and those large dark eyes set in such a delicate face. She looked the bright ingenue, but was she deranged? He had really become convinced that it would be far easier to draw a deranged lady into *Operation Sadly Hopeless* than a not deranged lady. At least, so claimed Magnon and Wiles, mostly because they thought he was himself becoming deranged.

This woman did not look deranged. For that matter, the duke did not look particularly deranged either.

Of course, he was not positively certain what derangement looked like in every case. All he had to go by was Lord Bakerston from his own neighborhood. That old fellow liked to ride round on his horse shouting at people. All the things he complained about seemed to center around "they." Nobody knew who "they" were, but supposedly "they" were after his money, his coveys, his horses, his silver, his wine cellar, and sometimes his wife, though that lady was long dead. Other than that, he was a cheerful sort of fellow and would come in for a cup of tea and be satisfied not to mention "they" once he'd been assured that all the doors were locked against them.

"The duke doesn't look deranged," Percy said.

The viscount snorted. "Oh really? Last he was in Town, aside from setting curtains afire, he stumbled, spilled a brandy on a baron from Cornwall, demanded satisfaction from the fellow though it was his own fault, and then slept through the appointed time. Apparently, when he was finally roused, he said he could not be bothered with it. Go and talk to him. Then you'll see."

"I believe I will. Where has Lady Westmoreland got off to—I must get on the card of the deranged duke's daughter."

"Very spirited, Percy," his mother said. "God speed."

Percy hurried off and was not long in locating Lady Westmoreland. That pleasant lady had rather a soft spot for him, as she did like a gentleman who was a cooperative guest and Percy was strict in his manners. He made sure to always turn up in good time and he made himself available to escort a lady round a dance floor when needed. He would keep his eyes open at a musical evening and look appreciative. He would partner at whist, though he did not particularly enjoy the game. He was, as one hostess had aptly put it, handy to have around.

Lady Westmoreland's permission to put himself down on the duke's deranged daughter's card was happily yielded. He was also in receipt of the information that her given name was Lady Felicity.

He swerved his way across the crowded room and presented himself forthwith to the duke and his daughter.

"Your Grace, Lady Felicity," he said. "Mr. Percy Stratton. Lady Westmoreland has graciously given me permission to put myself down on Lady Felicity's card, if she is agreeable."

The duke looked him up and down. "A *mister*, is it?"

"I am the eldest and only son of Viscount Denderby," Percy said, to assure the duke that he would have a title someday.

"Mister for now though, eh?"

Percy was not sure where this was going. It was no surprise that he only being a mister at this point in time had been noted. It *was* surprising, however, that it had been said out loud.

"Denderby? Who is Denderby? Never heard of him," the duke said.

Again, how was one to answer?

"Well, I suppose I must keep my eyes on the goal," the duke went on. "Launch this daughter out of the house and into somebody else's as fast as possible. Then it's just six more to go—my dream is within reach!"

"Really, Papa," Lady Felicity said. "Mr. Stratton, my father likes to jest."

"I do not jest, I mean every word. Seven daughters bleeding me dry, what else am I to wish for?"

"I'm sure I do not know," Percy said weakly.

Lady Felicity handed over her card. "You'd best put your name down and begone before my father explains how he plans to bar the door against his daughters at Christmastime."

Percy hurriedly scribbled his name down. He was hardly cognizant of the idea that it was the dance before Almack's wretched idea of a supper. His thoughts were too full of the understanding that the duke really was deranged. He'd had his doubts—after all, the *ton* was fond of exaggeration. But in this case, it seemed the *ton* had not gone far enough in their descriptions of eccentricity.

Lady Felicity might very well be deranged too, though it was too soon to say. It had been very strange that she'd found her father's comments somehow amusing. Another lady would have sunk through the floor to hear her father espouse such ideas.

And then, what was she talking about when she pointed out her father would bar the door against her at Christmas? Somehow, she thought that funny too.

She certainly seemed as if she might be deranged, which was both convenient and a pity. It was too bad that such a lovely lady should be not quite right in the mind. On the other hand, it was essential to his plan.

As his thoughts began to settle, he realized that the dance he'd put himself down for was ideal. He would lead Lady Felicity into supper, and it would give him time to fully outline *Operation Sadly Hopeless.*

He could not say where it would all go, but he instinctively felt that he had a better chance with Lady Felicity than he did with the other rather staid ladies he would dance with. After his encounters with Miss Sprig and Lady Jane, he would have to be careful in assessing the lay of the land. If he told too many ladies of the plan, it would likely get back to his father.

As for the Duke of Pelham, well, one need only keep well clear of that interesting individual. Percy would certainly work to keep his father away from the duke. A prickly viscount and a highly eccentric duke coming together could not be good for anybody, and his father had already expressed disappointment that the duke was not dead on the moors.

Percy made his way to Lady Violet for the first, all the while keeping his eye on Lady Felicity.

She was collected by the Earl of Rustmont. He hoped she would not be bowled over by that gentleman. He was a Corinthian of the first order. Percy found him really rather annoying, what with showing off his skills at everything, and being a handsome sort, and being an earl, and being ungodly rich, and pulling off the Oxford raised brow that Percy could never get the hang of.

As the raised brow was free and appeared urbane, Percy had spent a deal of time trying to work out how to get one brow to raise ever so slightly while the other remained where it was. His brows insisted on working as a team so whenever he tried it, he only ended up looking surprised.

Certainly, she would not be impressed by Rustmont's title, his money, or his single brow-raising. Lady Felicity was looking like his best chance and he would not like her to drift in another direction.

CHAPTER THREE

FELICITY HAD ALWAYS congratulated herself on her good sense. She had assured herself of having a steady mind and rational temperament. She'd mainly measured things by her sisters.

After all, Grace went round practically unaware of her surroundings which so often led to a chance meeting with the floor. Patience never had the sense to wait, even when it was the only thing one could do. Serenity was always laughing or crying. Verity made up stories so full of holes they were no better than a sieve. Winsome always came to the worst conclusion. And then Valor, afraid of her own shadow.

As the eldest, she'd been confident of her steady rationality. Of course, she was known to have a temper from time to time, but only when it was really called for. Any sensible person had a temper when it was called for. In any case, she'd put a deal of effort into reining it in and controlling it, as any mature person would do, and only unleashing it when it was really necessary. As all rational people do.

But now, all sense and rationality were gone. They'd gone up in a puff of smoke. She'd taken one look at the Earl of Rustmont and nearly fallen over.

Lady Westmoreland had brought him to her, and as that lady chattered on, Felicity stared at this wonder of a gentleman.

What a man. He was tall and handsome, with chiseled cheekbones, hooded eyes, and a very determined chin. What really struck her, though, was that he had a certain aloofness she had not encountered before. He seemed to ever so slightly raise a brow, as if he found a condescending amusement with all the world. There was something alluring about it all. It felt as if to gain his approval would be a real accomplishment, as perhaps not everybody did.

Even her father must have noticed something singular about the earl's presence. He did not say any of the outrageous things he liked to say to amuse himself and discomfit a listener. Of course, that might have been because he had his back turned and was taken up with making faces at Lady Marchfield.

Lord Rustmont had put down his name for her first. After he'd taken his leave, there had been other gentlemen who came after to put their names down. All the while, she fairly toe-tapped, waiting for Lord Rustmont to collect her.

She could not help but to be disappointed that the earl had not taken the dance before supper as that would have extended their time together. But then, she was already engaged before he approached her. There was every chance that if she'd not been engaged, he would have taken her into supper. She would keep that firmly in mind.

As it was, a certain Mr. Stratton would take her into supper. She did not like to condemn a gentleman on short acquaintance, but she could not help but notice that he had not held up very well against her father's teasing. Mrs. Right had already explained that sort of thing would be due to unfortunate and prickly youthfulness. She hoped she would not find him callow, as that would be tedious. But there was no time to worry about that. The Earl of Rustmont, the glorious earl, had come to collect her.

He bowed elegantly. "Lady Felicity," he said, holding out his arm.

"Earl," she said, working to sound very casual and not as if she were calf-eyed over him. Though, she really was calf-eyed over him. She laid her hand lightly on his arm and hoped it did not do anything stupid, like tremble.

He led her to the ballroom floor near the top. Of course, a gentleman of his stature would be near the top.

The Duchess of Gordon would open the ball, accompanied by the Earl of Bladensfeld. She did not know the other couples comprising the top set of the room, but they all seemed middle-aged, or nearly so, and she presumed them highly placed.

A sudden and strong scent of roses enveloped Felicity as a lady and her partner joined them in the second set. She and Lord Rustmont were the first couple, their backs to the musicians, this lady and her partner took the opposite side as the third couple.

Felicity scrunched up her nose, as strong smells always made her sneeze. Flowers and vinegar in particular affected her. Why had the woman seemed to have bathed in her perfume? It was terrible.

"Do you enjoy your first foray into Town, Lady Felicity?" the earl asked.

"Yes, good," Felicity said, as that was all she could manage while fighting off a sneeze.

The earl glanced at her quizzically. "Are you quite well?"

Felicity nodded vigorously. And probably turned twelve shades of red. She had no choice but to scrunch and unscrunch her nose in an effort to stop the incessant itch. She began to wonder if she might quietly sneeze. But no, it was impossible. Her handkerchief was in her reticule, which was just now in her aunt's possession.

Lady Westmoreland announced the changes to be danced, the Grand Rond very predictably coming first.

Finally, the itch in her nose began to pass. Felicity began to regain her composure and reminded herself that she was a very creditable dancer, which would certainly overshadow any nose scrunching she'd done. Their dancing master, poor Monsieur Villeaux, had been rather harried by her father. However, Mrs. Right had soothed him each night with copious amounts of ale and brandy. That, the housekeeper had told Felicity and her sisters, was the only reason he'd lasted a year—he'd been either drinking or recovering from drink with no time to pack his things. Once he sobered up, he was out of the house like a shot.

For all that, Monsieur Villeaux had known what he was about and all the sisters, except possibly Grace, were very good dancers. Though in fairness, of all of them Grace had the most natural ear for music and tempo, and she was very good when she was not tripping over her feet.

The orchestra struck up and the Grand Rond began. As Felicity passed by where the Lady of the Roses had stood as part of the third couple, she was again assaulted by the lady's strong scent.

The stench of rosewater slipped up her nose and tickled it like the fur of a caterpillar. Felicity held her breath to keep it out. Then she gasped for air when she could hold it no longer.

They moved through the figures and changes, Felicity doing everything in her power to dance elegantly, all the while holding her breath each time she came near the Lady of the Roses.

And then, it was no use. A series of violent sneezes racked her and her nose began to run. It could not be stopped, it was like an out of control carriage careening downhill. Her nose had been assaulted and was fighting back with vigor to eject the offensive odor. Liquid poured out at an alarming rate and she could not sniff it back in and make it begone.

The earl, as well as the other couples, seemed genuinely alarmed. The earl handed her his handkerchief, which she took gratefully.

There was nothing for it—she would have to blow her nose on the ballroom floor of Almack's.

It was awful. It was also a relief. Her sneezes had been building for a half-hour and had finally been released into the world.

The dance came to a conclusion and the other couples of her set scurried in all directions like mice in a barn when the local stray cat paid a visit.

Felicity was nearly frozen in place. She did not know what to say. She glanced down at the crumpled handkerchief and mumbled, "Did you want this back?"

"Do keep it, Lady Felicity. I insist," the earl said gravely. He held out his arm. "I will escort you back to His Grace and Lady Marchfield."

And he did escort her back, entirely grim-faced. What an impression she must have made. She was certain that he thought she ought to have been able to control her sneezes, but she could not have done. It had been impossible.

"It was the scent of roses, you see," she said by way of explanation. "Roses and vinegar, I am very sensitive to them."

The earl nodded. "We all have our crosses to bear," he said.

They reached the edge of the ballroom, and reached two people who had clearly seen what had happened and took entirely different views of it. Her father was laughing heartily while her aunt was wide-eyed and purse lipped.

"Well, my girl, I'm not sure I've ever seen that dance done before," the duke said, snorting at his own wit.

The earl bowed. "Your Grace, Lady Marchfield. Lady Felicity, I thank you for the honor of a dance and I take my leave."

He turned and strode away. Very fast, Felicity noted.

"What on earth?" Lady Marchfield said.

"What was it?" the duke said. "Flowers or vinegar?"

"Roses," Felicity said dejectedly. "A lady has drenched herself in rosewater."

"Come now, girl, do not look so downhearted about it. I'm sure not so many people even noticed."

Lady Marchfield sniffed at the idea. "I would not put my hopes on whatever your father is sure about on any subject. It was an exceedingly odd display. *Here* of all places."

"She sneezed," the duke said. "Everybody in the wide world sneezes on occasion."

"Perhaps so, but they do not do it at Almack's outside of a retiring room," Lady Marchfield said curtly.

"Oh they don't, now?" the duke said. With a swipe of his hand, he pulled a long ostrich feather out of Lady Marchfield's hair and waved it under her nose.

Lady Marchfield, being hardly ready for such an operation, waved her hands to get it away.

"Roland!" she said in her usual accusatory tone.

"Look, she wants to sneeze but she's holding it in," the duke said, laughing.

Of course, Felicity was rather adoring of her father's efforts to soothe her, though she did notice that others had watched the duke assault her aunt's headwear and seemed rather surprised by it.

Felicity's second dance partner, Mr. Wiles, came to collect her. He looked rather frightened. He held out his arm and almost whispered, "Lady Felicity."

"Keep her away from roses, that's my advice," the duke said to Mr. Wiles, as he threw Lady Marchfield's ostrich feather over his shoulder.

Felicity handed the Earl of Rustmont's crumpled and damp handkerchief to her aunt, as she did not know what else to do with it. Lady Marchfield held it by her fingertips, staring at it as if it were alive. Felicity could not blame her for being put out—her aunt was down one ostrich feather and up one wet handkerchief.

Mr. Wiles led her away and Felicity could not help but notice the stares in her direction.

Gracious. Her aunt had told her time and again that the rules in Town were a deal more strict than in the Dales. Could it be possible that she'd caused talk about herself just for sneezing?

And what did the glorious earl think? The sight could not have been attractive, she was not a pretty crier or sneezer. But, it was only one small moment in time.

Perhaps he'd forget all about it. Or laugh about it. Perhaps she would herself forget all about it. Or laugh about it. Though both of those results felt rather far off. She'd made herself foolish in front of the one gentleman in the room she would have liked to impress.

As much as she would like to deny it, she felt in a bit of a temper.

Her temper was like a hot thing that came upon her, especially when she was embarrassed. It had always been so, though now that she was older, she was better at hiding it. She only wished she was better at stopping it coming over her.

Her temper was not much improved while dancing with Mr. Wiles. The fellow seemed to talk in riddles. What did he mean by asking her what she thought of being pursued by a gentleman she could never tolerate? What did he mean by inquiring into any derangement in her family line?

To the last, she'd said, "Mr. Wiles, considering your conversation, I would wonder what sort of derangements lurk in your own family line."

That, at least, had the effect of silencing that strange gentleman.

All the while, the Earl of Rustmont danced with a pretty young lady who did no sneezing whatsoever. It was very unfair.

PERCY HAD BEEN on the fence regarding whether or not Lady Felicity was deranged. No more. Not after what he'd witnessed on the ballroom floor.

Though he was decided on that point, he could not for the life of him figure out what it was she had been doing. At least with Lord Bakerston, one was clear on what was on his mind. Bakerston was worried about 'them.' Lady Felicity was more of a mystery.

She'd been guided to the floor by Rustmont and had looked all elegance. And then, things took a very strange turn. The lady had begun by making contorted faces, then she appeared to hold her breath and went red in the face, then she had some sort of fit that had brought everyone in her set to a standstill. Then she'd taken the earl's handkerchief and blown her nose and smiled as if there was not a thing wrong.

If that wasn't enough, after being returned to her father, she seemed to find amusement in the duke ripping an ostrich feather from Lady Marchfield's hair and smacking the lady in the face with it.

Really, anyone marrying into such a family ought to know that if they dared it, they would end with exceedingly strange children!

Fortunately for him, he had no plans to dip his toe into that morass of madness. He only wished to look as if he did.

He had watched Lady Felicity closely after that display, but she went on looking very usual. Though, he could not help but notice that Wiles ended his dance with the lady looking a bit frightened of her.

Percy began to be amused by the idea that she'd acted strangely only with Rustmont. That gentleman was a regular stick and would not take kindly to being part of an odd display. People would laugh about it, which would make him exceedingly uncomfortable.

Now, it was time for Percy to take his own turn with Lady Felicity. He dearly hoped she had no plans for a repeat performance. As it was, he could see very well that there were plenty of people keeping an eye on her, likely hoping she would do something else they could talk about on the morrow.

"Lady Felicity," he said.

"It's the mister," the Duke of Pelham said, apropos of nothing.

Percy really did not know why the duke went on with it. It had already been thoroughly established that he was not yet in possession of a title.

The duke slipped a flask out of his coat pocket and took a swig. He casually put it back.

Percy was speechless. Any of the patronesses would go mad if they knew there was drinking inside the hallowed walls of Almack's. It was one of the most tedious rules they had—weak tea and sour lemonade only. It was also the reason so many gentlemen came already drunk.

"What?" the duke said in retort to his stare. "Who drinks tea and lemonade at this time of night? Only a madman, that's who!"

Percy nodded and said, "Quite right," hoping to end the conversation.

"Papa," Lady Felicity said, "do not cause any trouble while I leave you on your own."

"Hah! We'll see," the duke said, making no promises.

Percy supposed they had conversations along those lines quite often. What a family. Nevertheless, it could be precisely the family he looked for. With any luck, there might even be a push and pull to the whole thing. Percy would claim he was set on Lady Felicity, despite her unusual qualities, and his father would attempt to talk him out of it.

That would be amusing, really. The viscount had set out to push his son into a church and would find himself trying to bar the doors lest he end with a deranged daughter-in-law, likely leading to deranged grandchildren. The family line, already fairly new, would be doomed.

He put his arm out and led Lady Felicity to the floor.

Now that she seemed to have recovered from whatever sort of fit she'd had while dancing with Rustmont, she was all elegance. How odd that someone could change their mien so entirely. Just now, she was rather wonderful to look at.

"Lady Felicity, are you enjoying your first visit to Town?" he asked.

She briefly glanced at the ceiling as if she found the question tedious. "It is too soon to tell," she said. "Though I feel I should compose a pleasant answer to that question as I have been asked it all evening."

Percy was more than taken aback. It was a well-known and accepted conversation starter. What else was he to ask her? Lady Felicity, are you enjoying your father being a lunatic? Lady Felicity, did you enjoy embarrassing the Earl of Rustmont?

He was still game to lure her into *Operation Sadly Hopeless*, but he was beginning to think she might be difficult to manage.

She was not difficult to manage on a ballroom floor, however. Her dancing was exquisite. He could not fathom how it was so. According to all he'd heard, the Duke of Pelham lived very remote, somewhere in the Yorkshire Dales. It was said very few people had ever even ventured there, so isolated it was and so strange it was when a person actually arrived. Where had they found a dancing master in that far-off location?

Clearly, they must have, though.

Lady Felicity did not enact the same sort of performance she'd gifted the Earl of Rustmont with, there was no holding of breath or odd fits, or blowing of noses. Percy found himself very grateful for it. He'd led Lady Felicity into Almack's dining room and a footman hurried to his side.

"Lady Felicity, would you care for tea or lemonade?" he asked.

The lady sighed. "My father said both are wretched, so I suppose it does not signify."

Percy glanced round to ensure none of the patronesses were within earshot. Of course, everyone knew the offerings were wretched, but one ought not say so aloud!

"Tea," he told the footman. "And the dry cake if you can get it before it runs out."

"Do you know the Earl of Rustmont?" Lady Felicity asked.

"We are acquainted," Percy said. He found himself irritated that the lady should mention that fellow.

"He seems a very refined gentleman," Lady Felicity said.

"He's a bit of a stick, did you not notice?" Percy said.

Lady Felicity appeared mortally offended by the idea.

"Lady Felicity, certainly you did notice," Percy said. "He seemed very taken aback by… by… whatever it was that happened."

Now the lady really had her back up. She positively glared at him. He supposed he should have expected it—derangement was never going to be predictable.

"It was a sneeze," Lady Felicity said. "I sneezed because a lady in my set was reeking of rosewater. I am sensitive to the scents of flowers and vinegar."

"Ah, I see," Percy said. "I suppose you explained all that to Rustmont? What did he say to it?"

"Never mind what he said to it," Lady Felicity said through gritted teeth.

As far as Percy was concerned, that was answer enough. Rustmont had been his usual stick about it, he supposed.

The footman returned with sadly weak tea and plates with none too generous slices of un-iced cake.

Lady Felicity glanced down at her plate. "My father was right—this is terrible."

Once more, Percy surreptitiously looked about him to ensure she'd not been overheard.

She had not been, thank the stars. Though those sorts of comments, with no thought as to who might overhear, rather cemented his idea of Lady Felicity.

"Well," she said, "I suppose I shall see the earl no end of places and will not be sneezing. The lady of the roses cannot be everywhere."

Percy sat back. Lady Felicity really could not get off the subject of Rustmont. It was both irritating, and perhaps presenting an opportunity. If he were going to lay down his cards, now was the time.

"Lady Felicity, let me tell you something peculiar about Rustmont. He is obsessed with having what other people want. If you plan to get anywhere with him, he must see that another gentleman is interested in you. You understand? You must make him envious."

The lady picked apart her cake with her fork.

"I see you consider it," Percy pressed on. "The difficulty will be in finding a gentleman willing to act a part in that particular play."

"Do you imply I would have trouble finding a gentleman

interested in me?" Lady Felicity said, gripping her fork.

Percy had high hopes she was not going to stab him with it.

"Of course not," Percy said, though he was not certain he believed it. She was an arresting beauty, but one must eventually talk to a beauty and that was where it would all fall apart.

"I am certain I could locate an interested gentleman with ease," Lady Felicity said.

"No doubt, but I would point out that there is the difficulty of finding a gentleman who is willing to only pretend at it to pique another gentleman's envy."

Lady Felicity seemed to consider that idea.

"Fine. I'll do it," Percy said.

CHAPTER FOUR

PERCY WATCHED WITH trepidation as Lady Felicity dropped her fork in reaction to his proposal to create envy in Lord Rustmont's breast. She turned to him. "*You* will do it?"

"Yes, why not? I do enjoy a good ruse now and again."

"Hm, well, it *would* be best if whoever the gentleman is, he is not of the slightest interest to me."

Though Percy was not at all interested in her either, it did sting to be brushed off so lightly. He was generally well-liked, and he had reasonable prospects, so it seemed a bit far to say not the *slightest* interest.

Lady Felicity, having noted his expression, said, "It is only your youth, you understand."

"My youth? Lady Felicity, I am a man, not a youth."

"Perhaps not yet," she said.

"What does that mean?"

"Well really, Mr. Stratton, you strike me as some combination of smarmy and callow. I am sure those qualities will have fled in a year or so. Our housekeeper has explained the situation with young gentlemen—it is not your fault, it is just the way of the world."

Percy's teacup clattered to his saucer. Smarmy and callow? According to her housekeeper?

"I see," he said. "As it happens, I find you eccentric and off-putting and I doubt *those* qualities will have fled in a year or so.

We shall make a perfectly hateful couple."

"Eccentric and off-putting? Do not be absurd, you are only lashing out over your hurt feelings. Furthermore, I have not yet agreed to this idea of making the Earl of Rustmont envious," she said.

Percy had never in his life wished to tip a lady off her chair, but he would not mind doing it at this moment. However, he must keep his goal in mind.

"Who else will you find that will pretend to be smitten with you while being no such thing?" he asked curtly. "You can be assured that I would be in no danger whatsoever of falling for your charms, whatever they may be. And wherever you may have hid them."

Lady Felicity entirely ignored that latest salvo. "Well, I suppose I could try it out. After all, if it does not work or becomes too irritating, I can simply call it off," Lady Felicity said. She said it to him, but it was as if she were saying it to herself.

It was promising that he'd gained her agreement, but not as promising that she could call it off at any moment. Or that she was insulting in the extreme. He would have to think about that.

"Very well, Mr. Stratton," Lady Felicity said.

"Excellent," Percy said, though he was not entirely certain he meant it at this juncture. "I presume you will attend Lady Jillerbey's candlelight picnic on Friday."

"I have no idea, actually. My aunt has confiscated all the invitations and is dictating where we go."

"Then you will go, I am sure. Lady Marchfield and Lady Jillerbey are as thick as thieves. Rustmont will go too, he always does."

"If the earl will be there, I am sure we will come."

What did that mean? He'd just said she'd go because Lady Marchfield and Lady Jillerbey were as thick as thieves.

From behind his chair, they were suddenly interrupted by Lady Felicity's father.

"Sick of this place yet?" the duke asked his daughter.

"Rather," Lady Felicity said.

"Excellent," the duke said. "I told your aunt if I stay one more minute, I will throw some of that wretched cake at somebody. Probably her."

Lady Felicity rose, and laughed while she did so. "I suppose she took that as well as can be expected."

"You know *her*," the duke said, putting his arm out for his daughter. "She doesn't take anything well. You could tell that lady the sun was shining and she'd throw up her hands in despair and call it wildly inappropriate."

Lady Felicity nodded, as if Lady Marchfield's temperament was settled between them. She glanced down at Percy and said, "Mr. Stratton."

The duke followed her gaze. "Goodbye mister!" he said jovially. With that, he led his daughter away and they were gone.

Percy sat back. What an evening.

He'd accomplished his aim; he'd got a lady to agree to his farce to put off his parents' matchmaking scheme. But what a lady he'd come up with! He hardly knew what she'd say next.

Of course, how could she be anything other than what she was with such a father to guide her? Had Almack's ever seen a gentleman throw insults in every direction, drink from a flask, rip a feather out of a lady's hair and hit her with it, and then threaten to throw cake at her in the dining room?

He was certain all of that could not have got by the Patronesses, and that was only what he'd seen himself. There was probably more.

However, that eccentric gentleman was a duke, so he suspected not much censure would come his way. Percy sometimes thought the idea of rank in England had led to some very bad behavior!

FELICITY WAS IN conference with her sisters, those six individuals piled on her bed as the sun rose over the rooftops. Patience had not let anybody sleep in and had shaken everybody awake and dragged them into her room.

"So it is absolutely confirmed," Grace said, "that the Earl of Rustmont is the leading man of London?"

"I must think so," Felicity said. "He is very handsome. Mind you, there were no end of handsome gentlemen about, so the leading man of London must bring more. Really, it is a certain air he carries about with him."

"Certain air?" Serenity asked, turning away from the sunrise that had just now brought a tear to her eye. Serenity was particularly affected by nature and claimed every sunrise was different, though Felicity couldn't see much in the idea.

"A certain air," Felicity said. "It is as if he has no need to be jolly or approve of all the world."

"Are you sure he is not a rogue, though?" Winsome asked.

"Oh Felicity," Valor said, gripping at the bedspread, "Winsome did warn you about the rogues, though nobody will tell me what they are."

"He is not a rogue, I am sure," Felicity said.

"I suppose he was very struck by you and came out and said so?" Patience asked.

That was a sticking point.

"Not in so many words," Felicity said. "You see, there was a regrettable incident—a lady dancing near me reeked of rose-water."

Her sisters knowing her so well, there was hardly a need for extensive explanation. They could well guess at the situation.

"Did you sneeze?" Grace asked.

"Violently, I'm afraid."

"I would have died," Serenity said.

"Nobody dies of a sneeze," Grace said. "But, was it very noticeable?"

"The earl was forced to hand over his handkerchief," Felicity admitted. "So, that was not a promising beginning. However, it will all turn out well."

"I see," Verity said, nodding knowingly.

"See what?" Winsome asked Verity.

Verity turned up her nose, declining to explain what she did or did not see.

"I was able to discover that the earl has a weakness," Felicity said. "It turns out he will go mad for me if he thinks another gentleman has gone mad for me. I have dug such a gentleman up—his name is Mr. Percy Stratton. He will pretend interest in me, thereby driving the earl to fly to my side."

"Why?" Winsome asked. "Why should this Mr. Stratton wish to involve himself?"

"Well… he did say he enjoyed a ruse," Felicity said. "I suppose that is why." Though, now that she was looking at it, perhaps it did seem a rather flimsy reason.

"That seems a rather flimsy reason," Winsome said.

"It is a perfectly well-known reason," Verity said, "as everybody knows."

"I did not know," Valor said.

"In any case," Felicity said, "the Earl of Rustmont will be at Lady Jellerbey's candlelight picnic on the morrow and the plan will unfold."

"Papa and our aunt had a shouting match yesterday about that picnic," Grace said. "First, Papa said he would not go, as an indoor picnic sounded idiotic. Then our aunt said she was glad he would not go, as he was likely to cause trouble. She would be happy to take our Felicity herself. Then of course you can guess what happened…"

"Papa has now insisted he will go," Felicity said.

Grace nodded.

Felicity was not certain when Lady Marchfield would ever figure out that if you wished to steer her father one way, you ought to suggest he go the other way.

Valor suddenly laughed. She said, "Papa told our aunt that

she would be lucky if he didn't overturn all Lady Jillerbey's candles and burn her house down. She clutched at her heart. It really was very funny."

They all laughed at the idea. Really, their father could be very amusing.

Mrs. Right knocked on the door and came in, followed by two maids with trays.

"Jenny told me you were all up and I imagined you were starving," she said. "I thought to have brought up tea and toast to hold you over until your proper breakfast."

"You did bring a cup for yourself, Mrs. Right?" Felicity asked.

"I should be heartbroken if you did not," Serenity said.

The housekeeper nodded. "I saw into the future and perceived that you will wish to tell me about Almack's, and I will wish to tell you about a certain butler who is set to arrive."

"A butler!" Valor cried, as if the idea were terrifying.

Of course, it might very well be terrifying to her youngest sister. Valor had been too young to remember the last butler who'd been in the house. She'd only heard the stories of that gentleman's final day, which may have been exaggerated for interest.

"Is it Mr. Herring come back?" Grace asked.

"No," Mrs. Right said grimly, directing the maids with the trays, "I reckon that fellow is weeping in somebody else's house these days. It is some fellow named Mr. Joseph Sykes-Wycliff."

"He has two family names," Valor pointed out, as if this were further reason to be frightened of him.

"Will his mind collapse like Mr. Herring's did?" Felicity asked, all curiosity. That had been a day of real excitement in the house.

Mrs. Right poured the tea and passed cups round. "No doubt," she said. "It is only a matter of when."

With that genial idea, they proceeded to have a very merry pre-breakfast.

THE LAST PLACE Percy would purposely find himself was in the breakfast room with his father at eight o'clock in the morning. However, the viscount had left strict instructions with his valet that he was to turn up at the appointed hour.

He busied himself at the sideboard, hemming and hawing and taking this or that thing and then pausing to reconsider.

"I can sit here all day if necessary," the viscount said.

Percy gave up his delay tactic and sat down.

"Well?" his father said. "You've been to Almack's; you've had a look at every eligible lady in Town. What's it to be?"

Now was his moment to spring the ruse on his father. He did his best to sound casual. "As it happens, I was very struck by Lady Felicity, the Duke of Pelham's daughter," he said. He gulped his coffee as that idea settled.

The viscount shook his head violently. "No," his father said, "it cannot be her."

"Why ever not?" Percy asked, hope growing by the moment.

"I simply insist. Anybody but her."

This was a very convenient stance, and delightfully not one Percy would comply with.

"You said, as long as her father was not coming along with her, it would be fine," Percy pointed out. "She is a duke's daughter, she's got a good dowry, and right in the beginning of this project of yours you demanded a lord's daughter with money who was pleasant to look at. Remember? Because you said the estate could do with an infusion and you could not abide homely children?"

The viscount, never liking his own words flung back in his face, as it was a particular habit of his viscountess, harrumphed.

"She is everything you asked for," Percy said.

"I know what I said!" the viscount shouted.

A footman clattered a plate on the sideboard, but Percy remained unperturbed. If a person was to be perturbed every time the viscount shouted something, that person would spend a great deal of their life dropping plates.

"Stratton," the viscount said, "I failed to take one thing into consideration because it is an outlandish thing to have to take into consideration. After what I viewed last evening, Lady Felicity is out of the question."

Percy presumed his father referred to the lady's unusual behavior when she danced with Rustmont. "It was only a sneeze," he said.

"You are so naïve," the viscount said. "Her father the duke is entirely mad, you would not believe the things I witnessed!"

Of course, Percy would believe it. But he did not say so. "One cannot condemn a person by what they think of a parent," he said. "That would be too unfair."

"They can if they can see very well that the daughter has inherited her father's tendencies. Do you see what that means? It is in the line—any children from a union with Lady Felicity will be just the same. I will not tolerate deranged grandchildren! We cannot have a deranged future viscount!"

Percy worked to keep the amusement from his expression. One, because most of the time they had a deranged viscount right now. Two, this was unfolding better than he'd ever imagined. He'd planned to be the hapless and hopeless suitor. Already, he'd convinced Lady Felicity to assist him. Now his father was gamely stepping in front of the footlights to engage in this farce of a play, turning his son into a doomed Romeo. The viscount would be Montague and the duke would be Capulet.

Percy was poised to be hopelessly smitten with a lady his father would not accept, even if she could be convinced to accept, which she could not. Unlike Romeo and his completely stupid situation, Percy Stratton was as safe from matrimony as a fish swimming free in the sea and would not need to kill himself over it.

"Father, I am entirely set on Lady Felicity. I did not sleep at all last night for thinking of her. I will not have anybody else. My heart is no longer my own."

"Your heart is… get it back, you scoundrel!"

Percy shook his head sadly. "What you ask is impossible. There are things in this world that are beyond our control. Love will not be ordered to retreat at will."

Percy bit his lip. He sounded very much the vapid philosopher with that idea.

"I forbid it. I forbid a match between you and Lady Felicity. I will not sanction it. I'll cut off your funds!"

"Ah, that would be terrible," Percy said. "I will be left to mope about the house day after day. However, I will persevere! I will not give up on love! Also, if I am destitute, I will be here in the house rather than out and about in the company of the *ton's* ladies. You know, those other ladies you hope will catch my eye. But it matters not! I am all in for Lady Felicity!"

The viscount rose from his chair, knocking over a glass of orange juice as he did so. He whipped round to the butler, who was fussing with the sideboard as if he'd heard nothing at all untoward.

"Tell the viscountess I will see her at her earliest convenience!" he shouted.

His father stormed out of the breakfast room and stomped up the stairs.

Percy leaned back and sipped his coffee. *Operation Sadly Hopeless* was off to a rousing start.

Mrs. Right had thought long and hard on how to outfox Lady Marchfield's idea that the house required a butler. They'd all got along just fine without Mr. Herring for the last five years and there was no need to upset the equilibrium of the house.

The problem with a butler was that he was bound to be a bit

too impressed with himself. Mr. Herring had made that clear enough. How many hours did he drone on about standards before she'd put a stop to it? The servants' table back in those days had been a dreary place indeed.

Now, she sat at the servants' table in Grosvenor Square and there was Mr. Joseph Sykes-Wycliff sitting in *her* rightful place at the head and droning on just the same as Mr. Herring had always done.

"Naturally," Mr. Sykes-Wycliff said, stroking the rather ridiculous tuft of hair on his chin, "I must be concerned that there has been no butler to lead the staff forward for over five years. I am certain there will be much work to do to reestablish standards."

"In all fairness," Mrs. Right said, "we did always hold out hope that Mr. Herring would be found and returned to us safe."

"Found?" Mr. Sykes-Wycliff asked. "I understood that gentleman resigned his position."

Mrs. Right covered her mouth and made a great show of looking as if she'd accidentally allowed a secret out. The rest of the staff, who'd been thoroughly briefed and did not want a butler any more than she did, all looked away from Mr. Sykes-Wycliff.

The butler began to look alarmed. "If you say you hoped he was found, do you then imply he was somehow lost?"

"The moors are a vast place, Mr. Sykes-Wycliff," Mrs. Right said. "And the duke... well, less said the better about that."

"What about the duke?" Mr. Sykes-Wycliff asked, a note of anxiety creeping into his voice. "I have not even met His Grace yet, Lady Marchfield is to introduce me when she arrives to the house."

"All I say," Mrs. Right said, glancing round the table, "is lock your bedchamber door at night and do not be fooled into opening it up by any soft knocking you hear."

As Mr. Sykes-Wycliff stared at the rest of the servants, they all nodded sadly.

"Soft knocking," he whispered. "Lady Marchfield said nothing about soft knocking."

"No offense to Lady Marchfield," Mrs. Right said, pleased with how worried the fellow was beginning to look, "but she don't know the workings of the household. Just think, when we return home, we'll be miles and miles from another human soul. A person might scream as loud as they liked on them moors with nobody but the circling buzzards to hear."

"Why would someone scream? What buzzards?" Mr. Sykes-Wycliff said, his tone going up an octave.

Mrs. Right shrugged. "The Dales are not for everybody, alas."

"I am not at all clear what you hint at, Mrs. Right, but I intend to demand answers!"

Everyone at the table lost their composure and guffawed into their tea.

"Demand from who, Mr. Sykes-Wycliff?" Mrs. Right said, shaking her head at the foolishness of the notion. "Demand answers from who?"

The butler did not look as if he knew.

Mrs. Right, rather a master at painting horrifying pictures in a person's mind, was also rather good at the timing of the thing. She'd made a good start with Mr. Sykes-Wycliff. Now, she would let him stew in it for a while.

She rose and said to the rest of the staff. "We'd best get to our work. We all know the duke's moods in the early evenings."

Everybody hopped up and scattered. Mrs. Right left the butler to ponder precisely what the duke's moods were in the early evenings.

If she knew anything about the Duke of Pelham, His Grace would assist in the effort to drive this new butler from the house. She could not guess what he'd say or do, nobody ever could, but whatever it was, it would be alarming to Mr. Sykes-Wycliff.

CHAPTER FIVE

FELICITY HAD DRESSED carefully for Lady Jellerbey's candlelight picnic. As far as she understood it, the lady would have the lighting of her house rather low. Sideboards would be placed throughout the rooms, and one was to go staggering about in the dimness, filling their plate on their own.

Felicity had concluded that her crème silk was the best choice, as a darker color might cause her to fade into the woodwork under low light. To go with it, she had taken out her emerald necklace as it was large and would catch the light, further drawing attention to her location. She also thought the color was a subtle nod to her plan—green, the color of envy.

It would be crucial that the Earl of Rustmont observed that she was being trailed about by Mr. Stratton. It would do her no good at all if he could not make her out in the low light.

She hurried down the stairs to find her aunt introducing the new butler to her father.

"Mr. Why, is it? I might ask why myself," the duke said, eyeing the butler.

"Sykes-Wycliff, Your Grace," the butler said.

Felicity pressed her lips together to stop her laughter. Her aunt would know as well as she did that her father was in no confusion over the man's name.

"I've told my sister a hundred times that Mrs. Right takes care of everything," the duke said.

"Roland, do stop being ridiculous, a member of the nobility must have a butler and that is that."

"Oh really? If I must have one, then where did that rascal Herring get off to? Just disappeared one day, didn't he? Never to be seen or heard from again."

Mr. Sykes-Wycliff appeared stricken to hear the name of Mr. Herring. Felicity wondered what Mrs. Right had told him about that nervous fellow's final hours as the duke's butler.

Lady Marshfield turned her gaze to Felicity. Then her gaze dropped and settled on her emerald necklace. "Do change that necklace, Felicity. It does not suit a young lady—it is too presumptuous. Choose a simple gold chain, or pearls if you must."

"That necklace was given Felicity by me," the duke said, "after her poor mother bid us her final adieu and made her way to the great beyond. I divided up all the jewelry between the girls."

"That is all well and good, Roland, but a stone of that size is more suited to a married lady."

"Ignore her," the duke said to Felicity. "Your aunt would have liked to get her hands on every piece, but I gave her nothing! Not even that horrific enameled parrot brooch Valor insists on wearing all the time!"

The sound of the carriage rolling to a stop outside prompted Mr. Sykes-Wycliff to race to the doors and open them, likely in a bid to end his first interaction with his new employer.

"Never mind anything the duke says," Lady Marchfield counseled Mr. Sykes-Wycliff, "simply carry on with your duties. According to your references, you are an exceedingly regular sort of person, which is precisely what this house needs."

Her father appeared resigned that this new person was to be in the house for a little while at least. His parting advice was, "Follow Mrs. Right's direction in everything—she knows the house and she knows *me*."

One would suppose that a recently arrived butler would be grateful to receive direction on how to proceed. If Felicity could read Mr. Sykes-Wycliff's expression, though, she rather thought he was terrified of Mrs. Right.

So soon, too! She suspected that whatever was to go on between their dearest long-time housekeeper and this new butler, it would be vastly interesting.

Felicity hurried out to the carriage behind her aunt and her father. She had presumed Lady Marchfield would go in her own carriage, as she must have come in it, but the lady climbed into the duke's carriage.

She supposed that meant there was to be a lecture on the way to Lady Jellerbey's candlelight picnic, rather than the jolly time she and her father might have had.

After they were all settled, the duke said to his sister, "Might I inquire why I find you in my carriage?"

"Lord Marchfield has gone on to his club. He deposited me here on his way," Lady Marchfield said.

"Deposited you, has he?" the duke said. "No doubt he's tried that gambit before—depositing you somewhere in the hopes that you can't find your way back. He'll be fingers crossed all night! Well, if he thinks he will pawn you off on me…"

Felicity covered her mouth to suppress a snort of laughter. One of her father's favorite pastimes was to speculate on how much Lord Marchfield would like to be rid of Lady Marchfield. None of it was true, as far as she could see. Lord and Lady Marchfield seemed very cordial toward one another. Of course, what was true did not often trouble the duke.

Lady Marchfield sniffed and said, "I will not even dignify that diatribe with a response. I have other matters on my mind. Felicity, you presented yourself exceedingly odd at Almack's. This evening will either cement that opinion of you or turn it on its head. You must be everything graceful and demure. Say nothing odd, do nothing odd. With any luck, it will be thought that whatever anybody believed they witnessed at Almack's was just first-time out jitters."

"Jitters?" the duke asked, his tone incredulous. "You want

people to think that one of *my* daughters got the jitters?"

"Since when do you give a toss for anybody else's opinion?" Lady Marchfield asked her brother.

"I am afraid my aunt has you boxed in there, Papa," Felicity said, laughing.

"I'd box his ears if I could," Lady Marchfield muttered.

"I heard that!" the duke shouted. "I've a mind to deposit you on the road, just like your beleaguered husband did. With any luck, you'll wander into the Rats' Castle and never be seen again. Find the Seven Dials and walk straight ahead! That's my advice."

Felicity thought she'd better turn her father's and her aunt's attention to another matter before they ended wrestling in the carriage. She would not like her dress to be rumpled in a fray.

"Aunt, you are to know I have a particular plan for this evening. I will make the Earl of Rustmont wild with envy, so he will be driven to claim me as his own."

Interestingly, this news seemed to drain the color from her aunt's cheeks. "The earl? What? Envy? What do you mean by that?"

"My God, woman," the duke said, "can you not even understand simple sentences anymore? She said she's to make Rustmont jealous. Simplest thing in the world to comprehend."

"Felicity," Lady Marchfield said sternly, "I do not know what has got into your head, but I strongly caution you to do nothing at all like… whatever it is you are thinking. If you have any inclination in the earl's direction, I applaud it. But you must realize that Lord Rustmont is an exceedingly proper gentleman and will not tolerate any odd behavior or effrontery."

"Then he's come to the wrong family, hasn't he?" the duke said, snorting at his own wit.

"The point is," Lady Marchfield said, "he has *not* come to the family. He has danced with Felicity one time, and a very strange dance it was. I do not imagine he will venture near her again if there is even a whiff of anything else strange."

Felicity did feel the sting of that opinion. Certainly, the earl would not avoid her over a sneeze. Or series of sneezes. Of course he would not. He just needed to be propelled to her side.

"He has a weak spot though," Felicity said. "You'll see. He will be mad with envy and fly to my side because Mr. Stratton will pretend to be overcome by my charms."

"Mr. Stratton?" Lady Marchfield sputtered.

Felicity waved her hands. "Do not fear, Aunt, I do not have the slightest interest in Mr. Stratton—he is smarmy and callow, though he may outgrow it with time."

Lady Marchfield seemed silenced by this news. Though, Felicity did notice the lady gripped her reticule as if she wished to choke the life out of it.

The duke erupted in loud laughter that filled the small confines of the carriage. "Here I was, thinking it would be all drudgery to launch all these girls out of my house, and now I see I am to be vastly entertained!"

Before Lady Marchfield could respond to that comment, the carriage rolled to a stop. Whatever was to be this evening, it was set to begin.

PERCY HAD WORN his best coat to Lady Jellerbey's candlelight picnic, primarily in a bid to convince his father that he was set on Lady Felicity and could not be moved by any recent complaints.

The old soldier had tracked down his viscountess and closeted himself with that lady for most of the morning. Under cover of the occasional shouts of "I warn you!" Percy had slipped out of the house and taken his horse on a long ride round the park.

He'd found his mother waiting for him when he tried to slip in again to change before heading off to his club.

"Do sit down, Stratton," his mother said, waylaying him the hall and ushering him into the drawing room.

He did as he was bid, preparing to fight off whatever she was intent on hurling in his direction.

"Your father is in a state," the viscountess said.

"Father is always in a state," Percy pointed out.

"Yes, well, he has a rather volcanic temperament," the viscountess admitted. "Inherited by his ancestors in trade, no doubt."

His mother delighted in assigning blame to his tradesman ancestors for any and all difficulties.

"This time, though, he has reached a new pinnacle of hysteria," the viscountess said. "I hardly knew what to do with him. Now really, my darling, why must you be set on this Lady Felicity?"

"Why did you become set on my father?" Percy asked by way of an answer.

The viscountess seemed pensive. "That is becoming more and more a mystery," she said softly.

"And there you have it," Percy said. "Love is mysterious."

"Come now, I do not think you will find it at all comfortable to wed a lady with her… peculiarities. Those sorts of things lurk in the family blood, you see. Think of the children of such a union!"

"Nonsense," Percy said. "The duke may be mad as a spring hare, but Lady Felicity is only a touch mad. Just think, mother, have *I* inherited *my* father's temper?"

"Well, no. Goodness no, your cheerful temperament comes from my side."

Percy had hopped up and kissed his mother's cheek, as really there was no benefit to continuing the conversation. "I am certain that my children with Lady Felicity will all take after me and I know you are fond of me. You will like them exceedingly well and it will all work out splendidly. *If* the lady can be wooed. That is what I do not yet know."

He hurried from the room before his mother could reply.

Now, he was drifting round near Lady Jellerbey's front doors, making a great show of looking as if he were pining for Lady

Felicity. His father glared at him from the other side of the hall and his mother patted the viscount's arm to keep his volcanic temper in check.

The one thing that had begun to weigh on his mind was how long he could keep the whole ruse going. What if Rustmont did not cooperate? After all, Percy had invented the idea that Rustmont must be made envious. What if the earl ignored whatever display he and Lady Felicity would put on for his benefit?

Percy gave his shoulders a little shake. He could not contemplate defeat when the game had just begun.

There. There she was. Lady Felicity was looking smashing in a crème silk dress with the light adornment of a subtle braid at the bottom of the cap sleeves and along the neckline. She wore a rather large emerald round her neck. Very large actually. Why did that seem daring?

He supposed he was so used to young ladies hardly adorning themselves at all—a gold chain, a small cross, maybe a string of undersized pearls. Here was a whopping stone any duchess would be pleased to call her own. She was not a lady who wished to hide in the shadows.

Percy hurried over, and as he did so he saw Lord Rustmont just coming in the doors. Was that inconvenient or perfect? On the one hand, it was Lady Felicity's fever dream to make that stiff fellow envious, so that was perfect. The lady would play her part and that would help him on the other side—convincing his parents he was set on her.

Of course, it would be very inconvenient if the lord paid no notice of their charade.

"Lady Felicity," he said, with a sweeping bow. "Lady Marchfield, Your Grace."

"It's the mister again, eh?" the duke said.

Percy nodded, as it seemed to be the sum total of what the duke knew about him.

"Mr. Stratton," Lady Marchfield said through pursed lips.

"He's Stratton? What ho? This is the game, is it?" the duke said, laughing so heartily he clutched at his rather round stomach.

As Percy had not the slightest idea what the duke meant, he just smiled. In his experience, smiling was generally suitable for every occasion but for a deathbed or funeral.

"Really, Papa," Lady Felicity said.

Percy did not know if Lady Felicity understood her father's cryptic remarks either, but as was beginning to seem usual she was clearly amused by him.

Behind him, Percy heard his father say, "Stratton, do come away and see what's on the sideboard in the library."

The sideboard in the library? If that was not a pathetic gambit, he did not know what was. His poor viscount was attempting to be sly and lead him away from Lady Felicity. Whatever his father was, sly was not on the list.

Percy turned and found his father red in the face as if he'd run across the great hall. His mother had stayed behind and was just now wringing her hands from across the room.

"Your Grace, Lady Marchfield, Lady Felicity," Percy said, "my father, Viscount Denderby."

"The duke and I are acquainted," the viscount said.

"Are we?" the duke said, looking puzzled. "When? How? Remind me."

Through rather gritted teeth, the viscount said, "The last we met was in Lady Vanderwake's drawing room some twenty years ago."

The duke shrugged. "Not much to go on, if you ask me."

"The lady's curtains were set afire?" the viscount said.

"The curtain fire! That's right, it's all coming back to me. I was playfully keeping the candle away from Lady Margaret, as she claimed she wished to read. Well! These things happen."

Did those things happen?

"But say," the duke went on, seeming very jolly to recall the curtain fire, "you're the sire of this jackanapes mister, are you?" He'd pointed in Percy's direction to make clear who he referred to.

Percy's eyes widened. He never understood much of what the duke said, but why on earth should he be called a jackanapes?

Unless Lady Felicity had informed her father of the ruse, a circumstance that he'd not foreseen. He'd been too wrapped up in what a usual father would think of such a thing. It seemed the duke thought it a very good joke.

Percy only prayed that the duke would not give the game away to his father.

"Jackanapes?" the viscount asked.

"Yes, yes, very amusing. Look, there's Rustmont. Let us get this thing off the ground."

Lady Marchfield laid a hand on her brother's arm. "Roland!" she said in a warning tone.

It was a tone entirely lost on the duke. Rather, he shouted, "Rustmont! Get over here."

Lord Rustmont looked exceedingly surprised to be shouted at. Percy saw the flicker of annoyance in his expression that was speedily covered over with a tight smile.

He did make his way over, as Percy supposed he knew not what else to do after a duke had yelled those particular instructions.

After the introductions had gone round, which included the duke pointing out that he had not laid eyes on Viscount Denderby since he'd set Lady Vanderwake's curtains on fire, Percy noticed Lady Felicity blushing rather prettily.

Why should Rustmont have such an effect on the ladies? It was deuced unfair—the fellow was a stick.

"Come with us, Rustmont," the duke said. "Denderby here is going to show us something spectacular on the sideboard in the library."

"I never said spectacular," the viscount said.

"What did you say it was?" the duke asked.

"I didn't say," Percy's father said, beginning to look vastly uncomfortable.

As well he didn't, Percy thought.

"Well, let us go and discover it," the duke said.

Percy put his arm out and Lady Felicity laid her hand on it.

As an added touch, she said, "Gracious, Mr. Stratton, you are always very insistent in holding out your arm."

Percy surreptitiously glanced at Lord Rustmont. That fellow looked a bit dejected. He supposed Lady Felicity would take that as a compliment. Percy rather thought he was dejected over having been pulled into this ridiculous party that was to set off to examine a sideboard.

No matter, they would arrive to the library and see what the viscount could pull out of his hat regarding the remarkable thing he claimed he'd seen.

CHAPTER SIX

FELICITY FELT EVERYTHING was going remarkably well so far. She had taken Mr. Stratton's arm in full view of Lord Rustmont and now they were all traveling together to the library to see a spectacular item on the sideboard. She had high hopes it was a pineapple, as she had heard them described and viewed drawings of that interesting fruit, but she had never seen one with her own eyes. At home, they were always fairly drowning in Hunthouse apples, and then of course they went on bilberry forages on the moors and other various fruits turned up here and there. A pineapple, though, would really be something.

As Felicity drifted down the corridor on Mr. Stratton's arm, she hoped Lord Rustmont noticed that there was something romantic about the atmosphere of the candlelight picnic. The chandeliers overhead had been left unlit and candles were placed on every available surface. The lighting was really very favorable to a lady, even her aunt's features appeared softened.

They found the room housing Lady Jellerbey's books and made their way to the sideboard located in that room.

As Felicity gazed up and down the length, she could not pinpoint the item Lord Denderby had pegged as spectacular. There were savories and sweets, very usual fruits, a tea and coffee service, punch, bottles of wine labeled as to their type, and port and brandy for the gentlemen.

"Well, Denderby?" the duke asked. "I see nothing spectacular here at all. If this is your idea of a spectacular sideboard, one wonders how you live."

"Roland!" Lady Marchfield whispered.

Felicity well knew her father was only saying what everybody was thinking. Mr. Stratton, for once, was looking very amused by the duke.

Lord Denderby's eyes twitched and blinked. Then, as if he'd suddenly recalled something, he said, "My god, it's gone!"

"Gone, Father?" Mr. Stratton asked, his lips twitching at their corners.

"Was it a pineapple, Lord Denderby?" Felicity asked.

Lord Denderby paused, as if searching his memory for the recollection of what was gone. "Yes! Yes, that is what it was. An exceedingly large pineapple. It seems someone has made off with it."

"If it was large," Lord Rustmont said, "I do not imagine they will get far with it. Rather hard to hide."

"Who knows what people get up to, though," Lord Denderby said. "How should I know what happened to it!"

Felicity thought Lord Denderby was exceedingly upset by the missing pineapple. After all, it was not *his* pineapple that had gone missing.

"I will alert Lady Jellerbey," Lord Rustmont said. "I need to find her and pay my respects in any case."

"Don't tell her!" Lord Denderby cried. "You'll only upset the lady! It would be very cruel."

"What do you propose, then?" Lord Rustmont asked.

"Perhaps we ought to search for it?" Felicity ventured.

"Yes!" Lord Denderby practically shouted. He pointed at Felicity. "She knows what's what. We'll just have a look round. Who knows, maybe somebody hid it behind a pair of curtains!"

"Good luck to you," the duke said. "For myself, I'll pour a glass of brandy and find a comfortable chair. Let me know if you track down that spectacular pineapple—I'll be up out of my seat like a shot."

The duke sauntered off, leaving the rest of the party staring at one another. Felicity supposed nobody really knew how to start a search for a missing pineapple.

Lady Denderby hurried into the room. "Ah, there you are," she said to the viscount. Seeming to notice that something had occurred, she looked enquiringly at Mr. Stratton.

"We are poised to begin searching for a missing pineapple, Mother," Mr. Stratton said. "Father saw one on the sideboard, a large one mind you, and now it is mysteriously gone."

"Goodness," the viscountess said. "Perhaps we ought to inform Lady Jellerbey."

"Everybody stop talking about informing Lady Jellerbey!" the viscount said.

"I propose we split up and go from room to room," Mr. Stratton said. "I will insist, of course, on keeping Lady Felicity on my arm."

Felicity thought that was a very good turn of phrase. She glanced at Lord Rustmont to see how he was affected by it.

She could not read his expression. It seemed to be ever changing, bit by bit, though very subtle. She began to think he was a very deep personality.

Lord Rustmont turned to Lord Denderby. "You are certain you saw a pineapple?"

"Of course I am certain—I am not blind!"

Lord Rustmont sighed. "Very well." He turned on his heel and strode out.

"Let us follow," Felicity whispered to Mr. Stratton.

Mr. Stratton nodded and they set off. As they reentered the hall, Lord Rustmont had disappeared. Felicity did not know which direction he'd gone.

In a low tone, Mr. Stratton said, "You do realize there is no pineapple?"

"There is no pineapple?" she asked, turning to him.

"No pineapple," Mr. Stratton said laughing. "My father used the interesting item on the sideboard gambit to lure me away from your side. Then of course he had to invent something. He leapt at your suggestion of a pineapple like a man lunging toward a life ring."

"Gracious," Felicity said. "That sounds like something my father would do. He will be very amused by it. But wait, why should *your* father be intent on dragging you away from my side?"

"He does not care for any madness in the family," Mr. Stratton said.

Madness? What on earth was he saying? "I am sorry, do please explain that point," Felicity said, her temper beginning to rise.

"Well, *you* know," Mr. Stratton said, as if it hardly need be explained. "Your father, then you having that fit on the ballroom floor. He's got ideas from it, that's all."

They had turned into a large music room that was full of lit candles but rather empty of people. The various instruments housed there had almost a ghostly look in the dim light.

"I sneezed," Felicity said coldly. "And as for my father, pray, what can Lord Denderby accuse him of?"

Mr. Stratton looked at her with some surprise. "Well, I suppose he noticed the duke pulling an ostrich feather from Lady Marchfield's hair and smacking her in the face with it. For a start."

Felicity's temper was rolling through her like a kettle on the boil. "He was making a point to my aunt, about sneezing."

"Come now," Mr. Stratton said, "you cannot deny that your father is one die short of a dice set."

Felicity certainly could deny it. Yes, it was true that her father did not go through the world as perhaps other people did. But one die short of a set would hint at the duke being not very clever. The truth was, he was exceedingly clever. Why should Mr. Stratton be comparing him to a set of dice?

Her temper entirely boiled over and she said, "Perhaps, Mr. Stratton, you ought to look to your own family first. It seems to me that a gentleman claiming to have seen a pineapple that never existed might be one die short."

"Oh that? That's just my father."

"It is not in here?"

The voice behind them was unmistakable. Lord Rustmont. Felicity whipped around. "I am afraid not."

"Very well," Lord Rustmont said, "I'll go and have a look round the other rooms."

Felicity did not at all wish for him to hurry off when she'd just found him again. "Lord Rustmont, I've had an idea as to where it might have gone."

"Have you?" Mr. Stratton asked, looking very amused. As well he would, as they both knew there was no pineapple to begin.

"Indeed, I have," Felicity said. "It is my understanding that pineapples are often rented for a particular party by the hostess. Perhaps the person who rented it out had to come to collect it for another party. Perhaps it was only rented for a certain number of hours."

Lord Rustmont rubbed his chin. "You could be right. If that is the case, I would not wish to mention it to Lady Jellerbey and cause her embarrassment. Everybody knows pineapples are almost always rented, but everybody pretends they do not know it."

"My thoughts exactly," Felicity said.

"Excellent," Lord Rustmont said. "That will free me to seek out Lady Mary and her mother—I said I would at my earliest opportunity and have been shockingly remiss."

The lord bowed, turned on his heel, and strode from the room before Felicity could think up something to stop him.

"Who is Lady Mary?" she asked, noting the tone of outrage in her voice. She had not expected to hear it, but there it was.

"Lady Mary Kettleton, daughter of the Earl of Gentian."

"Why should Lord Rustmont be running round looking for her when he is supposed to be envious of the attentions you have paid me?"

"How should I know?" Mr. Stratton said. "It is only our first go at it. I had thought you were a rather stalwart sort of lady, but if you are willing to give up so easily, well…"

"I am perfectly stalwart, Mr. Stratton. Now, let us go and have a look at Lady Mary. I would like to know what we're up against."

The search for the nonexistent pineapple was given up and they traveled from room to room until they tracked down this Lady Mary that Lord Rustmont thought he must go and see.

They found Lord Rustmont attentively waiting on what Felicity supposed was a pretty lady. She was tall and lithe and had a pile of elegant blond curls. Her complexion was very much an English rose and her eyes were very blue. Lord Rustmont was not the only gentleman there either. She was all but surrounded.

"What am I seeing?" Felicity asked.

"A diamond of the first water," Mr. Stratton said. "Every year, one comes along and men fly to her side like bees to honey. It becomes a competition of sorts, as to where she will bestow her attentions."

"I see," Felicity said curtly. "Just one comes along each year?"

"Seems that way."

"So am I to understand that I am *not* a diamond of the first water?"

Mr. Stratton looked rather cornered by that question. "Oh, as to that, a lady should not dwell on such things."

"But I am dwelling on it."

"Well… you could be a diamond of the second water, I suppose."

The second water. He supposed.

Felicity was really taken aback by this information. She had no idea that each season brought one lady who ruled the town. Furthermore, had she known it, she would wonder at it not being her.

Why was Lady Mary to be the diamond and not herself? What was so exceptional about her? Was a gentleman to actually be taken in by a pretty complexion and blond curls?

Just then, Lady Mary lightly tapped her fan on a gentleman's arm and said something, which all in her sphere seemed to find wildly amusing.

Felicity could be wildly amusing. If she tried. As for the fan-tapping, she could take that up at once.

She had a feeling coming over her that she'd never felt before. It was some feeling of not measuring up. It was awful, and she did not know what she could do about it.

"We stay steady on our course," Mr. Stratton said. "That is the only move to make."

Felicity stared at the gentlemen leaning in to hear what this Lady Mary individual would say next. It was infuriating.

She would not stand for it. Steady on the course, indeed. Mr. Stratton was sadly lacking in imagination.

"No," she said.

"No?"

"No, Mr. Stratton, we must redouble our efforts, and when I say redouble, I mean double. Having one gentleman following me about has not proved sufficient. Of course, I cannot know if Lord Rustmont's head has not been turned because I have only one gentleman, or that gentleman is deemed not particularly significant. Let us be positive and assume it is because you are only one gentleman."

"What?"

"We will require another gentleman. Then, there will be a pair of suitors following me about. That is certain to catch Lord Rustmont's eye. I see now that he is only drawn to Lady Mary because other gentlemen seem as if they are. I must increase my retinue, as it were. Who can you get?"

"Who can I get?" Mr. Stratton said weakly.

"Yes. Who can you get? What about Mr. Wiles? I danced with him at Almack's. As far as I can see, he cannot have much going for him. He's bound to do it, as it would at least appear as if he's doing *something*."

"Mr. Wiles?"

"Mr. Wiles," Felicity repeated. She was beginning to think it was Mr. Stratton who was short a few dice—he was remarkably slow at following her.

Gracious, there was much work ahead. He really would need to keep up.

PERCY DID NOT often find himself positively stupefied, but that was exactly what had happened to him last evening. Everything had been humming along at the candlelight picnic until his father tried out the missing pineapple gambit. Things had gone downhill from there.

Lord Rustmont was not being very cooperative to Percy's plan. It seemed that fellow did not have the least interest in Lady Felicity and was all in for Lady Mary.

Percy could not understand it, if one were strictly speaking about looks. He found Lady Mary's looks just a little bit insipid and pale. As for Lady Felicity, well, not every lady had such wonderful hair or big brown eyes. She was much more compelling to look at than Lady Mary. He seemed to be entirely alone in that opinion, though.

Or perhaps Rustmont just could not get past the sneezing fit at Almack's. Or the things she said. Or her father.

Then, Lady Felicity had insisted he bring Wiles into the whole thing. How was he to get Wiles to agree to it? That question remained unanswered.

No sooner had Lady Felicity taken his silence as a tacit agreement to drag in Wiles, than the duke turned up to collect his daughter.

"Eh, Mister," the duke had said to him, "no sign of that stupendous pineapple that was to knock us flat with amazement?"

"No, Your Grace," Percy said, certain his face had gone red.

"It was all invented, Papa," Lady Felicity said laughing. "Lord

Denderby made the whole thing up."

"Did he now?" the duke said, appearing very amused. "Rather eccentric of him. But then, some of those in this town *are* exceedingly odd."

Percy had attempted to keep his expression neutral. If anybody lacked in self-awareness, it was the Duke of Pelham.

"Now my girl, are we done staggering around in dim rooms?" the duke asked. "Can we go?"

Lady Felicity had nodded and said, "Yes, I believe everything that can be accomplished this evening has been. Mr. Stratton? Do not forget our conversation."

As if he had any hope of forgetting.

Not a half hour later, just as he'd found a quiet corner and was soothing himself with a whopping glass of brandy, Lady Marchfield suddenly appeared in front of him.

He rose. "Lady Marchfield."

"Mr. Stratton, have you seen Lady Felicity and the duke?"

"Oh, they've gone," he'd answered.

"Gone!" she'd nearly shouted. "When?"

"Um, I suppose a quarter-hour past?" Percy said, nonplussed at what upset the lady.

"A quarter-hour—they may still wait for the carriage," Lady Marchfield muttered.

The lady spun round and actually jogged from the room.

Percy put his brandy down and followed her out. He could not account for what had upset the lady, but such was her upset that he was curious to find out. Perhaps Lady Felicity had borrowed that enormous emerald round her neck and Lady Marchfield was determined to get it back before it disappeared into the duke's household forever.

In a matter of moments he was on the lady's heels, headed out of doors. That was when he witnessed the capstone to the whole evening. And what a capstone it had been.

Lady Marchfield had flown out the doors without even collecting her wrap. Outside, she ran down the pavement after the duke's carriage as it trotted away, shouting, "Roland!"

First the carriage sped up, then it slowed and came to a stop. The duke opened the carriage door and, loud enough for anybody on the street to hear said, "I'll drop you at the Seven Dials, or the nearest gin shop, whichever you prefer!"

Lady Marchfield climbed into the carriage, the door shut, and they trotted off as if nothing at all had happened.

As far as Percy could guess at it, the duke had brought Lady Marchfield and then thought it would be amusing to leave her there. Then, when she caught up to him, it further amused him to claim he'd leave her at a rookery.

And Lady Felicity and the duke accused *his* father of being eccentric for inventing a phantom pineapple!

She was exceedingly eccentric herself and insulting too. His ears still burned over her idea that perhaps he alone was not enough to pique Rustmont's jealousy because he was not particularly significant. Percy Stratton was most definitely significant!

Just now, he headed into White's. It was still early, but he knew that Wiles usually came in first thing for coffee and to read the newspapers. The gentleman had a houseful of sisters who he claimed made a racket day and night and made it hard to think. White's was his refuge.

Percy had not yet devised a plan to lure Wiles into this farce, but he was sure something would come to him.

On his way in, he glanced at the bet book. Then he glanced at it again. Then he stopped.

Will Lady F require any more emergency handkerchiefs this season? Bets end in a fortnight.

Apparently, Lord Hardwick had come up with it. The gentleman had witnessed Lady Felicity's fit at Almack's and decided to make a game of it. Percy knew why, too. Hardwick and Rustmont were like oil and water. Hardwick was a jokester and Rustmont was often seen frowning at him or claiming he'd gone too far. For his own amusement, Hardwick decided that Rustmont should not be allowed to forget what they'd all seen on the ballroom floor that evening.

The betting appeared to be split down the middle.

Percy dearly hoped Lady Felicity did not get wind of it. Who knew what she'd think to do about it. The lady was highly unpredictable! And then the duke might be offended too. Perhaps he'd issue a challenge to Hardwick over the slight.

Though, that probably would not be too much of a danger. His father had already explained that the duke had not even bothered to turn up after challenging a Cornwall baron.

He went into the coffee room and found Wiles at a table near the window. He sat down and motioned for a coffee.

"Do you want a newspaper?" Wiles asked.

"God no," Percy said. "Whatever disasters in the making our government are up to just now, I'd rather not know."

"It does not serve to stay willfully uninformed."

Percy did not answer, but was of the opinion that was Wiles' opinion. "What's say we have a quiet game of cards instead?"

"Absolutely not," Wiles said. "I'm already in too deep on the gambling front. I owe you forty pounds and Magnon another twenty."

Like a bolt of lightning, Percy realized how he would get Wiles to join him in *Operation Sadly Hopeless*. He'd never really thought Wiles would get round to paying him, and now the fellow could pay him with service, rather than money.

"I tell you what," Percy said, "I'll erase the debt if you do me a favor."

Wiles lowered his newspaper. "What favor?"

"A small favor. Simply join me in escorting Lady Felicity about the town."

"Why?"

"Well, it's not my idea, but the lady is intent on having two gentlemen suitors. You know, to make Rustmont burn with envy."

"What's in it for you? Isn't the whole plan to make your father think you are set on having a lady who will not have you?"

Percy had indeed thought through what was in it for him. "Yes, you see, this works perfectly. I'll make it out as if Lady Felicity is leaning in your direction, but I am determined not to give up."

"This is a rum situation."

Percy nodded. "Now you're on to it—it could not get any rummer. However, I believe I can state with confidence that it is worth forty pounds of debt. Who else would offer you such a ridiculous proposal?"

"Nobody," Wiles said. "Because nobody else I know would embroil themselves in such a ridiculous situation."

"Yes, but you know why—I will not be chained!"

CHAPTER SEVEN

MRS. RIGHT WAS slowly but surely working Mr. Sykes-Wycliff right out the door. Of course, she did not work alone. The entire staff were enthusiastic participants and the duke played his own part whether he realized it or not.

Now all she need do is stay on course and bring in the final reinforcements.

She'd hurried into Felicity's room and congenially found all the sisters there, but for Valor, who was still asleep. That was well—Valor did not have a strong stomach for intrigue and she was too young to keep a secret for longer than ten minutes.

"Mrs. Right," Serenity said, "Felicity was just telling us of Papa leaving our aunt at the candlelight picnic and how she had to run after the carriage."

"It really was very funny," Felicity said. "As soon as Papa saw her, he ordered the carriage to speed up. I did feel sorry for her though, so I convinced him to stop and let her in. She was very out of breath, and then when she regained it she gave Papa a rousing what-for. She said he was no better than a toddler. Then he threatened to drop her off at the nearest gin shop, so she finally gave it up."

"She ought to have known how it would be, though," Mrs. Right said, shaking her head. "She should have kept her eyes firmly on the duke at all times. Now my girl, how did you get on with defeating Lord Rustmont?"

Felicity nodded. "I have not yet succeeded but I know why and what I will do. I am to have two suitors chasing after me. I should have known right from the start that one gentleman pining over me would not be sufficient. The odious Lady Mary had at least five last evening."

"She sounds horrible," Mrs. Right said, perfectly amenable to despising Lady Mary, though she'd never set eyes on the woman and knew not a thing about her.

"I rather think she *is* horrible, though I have not been introduced to the lady," Felicity said. "The important thing is that an elevated individual like Lord Rustmont cannot be overcome with just one supposed suitor. I am only glad I realized it. Mr. Stratton is to bring his friend Mr. Wiles into it."

All the sisters seemed well satisfied with this development.

"Just be careful you do not fall in love with either of those two fellows," Winsome counseled.

"Impossible," Felicity said. "Mr. Wiles is exceedingly strange and Mr. Stratton, well… he thinks Papa is strange!"

Mrs. Right thought Mr. Stratton probably had his head screwed on right. Anybody who didn't perceive the duke as strange did not have their eyes open. It did not preclude one holding a vast affection for the man. It was just sensible to face facts.

"I suppose neither of your two gentlemen is particularly handsome," Verity said. "As far as I know, gentlemen like that never are."

"You don't know anything about it," Winsome said, always ready to challenge what Verity did or did not know.

"Felicity must settle the question," Grace said, "as she is the only one of us who positively does know."

Felicity chewed on a biscuit from the jar on her bedside. "Mr. Wiles can be dismissed immediately—he is far too nondescript. As for Mr. Stratton, well for one, his given name is Percy, which I cannot like. If I owned a goldfish, I would name it Percy."

Verity nodded and murmured, "Very common name for a

goldfish."

"But what does he look like?" Winsome asked.

"Well, he is rather tall, I will give up that point. He has dusky colored hair, dark blond I would call it, and blue eyes. They are a very dark blue, which I do find superior to light blue in a gentleman. His clothes are really very good—I do not believe any gentleman could have bested his knot last evening. And then, I've noticed there is something in his expression that makes it seem as if he meets the world with good nature. I suppose there are some who might think his looks were rather suave."

"That is quite a lot of good things, Felicity!" Serenity pointed out.

"Is it?" Felicity said, looking a little perturbed to hear it. "Of course, whatever charms he may have are mightily outweighed by other less attractive aspects of him. Mr. Stratton is the sort of gentleman best admired from afar and not spoken to directly."

"I look forward to getting a look at him next season when it is my turn," Grace said.

Mrs. Right noticed Felicity seemed very struck by that idea. Perhaps her dear girl was not quite as immune to Mr. Stratton's charms as she imagined.

"Now, Mrs. Right," Felicity said hurriedly, "what goes on below stairs with the new butler? Will you tell us?"

"We are well on our way to being rid of him," the house-keeper said. "I hope I can count on my girls to play their part?"

As all the sisters nodded vigorously, Mrs. Right proceeded to outline what had been done so far to convince Mr. Sykes-Wycliff to pack his bags and begone. Then, she explained the girls' role in the operation.

They were to drop hints to the butler that he'd have little chance of encountering old age if he were to travel to the duke's seat in the Dales. In particular, they were to warn him never to agree to participate in the servants' hunt. It might *seem* amusing to have the staff running round the moors while the duke hunted them all with his fowling piece. However, the duke was a very bad shot and often hit things he did not mean to, like a footman the year before. That poor lad was back living with his mother in the village as he still had a limp. Of course, they were all thankful it was his leg hit, rather than his heart or his head.

"That is a jolly good idea, Mrs. Right," Grace said.

Felicity nodded. "I am certain we can frighten him into leaving."

"It's for his own good," Patience said. "He will feel better about himself if he goes to a house that actually needs a butler."

They all nodded at Patience's rather thoughtful assessment.

"Aye, it's a kindness," Mrs. Right said. "Now, we should not bother Valor with these ideas, as she would be up with night terrors, fretting over a servants' hunt that never was. Never mind her inability to keep it to herself, the dear little mite."

"She ought not know of it," Serenity said. "She's already terrified of Mr. Sykes-Wycliff on account of the stories we told of Mr. Herring's final hours in the house."

Mrs. Right pressed her lips together. There had been no 'we' about it. Verity had been the author of a wild tale that included Mr. Herring attempting to set the house on fire and burn it to the ground, but for it being a damp sort of day and he could not get a flame going. Poor Valor still had night terrors over the idea that he might slip back inside in the middle of the night on a drier sort of day and finish what he started.

No matter. Her plan was unfolding perfectly and Mrs. Right was certain they'd be rid of Mr. Sykes-Wycliff by the end of the week. Then, she would begin to tie Lady Marching Orders in knots so she had no time to dig up another butler.

She had not worked out her whole strategy for that harridan yet, but she had by happenstance come upon one idea already. Lady Marchfield was in the habit of taking all the invitations from the front hall salver and examining them to decide which would be appropriate to accept. Then she would write out her responses and leave them for a footman to deliver after noting them in the duke's calendar.

Mrs. Right had noticed she'd not got to them this morning and had a look herself. She'd gone through them and found something delightful. It was called a Cyprian's party. The description of it was. "A genial place where a gentleman could encounter certain ladies of sophistication, wit, and passion in a private and confidential setting."

A pile of courtesans looking for their next benefactor—of course they'd invited the duke. And of course, Lady Marchfield would throw it right in the bin.

Mrs. Right wrote out an acceptance to the invitation for the duke. Then, careful to imitate Lady Marchfield's handwriting, she put it in the duke's calendar as Lady Cyprion's dinner, confirmed for the duke, Lady Felicity, and Lady Marchfield, along with the time and address.

"Now Felicity," Mrs. Right said, "you know how sometimes I might ask you girls to trust me without explanation?"

Felicity nodded. "You have never steered us wrong," she said.

"No never," Serenity said. "Why, remember when you told us to take our fowling pieces up to the attics and fire out the windows when we caught sight of Mr. Weatherby coming to court you on your afternoon off? We never saw that fellow again."

"It was quite necessary," Mrs. Right said, "though I did not like to say why at the time. That person was very pushy. He would attempt to steal me from you."

"Just so," Patience said. "We did not know why we fired over the head of Mr. Weatherby, but it turned out to be for a very good reason.

"What is it we're to do this time, Mrs. Right?" Grace asked.

"This is just for Felicity. On Tuesday next, Lady Cyprion is to hold a dinner. I wish you will pretend at planning to go until the very last minute, and then claim a headache. I wish the duke to take Lady Marchfield alone."

"Gracious, it's so mysterious!" Winsome said. "We might never work out why, like we did with Mr. Weatherby."

"Oh, I expect you'll know why, when all is said and done," Mrs. Right said.

"You can count on me, Mrs. Right," Felicity said.

Mrs. Right sighed contentedly. Her girls were really very good sorts. As a further cheer, Lady Marchfield would shortly find herself surrounded by courtesans.

It was very pleasant to think about.

PERCY'S VALET HAD taken his time with his clothes and accomplished the rather spectacular knot he called *The Radcliff*. Of course, he named it *The Radcliff* since his name was Radcliff. His valet's sole ambition in life was to inspire envy and he wanted all the envious to know that his knot was invented by him. Percy might have thought the notion rather conceited, but for the fact that it really was well-done, and he appreciated the looks at it he got from other gentlemen. It was a Mail Coach somehow ending in a Barrel Knot—complicated and elegant. Nobody but Radcliff could understand how it was done, least of all Percy.

While Radcliff was working his magic with Percy's neckcloth, he'd chattered on about the latest gossip he'd picked up from who knew where. According to the valet, news of Lady Felicity's odd performance at Almack's was widely spoken of. There was speculation that she was prone to fits of the inherited variety. Radcliff had even heard that there was betting regarding whether there would be a repeat performance.

Percy just hoped none of this talk reached Lady Felicity's ears. She seemed to have a bit of a temper and it was not as if her father would rein her in. Percy could not imagine what she would do. After all, it was not as if she was well acquainted with reality and facts. He'd been surprised over *her* surprise when he'd mentioned the duke's eccentricity. How did she not see it?

Now, he was roaming round Lady Albright's annual rout—a

rather eccentric event itself. The lady kept a menagerie of animals, some in enclosures and some roaming free, some inside and some out of doors.

Percy recalled that last year her Tamarin monkey, Hugo was his name, had decided he was fed up with the crowd and its associated noise. In retaliation, he'd leapt from a chandelier into Lady Annabelle's rather elaborately done hair. The monkey proceeded to tear at it as if he were determined to get to the bottom of it. As the lady screamed and pins flew in all directions, Lady Albright only admonished Hugo for being a mischievous imp before luring him away with a slice of pear.

Percy doubted Lady Annabelle would make a second appearance. He did, however, think that Lady Felicity would make an appearance. She'd told him that her father, the duke, would bring her, as he said it sounded hilarious. Her aunt, Lady Marchfield, had counseled against it and refused to accompany them. That had seemed to be no matter as apparently the duke did not like his sister much.

Percy could well believe it, considering what he'd witnessed at their departure from the candlelight picnic. For all he knew, Lady Marchfield was just now wandering round the Seven Dials, the duke having pushed her out of his carriage.

"I still do not see what precisely we are meant to do," Wiles said, brushing a red squirrel off the sideboard and pouring himself a glass of hock.

"Where is the confusion?" Percy said. "Lady Felicity will arrive and we'll follow her about like two lovesick lotharios. If Rustmont turns up and sees it, wonderful. But the real point is that my father sees it and becomes convinced I am set on Lady Felicity even though she prefers you."

"Does she know she is meant to prefer me?" Wiles asked.

"No, but she can barely stand the sight of me, so I think it should be obvious enough."

"Where is your old gentleman anyway?"

"He's around here somewhere," Percy said, watching Lady

Albright's red squirrel creep back on the sideboard and begin collecting grapes. "He got waylaid by Sir Reynolds, but he'll catch up to me as soon as he can—he tracks me like a hunter on a stag."

"Is that a deer?" Wiles asked.

Percy looked at his friend. "Yes. It's a male deer. How could you not know that?"

"No, I mean over there," Wiles said, hooking his thumb.

Percy glanced at the far corner of the room. Indeed, a full-grown doe had made herself comfortable on a settee, her wide eyes taking in the room. He shook his head and turned away.

"There she is, there is Lady Felicity," Percy said, looking toward the doors to the drawing room.

He waved, so he might look enthusiastic. One never knew if one's father was observing by peeking round curtains, he must be on his guard every second.

Lady Felicity was really looking terrific. He had noticed before that candlelight did something very well for her hair. There were so many different shades running through it—browns and golds, and even hints of red. He'd really never seen anything like it and it made other ladies' hair color seem rather flat and uninspired. And then, those big brown expressive eyes. He supposed if she came with a usual temperament and a usual family, Rustmont and his ilk would be at her feet.

Percy braced himself as her father escorted her toward him. "Your Grace, Lady Felicity," he said with a bow. "Lady Felicity, I believe you know Mr. Wiles. Your Grace, may I present Mr. Harry Wiles."

The duke eyed Wiles up and down. "Gad, Felicity, you are collecting an awful lot of misters."

"Mr. Wiles is the eldest son of Baron Davies, Papa."

"A baron, eh?" the duke said, seeming amused. "Just got your toe on the ladder! Well, it could be worse—you could be a baronet!"

As Percy had expected, Wiles looked ready to fall over. Encounters with the Duke of Pelham were always going to be unsettling. He should have warned him that all the duke would ever know about him was that he was currently a mister.

"Hah!" the duke said, looking at the squirrel on the sideboard Here we are always trying to keep those rascals out and Lady Albright has invited them in."

"Oh, and there is a deer, Papa."

The duke's eyes traveled to the settee. "If only I had my gun, eh? Then we'd have a good dinner on the morrow."

"I do not suppose Lady Albright would thank you for shooting up her drawing room, though." Lady Felicity pointed out.

Percy did not suppose any rational person would appreciate it, particularly not an animal lover such as Lady Albright. It was said she lived on fish and vegetables, as she did not care to eat the meat of anything with legs. Percy had always wondered if that meant crabs were out.

"I suppose she would not like it," the duke admitted. "A messy business, killing things. Your mother was very put out when a bird got into the drawing room and I shot it in midflight. She said I ought not be firing a gun around so many young children."

Lady Felicity nodded knowingly, as if it were simply a matter of course that a mistress of a household might object to gunfire in the drawing room.

"Indeed," she said, "A wood pigeon. I remember we buried it in the garden and gave it a proper funeral."

Wiles was rather wide-eyed. Percy thought he'd probably get used to it, though. He was, himself, not nearly as perturbed by the duke and his daughter as he'd been in the beginning.

"I wonder, Mr. Stratton," Lady Felicity said, "if Lord Rustmont attends this evening? He was so very helpful in the search for the pineapple. I would like to thank him for his efforts."

The duke snorted. "Probably doesn't know it was all for naught, though, does he? Looking for a pineapple that never was."

Percy decided to ignore that comment, as it was beginning to dawn on him that the best strategy for responding to a deranged duke was no response at all.

"I have not yet encountered Lord Rustmont," he said. "Perhaps we may stroll to the back garden? That is where some of the larger animals are to be found and he may well be there, admiring them."

"I wonder at a fellow admiring animals rather than ladies," the duke said, "but all right—let us see what sort of lunacy Lady Albright has got up to back there."

With that genial assessment, they set off.

FELICITY HELD EVERY hope that Lord Rustmont would attend Lady Albright's rout, and equally hopeful that Lady Mary of the frothy blond curls and piles of admirers would stay at home. Nobody needed a diamond of the first water flitting about the place.

Perhaps Lady Mary was terrified of animals. There were such women, she knew. Valor was terrified of an old bull in one of her father's far fields, convinced he would break down the fence and skewer her, though the bull never even looked her way.

Mr. Stratton had done as he was asked and brought Mr. Wiles into the ruse, though Felicity was not certain how convincing a suitor that fellow was. He looked ready to fall over even conversing with her father. He did not seem made of very stern stuff.

No matter. It was two gentlemen following her around and certainly Lord Rustmont would note it.

Mr. Stratton had put out his arm as they prepared to make their way to the gardens, though Felicity had been forced to hint to Mr. Wiles that he ought to take her other arm. He really was not much of a romancer.

Of course, her father found it hilarious and said to Mr. Wiles,

"A little slow to the mark, eh, Mister?

This seemed to discompose Mr. Wiles even further.

They made their way out to the hall and encountered Mr. Stratton's father, the viscount, on his tiptoes, peering round in every direction.

"Still looking for that spectacular pineapple?" the duke said jovially.

Viscount Denderby only stared at the duke. Then he stared at Felicity and her two accompanying gentlemen. "I was looking for my son, in fact," the viscount said rather coldly.

"Now you've found him," the duke said, "hanging on one side of my daughter while the other mister takes the opposite side."

"Lady Felicity," the viscount said, "I wonder if I might steal my son away. I have a notion of showing him something in the back garden."

"I bet it's another missing pineapple!" the duke said, laughing at his own wit. "Don't fall for it, that's my advice!"

"Papa, really. Perhaps we might all travel there together, Lord Denderby," Felicity said. "That is precisely where we were headed."

The viscount nodded, but Felicity could see very well he was not happy with the idea. Well, it was his own fault for thinking her father was deranged and herself eccentric in some manner. What an idea.

They went through the doors to the garden and found it well lit with torches placed throughout.

To the right was a very long sideboard that seemed to be a series of doors off their hinges laid atop brickwork. Two young stoats were making a terrific mess, running up and down it and pausing to help themselves to an item. It all seemed to be a game—there was plenty there for them to eat, but they seemed more interested in stealing away what the other one had in its mouth. One of them had just stepped on butter carved as a swan and left a very distinct footprint.

"Oh Papa," Felicity said, "they are so charming. Do you suppose we ought to get a pair of stoats of our own?"

The duke shrugged. "Ask Mrs. Right—she'll know if we ought to do it."

"Excellent notion, she is sure to know. Oh, there is Lord Rustmont," Felicity said, looking across the garden to the larger enclosures that housed Lady Albright's more interesting creatures. "Gentlemen, do escort me there."

"Ah hah!" the duke said, "the game begins! Eh, Denderby?"

Lord Denderby did not seem to know what the game was, and Felicity hoped her father would not inform him of it. The lord was so stiff and might not appreciate his son participating in a ruse to make another gentleman envious of the attention.

That idea was rather confirmed by the look on Mr. Stratton's features—he looked almost panicked.

"Let us go," Mr. Stratton said hurriedly, pulling her forward.

They made their way toward Lord Rustmont's party. He stood with three other gentlemen she did not know and was currently frowning, and one brow raised at one of them in that marvelous way he had. Felicity was glad Viscount Denderby had declined to accompany them. As she glanced behind her, she noted the lord just staring after them.

Of course, Mr. Stratton's father had made his dislike of her own father known, so she should not be surprised. Her dear father would remain unscathed by the viscount's low opinion, though, as he so rarely deigned to notice anybody's disapproval. Their local vicar was concerted in his efforts to avoid the duke, even though it was her father's living that fed him. The fellow sometimes went to such lengths as jogging in the opposite direction, but it was all water off a duck's back for her father. He was forever calling after the vicar as he sped away, shouting, "Cheer up, old fellow."

"Lord Rustmont," Felicity said, calling for his attention from his friends.

The lord turned and he looked positively glorious wearing his signature disdainful expression.

"Lady Felicity," he said gravely. "Your Grace, Stratton, Wiles."

"Rustmont," Mr. Stratton and Mr. Wiles said in unison.

"Yes, yes," the duke said, "everybody has said everybody else's name, what a palaver. Now, what have we got here?"

Lord Rustmont stood aside to reveal two enclosures. One was a simple wood fence, as one might find on any English farm. It was meant to keep in a magnificent looking beast—a stout horse, but a horse that was striped black and white.

Good heavens, Lady Albright had a zebra.

The other enclosure was far more secure. It seemed to be wholly enclosed by metal bars spaced close together and rising up to curve, forming a roof. There was a sturdy-looking gate on the front of it.

Felicity could not see anything in it, though. She hoped it was not a float of crocodiles. She had seen a picture of those beasts in a book once; they'd all been creeping up a riverbank while some poor fellow had his back turned gathering reeds.

"There is a tiger in there," Lord Rustmont said, following her gaze. "He stays well in the back, as he does not appear to enjoy the festivities."

"As well he would not," the duke said. "I don't suppose a beast dragged all the way here from the Far East would be enjoying himself in a London garden."

Felicity thought her father was right. It would be one thing to welcome into the house some local stoats who would be fully capable of departing it if they did not like it. But a zebra and a tiger? She supposed both must find themselves lonely and wondering where they were. Particularly the zebra, as she was sure they traveled in herds just as horses liked to do. Where is the lead mare? Where is the stallion and colts and fillies? It must be very confusing to feel as if there should be a crowd around one and yet be alone.

She could not actually say how social an average tiger was.

Now that she was really considering the matter, she concluded that if Lady Albright loved animals as she claimed, she would have left them where they belonged.

She shook off the idea, as it was something that would deserve consideration on another day. Then she shook off Mr. Stratton and Mr. Wiles from either arm. She took a few steps forward toward the tiger's enclosure to show Lord Rustmont that she was stalwart in the face of such a terrific beast. Felicity imagined such a thing must be seen as an alluring quality and assist him in imagining her as the mistress of his house. Anybody running a household must have iron nerves. She'd seen that well enough from Mrs. Right.

As she peered into the darkness of the enclosure, a voice behind her said, "Do smell this, Lady Felicity—Lady Albright's roses."

A handful of roses was waved in front of her face. Predictably, the scent ran up her nose and itched and tickled it relentlessly. What was this person doing? Who were they? She did not recognize the voice.

She did not dare turn round to find out, as she would not like Lord Rustmont to see her scrunching her nose again.

Behind her, her father laughed uproariously. "Trying to make her sneeze, are you? You'll be lucky if she doesn't clobber you for it, and I won't stop her either!" he said.

Whoever had attempted to make her sneeze was all too successful. The fit that was coming upon her was even more violent than what she'd experienced at Almack's.

She tapped on her nose, and then she pinched it, staying turned away from Lord Rustmont. He could not be a witness to another sneezing attack. He would begin to think it was an everyday occurrence!

It was hopeless, she could not fight it off. Her body wracked with sneezes to expel the offending odor, and she fell against the door to the enclosure.

The latch made a rasping sound and disengaged. The door

slowly swung open. Felicity stared at it, almost uncomprehending what she was looking at.

There was a sudden shout. "Close it! Close the gate!"

Felicity fumbled with it as men began to join in on the shouting. Ladies screamed. There was a stampede to the doors of Lady Albright's house.

Her hands shook and she could not get the latch to engage.

Then, two large, amber-colored eyes ringed in midnight black emerged from the shadows of the dim enclosure and stared at her, unblinking. The eyes were housed in a head that was larger than she could have ever imagined—four times the size of a man's own.

CHAPTER EIGHT

FELICITY STARED AS the terrible beast showed its teeth, its canines yellow and at least four inches long. She dropped the latch and backed away. Turning her head, she saw the garden had emptied, but for Mr. Stratton and her father. Both stood motionless behind her.

"Do not look at us," Mr. Stratton said, "never turn your back on a large cat. Just slowly back up."

Felicity did as she was bid and took two very slow steps back, as she had no experience at all regarding what one ought to do in such a situation.

Out of the corner of her eye, she saw the two stoats up on their back legs, motionless and still, as if hoping not to be noticed.

The zebra was still for a moment, then it bolted to the back of its fencing. Felicity could hear its heavy breathing. The heavy breathing of absolute panic.

The tiger's head whipped round toward the sound. Felicity gasped, certain Lady Albright's zebra was moments away from a terrible demise. Her gasp brought the tiger's attention back to her.

The beast pushed on the door, seeming curious to find it open. It pushed further and the gate swung fully open with a whine from the hinges.

"Stay very still," Mr. Stratton said softly.

That would not be very hard to accomplish. Felicity wished

to run, but she felt frozen where she was. She was paralyzed in terror, just like the stoats.

The tiger's two front paws were out of the enclosure. They were impossibly massive, like a terrible dream of a monster. The claws could not be seen, but Felicity knew they were there, ready to come out when they were wanted.

The beast looked round as if he was not sure what he ought to do next. Felicity thought he found himself surprised to be free. She did not think his hesitation would last long.

"Do not move an inch, I am taking your shawl," Mr. Stratton said.

Felicity's mind was not working very well, and she could not fathom why Mr. Stratton should choose this moment to require her India shawl. Nevertheless, it slipped from her shoulders.

The movement attracted the tiger's attention. He stared with a strange and intense focus.

Suddenly, the shawl sailed over her head and into the enclosure. The tiger was lightning fast after it. Mr. Stratton pushed her out of the way and slammed the enclosure door behind the beast.

He forced the latch closed. The tiger was contained once more.

Felicity's heart pounded as it had never done before. How had Mr. Stratton known that a cat that size would chase like a housecat?

It was a cat's instinct to chase what ran. That was how.

Then the idea of what would have happened if *she'd* run—it would have been after her just as fast as it had gone after her shawl. It would have been his instinct to chase and pounce on her, just like a housecat on a mouse.

Felicity felt tears spring up in her eyes. She felt like laughing or crying or both. Never in her life had she come so close to dying. One lunge from that beast would have done it.

Mr. Stratton sighed in relief and turned to her.

He suddenly lurched forward with a shout and Felicity was horrified to see the tiger's paw swipe through the bars, massive claws outstretched. A terrible ripping sound rent the quiet of the night and Mr. Stratton fell forward on the grass.

As he lay on the ground, Felicity could see the tiger had ripped right through his coat and his shirt. The blood seeped everywhere and was dreadful to behold.

At least, dreadful for her to behold. The tiger seemed to find it less dreadful and lifted its nose to the air, sniffing it. It smelled the blood. Seeming enraged by it, the beast crashed itself against the bars of its enclosure.

"No time to waste," the duke said. "Let us go from here before the creature takes another run at it. Felicity, help me get him up. Come on, mister, time to quit this party."

Mr. Stratton seemed to be in a state of shock, but he made a valiant attempt to rise. Felicity grabbed his arm on one side and the duke took the other.

Between them, they supported him to the door which, incredibly, they found locked. She supposed once people understood that a tiger was loose it was every man for himself. They'd been left to face the beast alone, with no means of escape.

The duke banged on it and shouted, "Open this door at once or I'll hunt down every last one of you and shoot you in the head!"

Felicity heard fumbling with the lock. The door cracked open and Lady Albright appeared, her face gone very white.

"Out of the way," the duke said, pushing the door fully open. "Send for a doctor, we'll get him up the stairs and take over one of your bedchambers."

"But what... what happened? Who let Tiberius out?" Lady Albright stuttered.

"My daughter fell against the latch after some idiot made her sneeze," the duke said, practically dragging Mr. Stratton forward. "One wonders, Madam, why there was not a lock on it!"

"The padlock? Oh dear..." Lady Albright said softly.

From this, Felicity supposed there was meant to be a lock on the door. Really, how careless must one be to forget to secure the lock on a tiger's cage?

Mr. Stratton was getting heavier and harder to hold upright.

Her father pointed at two stunned looking footmen. "Don't stand there with your mouths hanging open. Carry this fellow above stairs!"

The footmen hurried over and took Mr. Stratton from either side. Felicity was rather relieved to be unburdened, as she had not known how much longer she could have held up her side. Mr. Stratton was rather tall and slim, but there was a solidness to him that she had not expected. His arm had been heavy as iron.

Now that she *was* unburdened and in better light, she could see the extent of the damage to Mr. Stratton's back. It was as if someone had taken a sharp knife and cut him open in four deep lines.

He had bled a lot and seemed only barely conscious. The side of her dress where she'd held him up was dripping with his blood.

"You all right, girl?" the duke asked.

Felicity nodded, attempting to appear very brave.

"Right, I'll go up and see the mister squared away. Have a stiff brandy while you wait, that will set you up."

Felicity nodded, vaguely aware that Lady Albright was attempting ten things at once. She was directing the footmen who helped Mr. Stratton, sending the butler for the doctor, sending another footman to the stables to find the padlock that was supposed to be on the tiger's enclosure, loudly explaining how Tiberius simply did not know his own strength and would not have purposefully hurt anyone, outlining what the tiger had eaten for his dinner to point out that it was not as if he were hungry, explaining how the padlock had no doubt been forgotten when the tiger had been served that dinner, and finally hurrying up the stairs behind the patient.

The duke followed the lady and the patient up the stairs and Felicity had far more faith in her father's ability to set things right than Lady Albright.

The house had emptied, but for the servants and Lord Denderby. He rushed forward and Felicity could not think where he had been when the latch came undone. Where had anybody been? Where had Lord Rustmont been?

People had disappeared out of that garden like a magician's trick. As far as she could tell, they'd kept going right out the front doors. She could hear the distant sounds of carriages and people, but Lady Albright's house was eerily empty.

"My son!"

"He has been taken above stairs and a doctor has been sent for, Lord Denderby," Felicity said.

"Look what you have brought him to," the viscount said, fairly spitting the words out. "He is an only son! You are a family of lunatics, that's what you are."

The viscount headed toward the stairs.

"It was not my tiger, my lord, and it was not me who forgot to put the padlock on the door!" she called after him. "Furthermore, you hightailed it out of that garden without your son, I noticed. And even furthermore, the door was locked when we tried to get in the house—where was all your concern then?"

The viscount paused his race up and stairs and cried, "There was a tiger on the loose!"

Felicity crossed her arms by way of answer. The viscount turned and continued his ascent, disappearing down a corridor.

Felicity began to feel a bit wobbly on her feet as the shock of what had happened began to leave her. She thought she'd best follow her father's advice and drink something strong to settle her.

She wandered into the empty drawing room and grabbed the decanter of brandy. She did not bother with a glass, nor did she bother about sitting on Lady Albright's white velvet sofa in a dress soaked in blood.

Her mind felt rather blank, her ability to think flown off somewhere. All that would come to her was that she was glad to be alive, and she hoped Mr. Stratton remained alive too.

She took a long swig from the decanter, and then two more

for good measure.

PERCY HAD BEEN laid on his stomach in one of Lady Albright's bedchambers. It had all happened so fast! One moment, they were facing a tiger who'd just realized his door was open, the next the beast was tricked back inside and the problem solved, then the next the dastardly creature had swiped at him through the bars of his enclosure.

He could not see the damage done to his back, but he could feel it. At first, it had been more of a shock than pain, but the pain had set in by degrees. Just now, it felt as if he was on fire.

Somehow, Lady Felicity's father had taken charge of the sickroom. The duke was sending the staff in all directions for hot water, bandages, turpentine to clean the wounds, and a large brandy for the patient. Lady Albright seemed to be hovering at the edges, occasionally defending the tiger, who Percy now knew was named Tiberius.

Tiberius could make his way to the ninth circle of hell for all he cared.

"Well then, Stratton," the duke said, "the good news is you saved the day. The bad news is your wounds are looking… not very good."

Though Percy ought to have been considering the duke's assessment of his injuries, his mind settled on the fact that the duke had for once called him Stratton, rather than mister.

He supposed one must get oneself gravely injured for the duke to remember one's name.

"Lady Felicity," Percy said. "She is all right?"

"As right as can be expected. I advised her to dose herself with brandy and I advise you to do the same. Of course, I'll have to hear from her what upsets her more—facing down a tiger or turning round to notice that her precious Rustmont had flown the coop."

"He's a stick," Percy murmured.

"And a coward, as far as I can see. I expect it's all up with him—Felicity knows well enough that I can't have a coward for a son-in-law. I'd harass him to the edges of his sanity!"

Percy laughed, though the movement caused the burning on his back to surge.

"You seem a stalwart sort—why don't you make a run at her? At least I'd know she was safe from wild animals. Probably the best I can hope for."

Percy coughed and choked and worked to clear his throat. Why did not *he* take a run at Lady Felicity? That was a circumstance he'd not seen coming. He'd put all his effort toward convincing his father that he was set on Lady Felicity. He'd not thought of the duke at all in his plan.

"Uh, well, as to that, you see, the way I see it, I suppose…"

Before Percy had to elaborate any further by way of a string of random words, his father burst into the room.

"My god!" the viscount shouted. "He's an only son and look what's happened to him!"

"It was never going to be very sensible to own a tiger, in my opinion," the duke said matter-of-factly. "Something like this was bound to happen."

"The tiger was not a danger until somebody let him out!" the viscount cried.

"You really should get hold of yourself, old fellow," the duke said. "Hysterics won't help Stratton, here."

"I demand an end to this pursuit of that man's daughter!" the viscount cried at Percy, apparently unable to put aside his hysteria.

"Ah, that's the game is it?" the duke asked. "I did wonder. Well, I am agreeable, even though he's only a mister."

"You see what they are, Stratton! They are deranged lunatics!"

"Hah!" the duke said, laughing heartily. "I'm not the one

looking everywhere for invisible pineapples, am I? Do you often hallucinate about fruit that isn't there?"

"Why aren't you dead on the moors?" the viscount asked the duke, fury trembling in his voice. "We all thought you were dead on the moors and we were very relieved to hear it!"

"I do not know who the *we* could be that you refer to, Sir Pineapple, but most people find me delightful," the duke said.

Percy had the idea the old soldier believed it, too. Oddly, the duke was somehow growing on him.

Fortunately, the doctor came in before his father could respond to being called Sir Pineapple.

Dr. Redmond took charge of the room at once. He showed himself to be a no-nonsense sort of gentleman who was not the least bit awed by a duke and a viscount hurling insults at one another. He ordered the duke out and he ordered Percy's father to sit quietly in a corner else he would be put out too.

The doctor examined the wounds and pronounced them precisely what one would expect from a tiger's claw. "If you avoid infection, you ought to do all right," he said. "I'll dose you with laudanum and get it all cleaned up—I don't suppose a tiger keeps his claws very tidy. You'll be sore for quite a while, I imagine."

"If he does not die!" the viscount said. "He is an only son—if he dies, the title will go to my imbecile nephew!"

Percy heard Dr. Redmond sigh deeply. "I'll give your father a dose of laudanum too. I can't see what else will calm him down."

"I do not require being calmed down," the viscount said. "I will take my son home now. Somebody call my carriage!"

"You will do no such thing," the doctor said sternly. "He is not to be moved for several days. I will stay the night to ensure he does not develop a fever and then we will see where we are. Now, you get in your carriage, by yourself, and get out of my way."

There were various sputterings from the viscount's direction, but for once he could not find the words to respond. It made

Percy laugh despite it causing him pain.

He heard the viscount jump to his feet. "I have decided to depart. I will return on the morrow. First thing! I order you to stay alive, Stratton."

With that fatherly advice, he promptly stomped out of the room.

"All right, one problem solved," the doctor said. "Roll carefully on your side so you can drink down the laudanum."

Percy did as he was bid, though it was excruciating.

It was well worth it though. Once the laudanum took effect, his pain lessened remarkably and his spirits rose. After all, aside from his skin being torn to shreds, the evening had gone rather well.

To think, he would forever be known as the fellow who fought off a tiger. It would be very pleasant to go round being a tiger-fighter. He did not suppose Rustmont could claim to be a tiger-fighter.

Rustmont. He'd run away with all the others, like a hare from a fox. Like a frightened child. Like a fainting woman. Like a... not the high-flown Corinthian he pretended he was. He wondered what Lady Felicity thought about *that*.

Percy said, "Rustmont is afraid of a tiger."

"Everybody should be afraid of a tiger," the doctor said drily.

"I wasn't afraid of the tiger," Percy said boldly.

"Then you are one die short of a set," the doctor said.

This caused Percy to laugh. "That's funny—that's what I said about the duke and now it's me. And you know what? Lady Felicity isn't afraid of a tiger either. She was cracking brave!"

"She sounds stupendous."

"Gad, have you seen her hair?"

"No, I have not. Though I presume the laudanum has taken good effect."

"Rather."

The next hour was not so pleasant, as the doctor worked on his wounds. After that, the jolly fellow gave him another dose of laudanum and he drifted off imagining all the monikers he might have earned for himself—The Tiger, The Savior, Scar-Back, The Undefeated, Genghis Stratton, Master of the Beasts, Percy the Great—there were so many possibilities he could not imagine which one would stick. He wondered what Lady Felicity would think about *that*.

"Gad," he murmured, "have you seen her hair?"

FELICITY'S SISTERS HAD gathered round her in the drawing room, captivated by the tale of the tiger escaping its cage and Mr. Stratton getting it back in again, and then Mr. Stratton being horribly attacked.

At least, five of her sisters were captivated—Valor's eyes were wide and she was white as a sheet.

"I knew something like this would happen," the youngest Nicolet daughter murmured. "I've had night terrors of beasts dragging me away and tearing me apart."

"You are in no danger, Valor," Grace said.

"You don't know that, though," Valor said. "That tiger is still here, right in London, and it got out of its cage one time. It could get out another time."

"Everybody knows that if a tiger gets out one time," Verity said, "they get a better lock so it doesn't get out a second time."

"They forgot the lock altogether," Felicity said. "I suppose a lock not used is no good at all."

"And," Valor said, "it's a wild animal. Once it smells blood, it cannot be stopped. Felicity had blood on her dress. I bet the tiger can smell it."

That did give Felicity pause. She was all but certain that Mr. Stratton remained in Lady Albright's house, recovering from his injuries. If the tiger did get out and prowled the house, Mr. Stratton would be in no shape to defend himself and the tiger had already a taste of his blood. It gave her a rather sick feeling.

"Think how brave Mr. Stratton was," Serenity said.

"I believe all gentlemen are brave, when called upon," Verity said. "That is a widely understood point."

"You don't know that," Winsome said.

"I am afraid not, Verity," Felicity said, before Verity could dig her heels in on the subject. "There were many guests out in the garden at that moment and the only people who stayed were Papa and Mr. Stratton. Oh, and whoever was the last through the door locked it behind them."

"I am shocked that Lord Rustmont did not stay and fight the beast," Serenity said.

Felicity was rather shocked herself. Had anyone asked her about such a circumstance ahead of time, she would have assured them that Lord Rustmont would act very brave and it would be Mr. Stratton who would run away.

"Tell us about the blood again, Felicity," Patience said.

"I cannot bear to hear of the blood again," Valor said. "I will go and have a confidential conversation in my room with Mrs. Wendover."

Felicity nodded. Mrs. Wendover, the raggedy stuffed rabbit that Valor turned to in moments of worry, would be a willing listener. According to Valor, Mrs. Wendover was always full of sensible advice, most of which consisted of pulling one's blankets over one's head so that monsters could not see you.

Valor skipped out of the room, but before Felicity could give another detailed description of the terrible wound, the butler entered the room carrying a tea tray. One of the footmen followed behind with a tray of fairy cakes.

Though there had been so much excitement out of the house, Felicity had not forgotten her duty to Mrs. Right inside the house.

"Mr. Sykes-Wycliff," she said with a bright smile, "how do you settle in?"

"Very well, Lady Felicity," he said.

Though he said he was very well, he looked a deal paler and

worn out than he had done when he arrived at the house.

"Rest when you can. When we are in the Dales, things are a deal more… what would you call it, Grace?"

Grace, having been talked to beforehand, as had all her sisters, nodded knowingly and said, "Fraught? Is that the word you're thinking of?"

Felicity noted the footman press his lips together and turn away—he would be well-informed of the plan from Mrs. Right.

"Oh," Patience said, "you mean Papa going round knocking on doors in the middle of the night and then clobbering whoever opens for him? I suppose it's the country air that does it."

"Actually," Felicity said, "I was thinking of the servants' hunt. Mr. Sykes-Wycliff, you might claim a limp on the day and just refuse to go."

Verity nodded. "It's meant to be great fun, you see. What with all the servants running across the moors and Papa chasing them with his fowling piece."

"If only he had better aim," Serenity said sadly.

At this inconvenient juncture, Valor ran back into her room with Mrs. Wendover in her arms. "It was lonely up there and then Mrs. Wendover thought she might want a biscuit."

They had all hoped Valor would not be present for the ruse, as they did not like to give her nightmares. But there was nothing for it now—they had got started and must finish it.

"Accidents will happen, as poor Jimmy well knows," Grace said.

At this comment, Valor quite naturally looked entirely confused. She suddenly piped up. "That's what happened to Jimmy? He had an accident?"

Felicity nodded gravely. Jimmy, of course, had not been shot down by the duke. He'd left to become an apprentice in a town some hours away.

"You are not to worry, Valor," Grace said. "He was only shot in the leg and he continues his recovery."

"Though he's been very loud about refusing to ever come

back," Patience said.

"That's too bad," Valor said, "I liked him."

"He blames Papa, Valor, which is very unfair. Everybody knows our dear father cannot help it—he's not a very good shot!"

Valor nodded sadly, though she did not know the first thing about it.

With that, they put their attention to their tea and allowed Mr. Sykes-Wycliff to stagger out of the room.

CHAPTER NINE

PERCY HAD SPENT a further two days at Lady Albright's house in a manner he would not like to ever repeat. The doctor, a good sort of fellow, had kept him well-dosed with laudanum, else he would have gone mad.

It was not so much the pain of the wound, which was slowly lessening, but Lady Albright.

She came into his room at all hours of the day and night, talking and talking and talking. He was to know everything about the charming qualities of Tiberius. She'd had him since he was a cub and he'd been very cuddly then. She claimed she did not know how the padlock had been off the enclosure. She swore it was not her who locked the door to the house against him.

After those querulous arguments, she seemed to gain some confidence and did an about face. Suddenly, the diatribes were all about her velvet sofa. She had discovered it bloodstained and she could only lay the blame on Lady Felicity.

Why had that lady sat on her velvet sofa when she had blood on her dress? That was what Lady Albright wished to know.

Percy could make a guess that Lady Felicity had been fully aware of creating a stain on the lady's sofa and had not given a toss about it.

On day two, a flower arrangement of daffodils had arrived for him. It had been signed *Household of the Duke of Pelham*. The note had rather given it away though.

Tigers, eh?

Clearly, the arrangement was from the duke himself, which gave Percy pause. The duke had come right out and said Percy ought to "make a run" at his daughter.

He had convinced himself the duke had only meant to shock. Half the things the fellow said were meant for that purpose, he was sure.

Were the flowers some kind of pushing forward? A hint that the duke had been serious? He was not certain. Nor was he certain what he thought about it.

Lady Felicity had shown herself to be a woman of substance when facing down a tiger. He could only admire that. There had been no hysterics or faintings, and thank the gods there wasn't. She hadn't attempted to run. Anything like that would have done them all in.

He could only think that Rustmont was not worthy of her.

Yes, she was a bit eccentric, but really it only seemed so if one were to compare her to other ladies of the *ton*. There was a regularity to the ladies of society, as if they all had the same governess. Of course, one could not expect the duke's children could have had that governess, whoever she was. They lived too remote in the Dales.

As well, she was very pretty.

But, those ideas aside, he must stick to his purpose. He would not be chained! Not even to a lady who was beginning to seem like she had a lot of charms he had not initially been cognizant of.

The duke's flowers were not in his room long. His father had made a visit and been apoplectic over them, throwing them in the nearest bin. The note, *Tigers, eh*, was considered more proof of the duke's derangement.

Finally, by day three, the doctor pronounced him past the danger of a setback and fit to leave the house.

Percy found that as long as he stayed upright and did not lean back on anything, the pain was tolerable. Getting on his horse was not to be attempted though, and so he found himself the borrower of Lady Albright's carriage. He knew very well that his father would arrive in an hour to take him home, but he did not wish to go home.

He wished to go to White's. He wished to have a word with Hardwick. That gentleman had waved the roses under Lady Felicity's nose and was the author of the whole disaster. Percy thought he knew why—he wished to win the bet he'd started in the bet book.

Entering that institution, he went straight to the bet book. The bet on Lady Felicity had been whether or not she would have another sneezing fit. He scanned down the page. It was marked void. Below the bet was the following:

> *As it has been confirmed that Lord Hardwick:*
>
> *Did attempt to steer the outcome of the bet in his favor by assaulting Lady Felicity with roses,*
>
> *And that attempt created great danger to the Duke of Pelham, Lady Felicity, and Mr. Stratton,*
>
> *And caused grievous injury to Mr. Stratton,*
>
> *The bet is cancelled. All monies will be returned from whence they came, but for Mr. Hardwick's, which will go into the club's coffers. Mr. Hardwick has been asked to resign his membership and has proffered such. May he find his place at Boodles.*

Percy had been prepared to give Hardwick a severe dressing down, but there could be no firmer dressing down than a call for resignation and being directed to Boodles. It rather took the wind from his outraged sails.

He wandered into the morning room and found Wiles and Magnon at a table by the window.

"What ho, the returning conqueror," Magnon said.

Percy made his way over under the glances of everyone else scattered round the room.

"Well, you're alive," Wiles said, "that's something, I suppose."

"It *is* something, actually," Percy said. "You seem to have disappeared like a shot out of that garden."

Wiles shrugged. "As you should have done. There was a tiger."

"Who locked the door to the house?" Percy asked. "When we were finally able to get away, the door was locked."

"That was Lady Albright, I believe," Wiles said. "She absolutely panicked and forced everyone out the front doors and then carriages were coming, and well, considering she said that nobody can escape a tiger, I did think you were done for. You know, there was nothing more I could do for you."

"Nothing *more*, you say. You did nothing at all!"

"I was very sorry about you being trapped out there with a tiger, I did *that*."

Percy declined to answer Wiles' heroics by way of feeling sorry. "What was Rustmont doing, I'd like to know. Where was the brave Corinthian when he was needed?"

"Oh, he called Hardwick an idiot and skipped right out. I believe he may have knocked Lady Mayberry out of the way."

"I knew it," Percy said.

"Don't be so down in the dumps over it, Stratton," Magnon said. "You're alive and get to strut around like a big hero. I understand they're calling you Tiger-Slayer."

"I didn't kill the tiger."

"So what?" Magnon said. "Would you rather be called Tiger-locker-up?"

"Yes, so what?" Wiles said. "And as a further reason to be cheerful, guess who has not showed his face here since? Rustmont."

"Good. It's about time people saw him for what he really is. He's all show."

A waiter brought Percy a coffee and, oddly, a note on a salver.

He picked it up as Magnon said, "See, you're famous now, getting notes sent to you at your club."

"It's probably from my father. He would have gone to Lady Albright's to collect me and found me already left. I supposed he guessed where it was I went."

Percy unfolded the note, but to his surprise it was not from the viscount. He read it twice to be certain of understanding its contents.

Stratton—

Jolly good of you to come to dine this evening, considering… tigers, eh? As agreed, we will see you at eight.

Pelham

"Dinner? When did I agree to go to dinner?"

Magnon took the note and Wiles read it over his shoulder.

"The duke invites you to his house?" Wiles said. "I thought that old rascal could not even remember your name."

"But he saved the duke's daughter from a tiger," Magnon said. "That has to soften anybody's feelings. Clever he sent the note here, as your father would have torn it to shreds."

"I really do not remember having any conversation about a dinner," Percy said.

"Maybe you were delirious from your injuries," Magnon suggested.

"No," Percy said thoughtfully, "it was the laudanum. It really mixes a person up. Sometimes I would wake and wonder if it were dawn or sunset. Sometimes a footman would bring in a tray and I thought I'd already eaten. Or vice versa. I'd inquire if Lady Albright planned to starve me to death and then the footman would explain I'd eaten eggs, a pile of bacon, and three rolls just an hour before."

"Well, you agreed to this dinner, nothing to be done about it now," Wiles said.

"In any case, it will keep your old soldier on the back foot," Magnon said. "It will convince him more than ever that you are set on Lady Felicity."

"Yes, it would," Percy said. Though, that might not be all it would do.

It might encourage the duke, if he had any ideas of pushing him forward for his daughter.

Percy set his cup down with a clatter. What if Lady Felicity was having the same kind of ideas? It would follow that a lady who had just been saved from imminent death might develop feelings for her rescuer. What if that was where the duke was getting his ideas to begin?

"Oh no," he said, "I believe Lady Felicity may be falling in love with me."

Wiles looked rather slack-jawed. Magnon erupted in laughter. "Hoisted by your own petard, Stratton," he said.

Percy glared at him. He did not have time to compose a retort, though. Before he could say a word, his father's booming voice made him nearly jump from his chair.

"There you are! Scarpered out of Lady Albright's? Well I knew where I would find you. Come home. We are to have a quiet dinner this evening where we can rationally talk about your future."

As his father so little liked to talk in a rational manner, Percy thought that was a pipe dream. It would be a dinner full of rants and raves, his mother's taunts, and shouts of "I warn you!"

However, he had a way out of it. He picked up the sheet of paper that Magnon had set down on the table. "Unfortunately, I am already engaged. Otherwise, it sounds as if it would have been a delight."

The viscount snatched it from his hands. He very reliably began huffing and puffing.

"Why should you go to that lunatic's house? Why did you agree to it?"

"I have no idea why," Percy said. "I suspect it was the laudanum."

"Cancel it! Tell him you're not coming! Tell him you would never have accepted if you had not been drugged out of your senses!"

"It is too late to cancel attending a dinner, as you well know. In any case, I suspect I am just brought in to even out the numbers. As well, I am certain Lady Marchfield will be there and we would not like to offend her in the process of offending the duke."

"Harumph, I don't like it." The viscount said.

Of course, Percy knew he'd complain and complain about it, but in the end the viscount would have no wish to insult Lady Marchfield. Not even if he wished the duke would throw himself in the Thames. Or the oft wished-for idea that he would be discovered dead on the moors. There was something about being a fairly new-minted, titled gentleman that made one cautious about crossing a well-regarded matron. Especially a countess who was the daughter of a duke, even if that countess did not like the current duke very much.

As for his own opinion of apparently having accepted the duke's invitation, his feelings were rather mixed. He would not mind encountering Lady Felicity again after their recent adventure. Though, he ought not make it a habit.

Was his heart attempting to tell him something his head was not interested in hearing? No, that was ridiculous, He would not be chained. He'd said so many times.

MRS. RIGHT WAS well-pleased with how things were progressing in the plan to send Mr. Sykes-Wycliff screaming from the house. Her girls had seemed to have done their part, considering the questions she was just now being asked.

"Mrs. Right, I demand to know the full circumstances of what happened to this young footman—Jimmy was his name."

Demand, does he? All right.

"Very naturally, Mr. Sykes-Wycliff," Mrs. Right said smoothly, "I will happily answer any questions you may have. I am only trying to understand why there is a question. It was simply an unfortunate accident."

"So I heard. I want to know how it occurred, exactly. How does a footman get shot in the leg?"

"Well, I suppose we might have predicted it, in retrospect. As always, the men-staff had been given a head start and set out for the moors at dawn. An hour later, the duke followed, the idea being to hunt them down as they ran this way and that. When the duke spotted a servant, he was to fire over the fellow's head and then they were out of the game and must return to the house. All very amusing."

"How did it go wrong?" Mr. Sykes-Wycliff whispered.

Mrs. Right made a great attempt to peer at the butler as if he were not very fast on the uptake. "The duke became a bit too… enthusiastic. He was firing in all directions. Jimmy was situated on a cliff above the duke. So, when the duke attempted to fire over his head, he simply didn't aim high enough. Naturally, he put his gun down instantly when he heard Jimmy scream in agony. The duke was very sorry over it, I can tell you."

"I suppose he would be! I suppose Jimmy was rather sorry too! But certainly, Mrs. Right, after that disaster such an ill-omened activity would never be tried again."

"Of course you are right—the duke is nothing if not full of good sense. This year, he's only going to hunt the servants with his knives. The ones he would use to skin a deer. You know, the really big ones that look like they could chop down a tree."

"Large knives?"

"He's only to bring two—one for each hand. As long as everybody is quick on their feet, there should be no harm done."

"Quick on their feet? Do you mean running?"

"Just so."

"But Mrs. Right, I am not quick on my feet!"

Mrs. Right seemed to give that information some deep reflection. Then she said, "I know what you ought to do. You ought to practice. You could run round the square every morning after the duke has had his breakfast. That will build you up!"

As she watched Mr. Sykes-Wycliff actually consider this bizarre notion, Mrs. Right had great hopes that the neighbors of Grosvenor Square would very soon see the duke's deranged butler running round the square to no purpose.

With any luck, he'd keep running and never be seen again.

FELICITY HAD BEEN under the impression that they were to have a cozy family evening. It would not be as cozy as they were in the Dales, as Lady Marchfield was coming and would no doubt have a lot to say about Lady Albright's tiger, but she supposed they could sneak by a few things the lady did not approve of.

Grace might pitch a roll at their father's head and hit a footman with it instead, which would really cheer the lads. They had always been in the habit of laying bets regarding where the roll would land, and Felicity suspected it was one of the highlights of their evenings.

She also supposed their father would give his usual speech about getting his daughters out of the house as fast as possible and barring the door at Christmas. Then, they could all call him a liar and be very jolly.

They might even stay on at table to keep their father company while he drank his port. Lady Marchfield did not like the habit, but she had seen the results when the duke was left on his own with the bottle and she'd found it very uncomfortable.

All of that seemed very usual, so she was surprised when her father casually said, "By the by, I expect Mr. Stratton will turn up."

"Turn up?" Felicity asked. "For dinner?"

"Yes, dinner, what else? I sent him a note at his club. I pretended he'd already agreed to it, hah!"

"But why?" Felicity asked.

"Well now, he did come through with that tiger, after all. Mind you, I want all you girls out of my house as fast as possible, but being eaten by a wild animal is extreme, in my view."

Felicity looked down at her dress, feeling she might have made a different choice if she'd known there would be a guest outside of Lady Marchfield. She wore a neat but plain muslin that did not do anything particular for her.

Of course, there was no reason why she should concern herself over her appearance on account of Mr. Stratton. It was not as if Lord Rustmont was coming.

Felicity paused. Her feelings about those two gentlemen were so mixed up. Her first impressions had been muddled. Lord Rustmont had abandoned her to her fate with the tiger and she dearly wished to encounter him and hear an explanation that washed her doubts away.

Mr. Stratton had not abandoned her. He had saved her. Though that would have been the last thing she would have predicted. And then, she had to admit her feelings had softened toward that gentleman when she'd seen the injuries he had incurred in doing it.

"But Papa," Valor said, "won't Mr. Stratton know that he never did agree to come?"

The duke shrugged. "We'll see. I suspect that the doctor loaded him up with laudanum. If that was the case, he would have believed he could fly if someone told him so in a convincing manner."

"Do you suppose he will show us his injuries from the tiger?" Winsome asked.

"Certainly not," Felicity said. "They will be under his clothes."

Felicity felt a certain flutter at the mention of anything being under Mr. Stratton's clothes. It was highly ridiculous.

They heard carriage wheels rumble to a stop in front of the house.

"Well then," the duke said, "here is either Lady Misery, otherwise known as my sister, or it is the tiger-managing mister."

Felicity found herself unaccountably nervous. She really was making a cake of herself, even if she were the only one to know it.

Fortunately, or unfortunately, she really did not know which, it was Lady Marchfield.

"Roland," she said in her usual disapproving tone. "Felicity, I was told you were unharmed from that scurrilous evening at Lady Albright's. I did tell you both not to attend it. I do not see why anybody goes—first it was that stupid monkey assaulting people and now it is a tiger. Somebody ought to put a stop to it."

"Have a seat, Lady Misery," the duke said, entirely ignoring her diatribe and seeming pleased that he'd invented a new moniker for her. "We only wait for the mister."

"Do not call me names, Roland. You are no longer five years old. What mister?"

"Mr. Stratton, Aunt," Felicity said.

"Mr. Stratton? Why?"

"Because even though Papa wants us all out of the house as fast as possible," Patience said, "he does not care for the idea of one of us eaten by a tiger."

They all nodded gravely at this idea, though Lady Marchfield did not seem to see the sentiment in it.

"We were hoping we could have a look at Mr. Stratton's wounds," Winsome said, "but Felicity said no because they are under his clothes. We've never seen a man's back, under his clothes."

"I should say not!" Lady Marchfield exclaimed. She whipped out her fan and took to creating a windstorm on her face.

"We cannot be sure he will come," Valor said. "Papa only pretended to Mr. Stratton that it was already arranged, and now we have to see if he was drugged up enough to believe it."

"What?"

Fortunately, or unfortunately, Felicity could not tell which, a second set of carriage wheels was heard stopping.

"Oh Papa!" Patience said, "Mr. Stratton believed you!"

"I am very believable, my girl," the duke said jovially.

"Really?" Lady Marchfield asked, staring at her brother. "I find you rather unbelievable."

The duke snorted. Mr. Stratton was led in.

CHAPTER TEN

"MR. PERCY STRATTON, Your Grace," Thomas said with aplomb, leading that gentleman into the duke's drawing room.

Valor clapped for Thomas. The young footman had so little experience announcing visitors that he had been regularly practicing in the great hall, with Valor as his willing audience.

Though Mr. Stratton had so recently faced down a tiger and been wounded for his trouble, he was looking very well. His dusky hair looked a shade darker in the candlelight of the drawing room and his dark blue eyes were lively and full of fun. His neckcloth was superb—it was painstakingly complicated and yet full of elegant simplicity.

"Your Grace, Lady Marchfield, Lady Felicity," he said, accompanying it with an elegant bow.

"There he is, still alive, well done," the duke said. "I'd slap you on the back in congratulations, but I am not a monster."

Mr. Stratton looked momentarily perplexed, until Valor said, "Oh, because of the wounds. Papa does not want to hit your wounds. Well done, Papa."

"Very considerate, Your Grace," Mr. Stratton said.

"We are told we cannot see the wounds," Serenity said, "because they are under your clothes."

"Serenity!" Lady Marchfield hissed.

"It's true, though," Serenity said.

"It really is, Aunt. I heard it myself," Valor said nodding.

"You might as well be introduced to this pile of disappointments, Stratton," the duke said. "That's Grace—don't let her hit you with a roll! Patience and Serenity—twins, though you wouldn't know it to look at them. That arrival was quite the surprise, I can tell you. There's Verity—don't believe a word she says."

"Papa!" Verity exclaimed.

"It's true," Winsome said.

"That's Winsome, always trying to catch a person out," the duke said.

"*That's* true!" Verity said with a small smile toward Winsome.

"And there's the youngest, Valor. Afraid of her own shadow, though she might grow out of it," the duke concluded.

Valor shrugged, as if to say she had no particular plans in that direction.

"Now," the duke said, "if I can track down that butler Lady Misery here went and hired for me, we can go through."

Everyone looked expectantly toward the door. The duke shouted at it. "Mr. Why!"

Felicity bit her lip, as the name Why was very amusing. At the same time, she could not help but notice that Mr. Stratton looked pretty bowled over. She supposed meeting her entire family at once was a lot to take in.

Mr. Sykes-Wycliff appeared at the doors.

"Mr. Stratton," Lady Marchfield said, "I would like to clarify that this dignified butler's proper name is Mr. Sykes-Wycliff. Please disregard my brother's attempts at humor, which nobody finds funny."

Mr. Sykes-Wycliff nodded sadly. "Your Grace?" he asked.

"We will go through," the duke said, "no reason to stand around staring at each other in the drawing room."

The butler, who was looking very pale, nodded and led them through.

Felicity sat on the duke's right, and Mr. Stratton sat on Lady Marchfield's right at the other end.

Valor, being the youngest, was in the middle of the table, but they were not so many that they could not all talk together. Her youngest sister leaned forward and stared at Mr. Stratton.

"Can I ask you something?" Valor said.

"Brace yourself, Stratton," the duke said, "you never know what you'll be asked when it comes to this string of setbacks."

"I am braced," Mr. Stratton said.

"Well, it's just that, personally, I am terrified of tigers," Valor said. "I was even afraid of them when I thought they were all trapped in India. Now I'm even more afraid because one is in England. Is it even the only one? Are there more? So I was wondering, were you scared?"

The footman had just filled Mr. Stratton's wine glass with her father's excellent hock. He took a small sip and set it down. "I was petrified, Lady Valor," he said.

Felicity was rather surprised by that. He'd not seemed petrified. He had seemed very calm and confident.

Valor, for her part, nodded in commiseration.

"If you were petrified, why didn't you run away, then?" Patience asked.

"Never run from a cat," Mr. Stratton said. "Anybody with a housecat knows it."

"Do you have a cat?" Serenity asked.

Mr. Stratton nodded in the affirmative.

"What's your cat's name?" Winsome asked.

For some reason, Mr. Stratton seemed reluctant to answer. However, with seven young ladies staring at him and the duke laughing at the sight, he did not have much choice.

"Mind you," Mr. Stratton said, "I got him when I was young. Very, very young." Mr. Stratton fumbled with his napkin and said, "His name is Blueberry."

"You have a blue kit-cat!" Valor said, seeming very interested in the idea.

"No, I just liked blueberries. As I said, very young," Mr. Stratton said.

"Hah!" the duke exclaimed. "Wait until I see Denderby! I'll say, I understand you have a cat named Blueberry in your house. It's very eccentric, Sir Pineapple!"

"Papa!" Grace said, "Do not tease Mr. Stratton, or his father when you see him. You are very naughty!"

With that, Grace flung a roll. Felicity supposed it was meant to be sailing toward the duke, but of course it went very wide of the mark and hit Thomas square in the chest. He seemed delighted, and Felicity imagined he had won that bet.

"For heaven's sake," Lady Marchfield said. "Do attempt to recall, all of you, that you have a guest at table."

Most of the duke's daughters were relatively immune to Lady Marchfield's complaints. Valor, however, nodded gravely. "Tell me, Mr. Stratton, how are you finding the weather?"

Felicity bit her lip. They had all been advised, at one time or another, to consider the weather a safe and reliable topic of conversation. Mrs. Right thought it was a bit of nonsense, though. Any rube might look out a window to judge the weather for themself—no reason to ask other people what they thought about it.

Mr. Stratton did not laugh at the question, but gave Valor a very thoughtful answer, even comparing this season to the last. She appeared gratified to be taken seriously and nodded gravely throughout. It was really very kindly done.

Felicity was beginning to think she'd never understood Mr. Stratton. He appeared so different to her now. As well, she could not help but be a little charmed that he humored Valor. And that he had a cat named Blueberry.

Coming to Town was turning out to be far more confusing than she had imagined. She hardly knew what she thought about anything anymore.

Percy was fascinated by the duke's family. Of course, everybody had heard how eccentric they lived in the Dales, but in the usual case such gossip was exaggerated. At least a little.

Not so in this case.

Everything the duke did was done with his own particular… was it flair? Personality? Eccentricity? All of those things? The duke had managed, within a short space of time, to name his daughters as disappointments and setbacks, and they seemed not at all perturbed to hear it.

Of course, any person growing up in such a household must take on its habits. That idea was on full display at the duke's table. Why had Lady Grace thrown a roll at a footman? Why had she thrown a roll at all? As the duke had warned him about it, Percy supposed it was a regular occurrence. Nobody had seemed to pay any mind to it, and the footman who'd been struck had seemed delighted.

Lady Marchfield was the only usual person at table, and she seemed disgusted with them all.

For all that, the duke put on a very good dinner. The chicken fricassee was excellent and the savarin cake he'd just been served was first rate. Nobody would turn their nose up at his wine cellar either. And then, the conversation was a deal more interesting than most dinners he attended.

"Mr. Stratton," Lady Verity asked, "this may seem a strange question."

Percy braced himself. Every question coming his way had been on the strange side, so he must imagine Lady Verity was prepared to take things up a notch.

"Were you very drugged up from laudanum after the tiger tore you apart?"

"Uh, the doctor did dose me with it," Percy answered, perplexed over why she wished to know.

"I suppose after he dosed you, you would even believe you could fly, if someone told you in a convincing manner," Lady Grace said.

"I do not recall having the notion," Percy said. He could not help but to notice the duke chuckling softly to himself, though he was himself completely lost on the amusement.

"But you believed Papa when he wrote to you that you had prior agreed to come to dinner!" Valor said, laughing in fits.

The duke began laughing harder too. "That's right, you never did agree to it!"

So that was why he did not remember agreeing to it—he hadn't.

He probably would have, though. There was something fascinating about this family. Something fascinating about Lady Felicity too—she was a very different sort of lady.

All of the sisters, but for Lady Felicity, found the joke on him hilarious. Lady Felicity looked vaguely uncomfortable. Lady Marchfield was another story altogether, she gripped her fork and Percy thought the duke would be lucky if he didn't lose an eye to it.

"I believe the time has come to leave the gentlemen to their port," Lady Marchfield said through gritted teeth.

Lady Valor began eating her cake as fast as possible, as she was at imminent risk of being dragged away from it. There were various protestations from some of the younger daughters. Lady Patience said. "Aunt, you know our Papa gets too drunk when he is left alone."

Lady Marchfield countered that he would not be alone, and she would place her trust in Mr. Stratton's good sense. Then, through sheer force of will, she marched them all out.

The butler, and Percy could not remember what his actual name was since he'd heard him called Mr. Why, poured two glasses of port and set the bottle on the table.

"Do you smoke a cigar, Stratton?" the duke asked.

"No, Your Grace, I do not care for them."

"I care for them," the duke said, "but I had to give them up. Set too many fires, you see. One is always laying them down somewhere and forgetting all about them. Can't burn down the family pile of rocks, eh?"

Percy had no idea who went round losing track of lit cigars, but he nodded as if this was a very common problem.

"Your Grace," he said, wishing to get some answers to his questions, "was there a particular reason why you would have pretended that I'd agreed to come, rather than just asking?"

"The interest of it, I suppose. Will he come? Will he not? It passes the time in a pleasant manner."

"I see," Percy said.

"And then, as I told my girls, I want every last one of them out of my house as soon as possible, but mauled by a tiger is going too far. I would not prefer it."

Percy would like to know who *would* prefer it.

"And then," the duke went on, "I suppose Denderby's head nearly separated from his shoulders when he discovered where you were going. Sir Pineapple must have raved over it."

"He did, rather."

"Yes, he would, wouldn't he? Tightly wound. I remember him from when I very accidentally set Lady Vanderwake's curtains on fire all those years ago. From your father's shouts about it, you would have thought I'd murdered the king. The lady herself was not half as upset about it."

Percy snorted. "My mother says his temper is always at the ready for any and all occasions."

The duke picked up his glass of port, and the bottle too. "No way to live, to my mind. Well! We ought to rejoin the girls and that harridan who claims to be my sister. I'll bring the bottle in. I do not like my daughters to be too long in her company. I would not like any of them to take on her grim habits!"

They sauntered into the drawing room to observe Lady Marchfield at the tea tray, scolding the duke's daughters regarding their lack of table manners. None of them seemed much affected by it, but for Lady Valor. That poor girl looked some combination of stricken and overtired.

Lady Marchfield's attention was momentarily stolen away from the duke's daughters and settled on the bottle of port in the duke's hand.

"Roland. Is that really necessary?"

"Put your complaints in the icehouse, Lady Misery," the duke said. "I do what I like in my own household, and anywhere else for that matter. Furthermore, cannot you see Valor is overtired? Go on, my girl—Mrs. Right will take you up."

Percy looked round for the elusive Mrs. Right, but he saw no such lady.

The duke shouted at the door. "Mrs. Right!"

Nobody seemed the least bit alarmed, but for the poor butler. A stout middle-aged lady came to the doors, and Percy must only assume it was Mrs. Right and that lady was the housekeeper. He could not as easily work out why the butler staggered back at the sight of her, as if she were some sort of harbinger of doom.

Lady Marchfield did not seem any happier to see the housekeeper. She glared at Mrs. Right, and Mrs. Right glared back defiantly. Percy supposed there were hidden depths to Mrs. Right.

With a disdainful sniff, the housekeeper turned her attention to her young charge. "Come, my little love," she said to Lady Valor, "say your goodnights and we will have you to bed in a trice."

Lady Valor stood. In a very formal tone, she said, "Mr. Stratton, a pleasure to know you, sir. And I do feel the honor of being addressed as *Lady* Valor, nobody ever does it." She then enacted a pretty little curtsy, kissed her father, and was gone.

She was a rather charming little person.

"We ought to play Fact or Fib," Lady Winsome said.

"Ah yes, a very amusing game, Stratton," the duke said. "One of these bad dreams of mine thought it up."

"That is the first lie!" Lady Felicity said. "You are very fond of us, Papa."

"Nonsense, I can barely stand the sight of you."

As this interesting exchange was taking place, Lady Winsome and Lady Patience were counting out yellow and blue scraps of paper.

Lady Marchfield rose. "Mr. Stratton, I do not know why you have come, but expect you are sorry for it. Roland, I will see myself out, as I have no inclination to play this ridiculous game. I will see you promptly at eight on the morrow for Lady Cyprion's dinner, though for the life of me I cannot recall accepting it or who the lady is."

"Some stiff-lipped acquaintance of yours, I suppose. I'll have to get very drunk to put up with the company," the duke said.

Lady Marchfield ignored that threat. "I will guess she has an eligible son for Felicity—that must have been what I was thinking. Lord Marchfield will escort me here and I will go in your carriage."

Lady Marchfield turned on her heel and made her way toward the door.

"Old Marchfield is trying to give you the slip again?" the duke called after her. "Tell him, he cannot pawn you off on me by dropping you here and speeding off! If he tries it, *I'll* drop you at the nearest gin shop! Hah! Then the gin shop people will probably run you up to St. Giles! Who knows what that neighborhood will do about it. Put you on a boat at Portsmouth maybe. Watch out, Boston—things are about to go downhill!"

Lady Marchfield did not deign to respond to any of the various places where she might be relocated.

The duke's daughters were remarkably unaffected by this exchange between their father and their aunt. Percy supposed he could understand—he was rather unfazed by his own father's outbursts. When a person was outrageous on a regular schedule, it hardly caught one's attention after a while.

Lady Winsome put the pile of yellow and blue strips of paper on an ottoman and dragged it to the center of the room. "Now, Mr. Stratton, the game is simple—you will be asked a question.

When you answer you may tell the truth or tell a fib, and then the rest of us will guess at it before you reveal which it was. If you fool us, you get a yellow ticket, and if you do not, you get a blue ticket. Papa has already earned one blue ticket for pretending we are bad dreams and he cannot stand the sight of us. Don't worry, he always loses."

Percy supposed the duke *would* always lose, ranged against seven determined daughters.

"Now, if you get two yellow tickets, you win," Lady Verity said. "But a blue ticket cancels a yellow, so Papa already is in the hole."

Percy began to worry that this game of theirs might wander into dangerous territory, depending on what questions were asked of him. The questions might well be more embarrassing than having to admit he had a cat named Blueberry.

"I'll pull rank and start the game," the duke said. "Stratton, what would you say is Felicity's best feature?"

CHAPTER ELEVEN

PERCY STARED AT the duke. What would he say was Lady Felicity's best feature? This game was going to get very personal. Too personal!

Seven pairs of eyes bored into him.

"Uh, well, let's see, if I am pressed…"

Lady Felicity's complexion was growing redder by the minute. He assumed his own was following suit.

"The clock is ticking," the duke said, "our lives are draining away minute by minute."

"Her hair," Percy said.

"Fibber!" Serenity cried. "It's her eyes!"

Percy did not think he had a very good understanding of this game. Was it that he was to tell *his* truth or *their* truth?

"Well, I…"

"Never mind it, Stratton," the duke said, pouring himself another port. "You can't win with this army of hooligans. Have another port, it's really the only thing you can do while you rack up blue tickets."

Patience gave him his blue ticket, while the duke refilled his glass.

The game went on and Percy was grateful that there were so many daughters. Not every question was pointed in his direction.

Over the next hour, he discovered that the last sunrise Serenity had cried over had been that very morning. Apparently, she was very struck by sunrises.

Patience was asked how she fared with tea delayed for over an hour that afternoon, as there had been some sort of kerfuffle with the kitchen's stoves. She claimed she simply occupied herself with a book. Everybody, including the duke who had not even been there, named her a fibber and she was promptly given a blue ticket.

As it would turn out, Lady Patience had several times stomped on the floor over the kitchens. The cook, being well used to the family and impossible to rattle, had answered her by using a broom handle to whack his ceiling in response.

Winsome was asked when last she'd accused Verity of making something up. It had been only a few hours ago and was perfectly true.

Verity was then asked if she *had* made something up. She stuck to her story, which was that it was an accepted fact that she had grown an inch in the past month. As everyone had eyes and could see her, she was promptly named a fibber.

It was inquired of Grace whether or not she'd tripped over anything that week. She vehemently denied it, but covered a bruise on her elbow at the same time so she was caught out.

Finally, all eyes drifted toward Lady Felicity. Grace said, "Felicity, has your opinion of Mr. Stratton changed since he saved you from a tiger?"

There had been a long pause. Then she had said quietly, "I believe so."

She had been given a yellow ticket with no debate from anybody.

Percy could barely look in her direction. What did it mean?

He knew very well that she had begun by despising him and being bowled over by Rustmont. If her feelings regarding him had changed… well, he did not see how they could have got worse. If one is at the bottom of the barrel, one cannot go any deeper. The only way was up.

He must presume she had taken on a better opinion of him

than she'd begun with. Of course, it made sense—a lady who had been through the shock of a tiger on the loose was bound to rethink some of her opinions.

Percy was not certain how he felt about this warming of temperatures. He ought to be wholly against it—it had been very convenient that Lady Felicity despised him.

He could not say he was *wholly* against it, though. This evening had been rather pleasant, after all.

"I know my opinion has changed," Lady Winsome said. "It had been very low, if I'm to be honest, Mr. Stratton."

"I, myself," Lady Verity said, "always perceived Mr. Stratton's worth."

"Liar," Lady Winsome said.

"Do you say, then, Winsome, that Mr. Stratton has no worth?" Verity asked.

"That is not what I say and you know it."

"Do I?"

"Well!" Lady Felicity said, "I am afraid we have tired Mr. Stratton with our game."

Lady Felicity looked warningly at all her sisters and they seemed to have received the message.

"Only to be expected, Stratton," the duke said. "I live in a constant state of exhaustion, dealing with these people."

"Papa!" Lady Grace said laughing.

Percy rose, as he thought he ought to take his leave before any more probing questions were thrown his way.

The goodbyes and farewells were all prettily done. Except perhaps from the duke, who called after him as he mounted his horse. "If you see my sister on your way home, drop her off at the nearest nunnery!"

Percy laughed all the way home.

AFTER MR. STRATTON had left the house, Felicity and her sisters made a great show of being tired and left their father in the drawing room with his bottle of port.

All of them perceived that an immediate sisterly conference must be had to discuss impressions of the evening.

Felicity was most interested in hearing her sisters' opinions, as hers were quite a jumble. It had occurred to her that the Mr. Stratton she had met this evening was a Mr. Stratton she would have been most interested in if she were encountering him for the first time.

She was only not certain of the cause. If her feelings were to change so much on account of being saved from a tiger, it would be well to know it. Those feelings arose from shock and would not last.

Winsome pulled the bell for tea and biscuits and Mrs. Right, fully expecting it, was up in a trice.

The sisters ranged round Felicity's enormous bed while Mrs. Right took the chair by the fireplace and poured out cups of tea.

"Felicity," Grace said, "Mr. Stratton is so different from what you described. What I mean to say is, you described his looks very well—they are really very good, and nobody could beat that knot. I noted Papa glancing at it several times."

"But his temperament, Felicity," Patience said. "That is what seems different from what you described."

"It *is* different," Felicity said. "He seems changed, somehow."

"What won me over," Serenity said, "was how kind he was to Valor—calling her *Lady* Valor and discussing the weather with her. It was very well done, I almost cried I was so moved."

"Aye," Mrs. Right said, "the little mite told me all about it, she was very gratified."

"And he is so interesting, too," Winsome said. "Imagine, he has a cat named Blueberry."

"I was surprised that he admitted to being petrified of the tiger," Verity said thoughtfully. "It seemed brave to admit it, somehow."

"I really do not know what to think," Felicity said. "It is almost as if there are two different Mr. Strattons. The one I do not give a toss for… and the other one."

"Goodness, this is a circumstance we never discussed," Grace said. "We spent hours and hours talking about what might happen in Town, but never about a gentleman with two personalities."

"It is not quite that," Felicity said. "Though I cannot put my finger on it."

"No need to, my girl," Mrs. Right said comfortably. "Time is often the answer to a question. Just see what happens next—whatever your final opinion on Mr. Stratton is to be, it need not be settled this minute."

As always, Mrs. Right was full of sensible advice.

"That's very true, Felicity," Grace said. "When do you suppose you will see him next?"

"Lady Lewellyn's ball," Felicity said. "It is the day after next and he did say he would attend it."

"Or even sooner, Felicity," Winsome said. "You did mention to him that we were to go to Lackington & Allen on the morrow. If he were determined to see you, he would make his way there."

"I read a novel where the gentleman was determined to see a lady behind her father's back and began haunting all the shops," Verity said. "It seemed to be a very usual thing."

Felicity could not be sure if Verity had invented that or not. It certainly *could* be true. How would she view it if Mr. Stratton were seen lurking in Lackington & Allen?

Mrs. Right set down her cup and rose. "See what you think when next you see him, that's my advice. Now, I'd best go and keep your father company in the drawing room, else he drinks that entire decanter of port by himself. Mr. Sykes-Wycliff will find my presence shocking, which is another advantage."

"How does your plan to encourage him out of the house proceed, Mrs. Right?" Felicity asked.

"See for yourself in the morning. Mr. Sykes-Wycliff has taken to running round the square of a morning, to build himself up for the servants' hunt that never was. I keep telling him he's not near fast enough—and then I hurry away and laugh and laugh."

"That is excellent news," Grace said. "Perhaps we all ought to hint that he's going rather slow."

"Yes, do," Mrs. Right said, "every bit helps. Now, Felicity, do recall that you are to dress for Lady Cyprion's dinner on the morrow and then claim a headache at the very last minute. Right before you are all to get into the carriage."

"I remember," Felicity said. Of course, she would never let Mrs. Right down regarding one of her plans.

"There's my girl," Mrs. Right said. "We'll play lottery tickets in the evening, while your aunt is getting the surprise of her life."

With that interesting information, Mrs. Right departed the room to keep their papa entertained and stop him from getting too drunk.

After her sisters eventually left for their own beds, Felicity spent a good amount of time staring into the darkness and trying to work out her changed feelings regarding Mr. Stratton. She did not come to any firm conclusions.

PERCY REASONED WITH himself that he went to Lackington & Allen simply because he must have an escape from the house. His father had trailed him from room to room, asking questions and making comments about his dining at the duke's house the evening before.

"How was it that you accepted his invitation and had no memory of doing so?" the viscount asked. "Did he slip into Lady Albright's house in the middle of the night and shake a promise from you?"

"No, he made the whole thing up," Percy had answered.

"I knew it! Of course he did! Just like him to do it, too. Don't you see what this is? It's maneuvering. He's trying to maneuver you into Lady Felicity's clutches."

"I do not believe Lady Felicity wishes to clutch anybody, sadly. You know I am set on her, though she seems to prefer Wiles."

"What do you know about it—you're too naïve! The old lunatic is trying to get some sanity into the blood. That's what he's trying to do. He knows he's as mad as a horde of bees—he's thinking of future generations."

Percy did not let on that he found that theory wildly amusing. As well, he did not think his father knew who was to carry on the family line of the dukedom, as the duke had no sons—it was probably a cousin somewhere. He would not get sanity in the line through a son-in-law.

"Did he dare refer to me as Sir Pineapple?" the viscount asked. "If he did, I will see him on a green!"

"No," Percy lied. He did not see any benefit to being truthful, nor informing his father that he could expect further insults on account of the eccentricity of naming a cat Blueberry.

"If he ever calls me that again, well, he will answer for it!"

"I doubt he will answer for it. Did you not tell me right in the beginning that he was engaged to a duel twenty years ago and couldn't be bothered to get up and go to it?"

"True, true, you can't even box that fellow in with the idea of honor. He is shameless."

Percy had finally been able to escape the house when his mother took over jousting with the viscount. Though it was getting late in the afternoon, he suspected he would not have missed Lady Felicity—all of her sisters were going and getting that many people out of the house at the same time was bound to take most of the day.

Finsbury Square was its usually bustling place, with the bookshop, or the Temple of the Muses as it was called by literary types, dominating the southeast part of the square.

He'd been very surprised to find Mr. Lackington himself

milling round the front doors. The proprietor greeted him and then went back to staring intently out the windows.

"I perceive you must have a very elevated visitor set to arrive," Percy said. "I'd say it must be the prince, but forgive me, I doubt he reads very much."

"Gracious no, I do not suppose the prince is aware of my existence," Mr. Lackington said. "I have been informed that the Duke of Pelham's seven daughters will pay a visit. *Seven?* Can you imagine?"

"I can, rather. I dined with them last evening."

Mr. Lackington turned to him. "Did you? I was not informed whether the duke accompanies his daughters, but I have been told… well, I can hardly explain it."

"That the duke is very original, shall we call it."

"Yes, original. Very diplomatic word for it."

"I doubt you will see the duke," Percy said. "Though, you might see the housekeeper."

"The housekeeper? That's all right then."

"Is it?"

"Isn't it?" Mr. Lackington asked, his tone gone an octave higher.

"I cannot be certain," Percy said.

"Gad, what a situation. The note from the duke said his daughters are all exceedingly unpleasant, but that I was to afford them every courtesy. What am I to do with seven unpleasant ladies?"

Percy laughed. "They are not at all unpleasant," he said. "That is just the duke's originality on display."

Mr. Lackington rubbed his chin. "That's something, I suppose. But there *are* seven, that's really quite a lot."

Percy thought for a moment. He could understand Mr. Lackington's concern. In truth, the fellow probably ought to be more concerned than he was. He'd already seen Lady Grace throw a roll, who was to say she did not throw books too?

"You have that charming room upstairs, the one that overlooks the square," he said. "You could put them all in there and then just bring them books on the subjects they express an interest in."

"Yes, yes," Mr. Lackington said, rubbing his hands together. "Keep them all in one place, contained as it were, excellent idea."

"Do not tell them you have encountered me, if you please," Percy said. "I would rather come upon them by happenstance."

"I understand you, Mr. Stratton. I must have a half-dozen gentlemen every day, lurking the aisles and coming upon a lady by happenstance. The vicars of this town ought to be paying me for helping things on their way to a church."

This caught Percy entirely by surprise, as he had no notion of hinting at such a radical step. He hurried away and left Mr. Lackington fretting at the front doors.

He climbed the staircase to the first floor and took a place by the windows to watch for Lady Felicity's arrival.

He'd not had to wait long, nor could he have possibly missed it, as it took two of the duke's carriages to transport such a crowd. Out they came, one by one. He'd been right in thinking that the duke would not attend them. The housekeeper was herding them like sheep gone toward the wrong field.

The last out of the carriages was Lady Felicity, in a charming, printed muslin dress and a sarsnet pelisse in a sunny yellow, with a jaunty straw bonnet with a matching ribbon topping the whole thing off.

Mr. Lackington hurried out to the pavement to greet them and was soon surrounded like a lame antelope on the savannah. He somehow fought his way out of it and led them through the front doors.

Percy heard them all chattering up the stairs. Poor Mr. Lackington was making a heroic effort to hear them all, though they all spoke at once.

He'd really better rescue the fellow. He stepped out of the aisle he had concealed himself in. "Lady Felicity, how fortuitous that I encounter you here."

Lady Felicity went red as a ripe apple. Lady Grace said, "We did say we were coming, Mr. Stratton."

Of course they did say that, but a lady was not to point out the lack of coincidence in a coincidence.

"Indeed you did, of course I could not be sure of the time, so a happy turn of events. Do let me show you into a sitting room of sorts. There, Mr. Lackington will send for tea and you can tell him what you're after."

Mr. Lackington had given him a grateful look. They filed into the room overlooking the square as the proprietor sent one of his assistants off for a tea tray.

"Mr. Lackington," Percy said, "May I introduce you to Mrs. Right, Lady Felicity, Lady Grace, Lady Patience, Lady Serenity, Lady Winsome, Lady Verity, and Lady Valor."

"All the graces," Mr. Lackington said, with a flourishing bow.

All the graces indeed.

"Please do be seated and I welcome you to Lackington & Allen," Mr. Lackington said.

"Ought we to sit, though?" Lady Felicity asked. "Should we not be roaming the aisles?"

"No need, my lady! No need at all," Mr. Lackington said hurriedly. "Anything you require can be brought to you."

"Now that's a comfortable idea," Mrs. Right said. "I did won-der how I was going to keep track of all my girls."

"I tend to run off," Valor said matter-of-factly.

The ladies arranged themselves on the sofas. Mr. Lackington said, "Now, what are your interests? What sort of books are you looking for? Lady Felicity?"

Percy had been sure Lady Felicity would ask for a gothic novel of some sort. It was his understanding that was all the rage with young ladies—they liked to terrify themselves before retiring for the night.

"Do you have any literature on stoats, Mr. Lackington?" Lady Felicity asked. "We are thinking of acquiring a pair to join our household."

"We'd like to know what we're getting ourselves into on the stoats' front," Mrs. Right said.

That had been surprising. Though, the next few minutes brought fewer surprises. The ladies Grace, Patience, Serenity, and Winsome were all in favor of gothic novels. As Lady Grace explained, the more frightening the better. Damsels in fear of being murdered every moment, preferably in an old and dark castle, were preferred.

That just left Lady Valor.

"I do not wish for anything scary, Mr. Lackington," she said gravely. "Might you have something about fairies? Nice fairies, you understand. Or nice ponies."

Mr. Lackington said he was certain to find something for the young lady, and set off to locate a tome on stoats, four gothic novels, and one faerie book. Or failing that, nice ponies.

The tea tray came in and was expertly managed by Mrs. Right.

"I understand you will miss the Gandrians' rout this evening, on account of a dinner Lady Marchfield mentioned?" Percy asked Lady Felicity.

"Lady Cyprion's dinner," Lady Felicity said.

For some reason, this caused Mrs. Right to snort.

"Felicity is not going, though," Lady Serenity said.

"She will pretend to go," Lady Grace said, "and then claim a headache at the very last possible moment. They will have to go without her."

"We do not yet know why," Lady Patience said. "Though we think it will be very amusing—you see, our papa and our aunt are like Punch and Judy."

"Our aunt is often cross," Lady Valor clarified.

Percy had seen that well enough the evening before. He'd been casually acquainted with Lady Marchfield for some years but had never observed her temper before that.

But what could be the meaning of Lady Felicity pretending at a headache at the last minute, though nobody understood why she was meant to? He was not wholly against the idea, as Lady Marchfield had speculated that Lady Cyprion must have an eligible gentleman available for Lady Felicity. Whoever that fellow was, he could not be up to scratch, or Percy would have heard of the family.

"It is a mystery, you see," Lady Felicity said. "Only our Mrs. Right knows why I am to have a headache."

Mrs. Right bobbed her head up and down. "I'll say nothing for now."

"We do like a mystery," Lady Winsome said. "Except for Patience. And Valor."

"I don't like mysteries because you don't know what they're about. It's scary," Lady Valor said.

"I don't like to wait," Lady Patience said.

"All will be known soon enough," Mrs. Right said mysteriously.

"I hope it's to do with driving Mr. Sykes-Wycliff from the house," Lady Winsome said.

"Perhaps, in a roundabout manner," Mrs. Right said smiling.

"We watched him run round the square this morning," Lady Serenity said. "He was very out of his breath. He was clutching the railing of the park and heaving."

"I'm sorry—your butler was running round Grosvenor Square?" Percy asked.

"Oh yes, that's to do with—"

Lady Felicity cut off Lady Serenity before she could explain what it was to do with.

"Never mind what it's to do with," she said hurriedly.

"I have been assured that Jimmy is making a wonderful recovery," Lady Valor said, "if that makes you feel better, Mr. Stratton."

Percy was entirely lost. All he could gather was there was a mysterious dinner Lady Felicity would not attend, and it was indeed mysterious—he'd never heard of Lady Cyprion. Who on earth was she? As well, they were set on driving the butler from the house, which somehow involved him running round their square. And who was Jimmy? What was he recovering from?

Percy thought the butler might be well served to set off running and keep going from whence he came. Maybe he ought to take Jimmy with him!

Mr. Lackington came back with an armful of books. Lady Felicity was to be gratified in her wish to gain more knowledge regarding the habits of stoats, though Percy could not think it a wise choice to emulate Lady Albright on any matter.

It seemed there were endless choices regarding gothic novels, and the four sisters who requested them were to be scared out of their wits for weeks to come. Lady Valor was equally satisfied, as she perused a book called *The Gentlest Unicorn*.

"Well, ladies, I think Mr. Lackington has things well in hand," Percy said. "Lady Felicity, I hope to see you at Lady Lewellyn's ball."

Lady Felicity nodded prettily.

"I suppose you will insist on taking her first dance, Mr. Stratton?" Lady Serenity said.

Before he could answer that rather forward question, Lady Patience said, "No, Serenity, Mr. Stratton will wish to take the dance before supper. For extended conversation, you see."

"Oh yes, that does make sense," Lady Serenity said.

All eyes looked toward him, but for Lady Felicity's, as she had turned away.

"Perhaps Lord Rustmont will beat me to it," Percy said.

Why did he say that? What a stupid thing to say.

"Lord Rustmont?" Lady Winsome exclaimed. "I should hope not. He ran away, Mr. Stratton. At the critical moment, he ran away from the tiger."

"So he did," Percy said.

"Sisters," Lady Felicity said, "we do not yet know Lord Rustmont's explanation for why he… disappeared."

"*I* know," Percy said. "He's not the suave and heroic Corinthian he claims to be."

"I've never even heard of a suave and heroic Corinthian," Lady Grace said. "Just a regular Corinthian.

"Well, in any case," Lady Felicity continued, "do not bother Mr. Stratton with these questions. He is not at all obligated to put himself down on my card for *any* of the dances."

"No?"

"Well, no."

"Maybe I will, though."

"Gracious," Lady Valor cried, looking up from her book, "the gentlest unicorn really is the gentlest unicorn!"

"Ladies," Percy said, bowing and fairly running from the room.

CHAPTER TWELVE

FELICITY HAD BROUGHT all of her dramatic skills to bear in getting almost to the carriage to set off for Lady Cyprion's dinner, and then coming to a dead stop and clutching her head. After it was agreed all round that she must have a headache, there was a brief moment of danger when Lady Marchfield said she would send their regrets.

Felicity had pointed out that it would be bad enough for a hostess to lose one guest at the last minute, but three would be impossible to manage. She added that her aunt speculated that Lady Cyprion likely had an eligible gentleman in mind for her, and it would be well if Lady Marchfield set eyes on him and gave him a good going over. That last point had tipped the scales, as Lady Marchfield viewed herself very skilled at giving a good going over. Her poor Papa had dejectedly got in the carriage with his sister and they set off.

After the carriage was safely away, they settled into the drawing room to play lottery tickets. A tray was brought in for Felicity, as she had not yet eaten since she was meant to be dining at Lady Cyprion's house.

Felicity did her very best to keep her mind on the game, but she could not help thinking of Mr. Stratton. He had come to Lackington & Allen very purposefully, as he had known she would be there. He'd claimed he had not known the time so it must be put down to happenstance.

It was true he had not known the time, as they had not known it themselves. They had meant to set off earlier, but somebody always seemed to need to go do something before they left. Grace had changed her bonnet three times. Serenity had wept over a dead bee in the garden. And then finally, a search of the house had to be made because Valor lost track of Mrs. Wendover, who would be upset if she did not say goodbye before she left. The raggedy stuffed rabbit was found under Valor's bed in its usual location, though it took some time to discover it, as Valor had sworn she'd already looked there.

Their late arrival begged the question of how long Mr. Stratton had waited. They arrived near four o'clock—he might have been there all day.

She was not such a fool that she did not see that it indicated a partiality. She was also not such a fool as to ignore a bit of partiality on her side too.

When she'd seen him there, she did experience a little flutter of something. And then, she did notice that she had not given Lord Rustmont a thought in quite some time. Her ideas went round and round and all she could settle on was that she was beginning to like Mr. Stratton. Very much, actually.

She did not wish her feelings to run ahead of reality, as she thought they might have done regarding Lord Rustmont. She silently vowed she would wait until Lady Lewellyn's ball to allow them to go any further. What would he do? Would he put himself down on her card? Would it be for a dance of any significance?

She would have to bide her time and see what came of it.

They had imagined their father would not return from Lady Cyprion's dinner until quite late, but it was not an hour before he was back in the door.

"Papa?" Felicity asked. "What has happened?" Then remembering she was meant to be abed with a cold compress on her forehead, she said, "Also, my headache is quite gone."

Felicity supposed her father would tell her why he'd returned so early if he could only stop laughing. Something had entirely set him off. Felicity had not seen him laugh so hard since Mrs. Biddleton's Christmas party. The decorative pine boughs on her mantel had been knocked over by her stumbling butler, fallen on top of Baron Richards' head, and made him spill his claret all over his shirt.

Just now, her father was quite out of breath with laughter and each moment it looked like he might have come to the end of it, he started up again. He was mopping his eyes and he was red in the face.

Though she loved her father dearly and thought his temperament quite perfect, she was cognizant of the idea that not everyone in the wide world perceived his charms. He was prone to doing and saying things he found amusing, which some others might not. In truth, what often amused him the most was seeing his listeners faintly shocked.

She could not imagine what he'd done at Lady Cyprion's dinner. Had the lady thrown him from the house? It was not out of the range of possibilities.

Finally, her father's laughter had run its course and quieted down to chuckles and snorts. Mr. Sykes-Wycliff remained standing by the doorway, staring in horrified fascination. Mrs. Right had brought the duke a glass of brandy, as he had been pointing at the decanter through his laughter, but the butler had not seemed to understand the message.

The duke took a long draught. "Never have I been more entertained in my life. Now Mrs. Right, you must own to being the author of this joke. Lady Misery would have never put that appointment in my book!"

"I, Your Grace?" Mrs. Right asked, eyes wide.

Felicity was quite sure Mrs. Right *had* been the author of whatever had happened. After all, it was she that had ensured that Felicity did not go.

"And you, Felicity!" the duke said with a snort. "Very clever to come down with a headache! Glad you did, wouldn't have been right to go."

"Papa," Serenity said, "you really ought to tell us what happened at Lady Cyprion's house. Was she very stiff-lipped and then you teased her and she went mad like our aunt does?"

"There is no Lady Cyprion," the duke said, wiping tears from his eyes. "It was a cyprian party." The duke paused. "Ah, you younger girls perhaps should not know anything about *that*. Let's just say there was not a stiff-lipped lady among them."

"Do you mean to say, Papa," Lady Felicity said, hazarding a guess at the situation, "that the ladies there were, well they were… of low morals?"

"The lowest!" the duke said with a snort.

"How did you know, Papa?" Valor asked.

"Never you mind how I knew," the duke said with a chuckle.

"Was it the ladies' clothes?" Valor pressed on. "The vicar always says that clothes can advertise your morals."

"I think the vicar meant the lack of clothes, Valor," Winsome said. "He's very determined that every lady wear a fichu."

"Yes, well," the duke said, "the clothes were definitely a tip-off—not a fichu in sight."

"I suppose our aunt went positively mad," Patience said. "I cannot imagine what she had to say to you in the carriage."

This, for some reason, sent the duke into a new round of heaving laughter. It was some minutes before he could recover himself. Then he said, "That's just it, I left her there!"

Felicity pressed her lips together to stop from laughing, though everybody else was not as successful. Particularly Mrs. Right, who was laughing behind a handkerchief, her shaking shoulders giving her away. Valor laughed along with everyone, though Felicity doubted very much she understood what she was laughing about. The only person not gripped with hilarity was Mr. Sykes-Wycliff, who stood clutching at the doorframe.

"Papa," Felicity said, attempting to control her laughter, "I think you are making that up. You did not leave our aunt. How could you have?"

"Simplest thing in the world," the duke said. "Knew what I was looking at in an instant and slipped right out before my carriage had time to pull down the street. I hope she's having a good time!"

That hope was punctuated by the loud crash of the front doors being flung open from the front hall.

Not a moment later, Lady Marchfield came through the doors. She was heaving in breaths and her bonnet was quite askew. This very naturally sent the duke into more paroxysms of laughter.

Felicity was quite sure Lady Marchfield was on the verge of giving her father the what-for of the century. Instead, her aunt turned her eyes on Mrs. Right. She pointed and shouted, "You!"

Mrs. Right threw her chin up and said, "Yes, your ladyship?"

"Do you think I do not know it was you who put that shameful appointment in my brother's book?"

"I cannot think what you mean, your ladyship," Mrs. Right said calmly. "*You* manage the duke's calendar."

"I would never accept an invitation to a party of that base nature. Never!"

Mrs. Right shrugged. "Everybody makes mistakes now and again."

"Roland, you must do something about this!"

"Must I, now? Seems to me you can't prove how that entertainment got into my book. It looks like your handwriting, after all."

"That is another thing! She forged my handwriting!"

"Prove it," the duke said jovially.

"And then, to leave me there, with those sorts of people! I was forced to hail down a hackney just to get away!"

"We understand none of the ladies wore fichus," Valor said. "The vicar would be shocked to his shoes."

Lady Marchfield stared at Valor. Then she turned to the duke. "If you are not careful, Roland, you will ruin your daughters' chances of a good match. What if Felicity had gone? What if word had got out that Lady Felicity Nicolet had been seen in the company of… those women!"

"Lucky she had a headache," the duke said. "She's right as rain now, though."

"Lucky…" Lady Marchfield said softly. From Felicity's view, her aunt was making rapid calculations in her head. "Do you suggest that your eldest daughter has been pulled into this by that wretched housekeeper?"

"Felicity was not pulled into anything," the duke said. "She had a headache and very sensibly stayed at home."

Lady Marchfield's hands were clenching and unclenching and Felicity thought her aunt would very much like to box her brother's ears. She turned to Mr. Sykes-Wycliff, who was just now blinking and unblinking his eyes in a nervous fashion.

"Call the duke's carriage!" she shouted. "I will go home this instant and inform my lord of what I have been subjected to this night. He will know how to answer this insult!"

"Bet he tells you the answer is in the Far East and you should go looking for it," the duke said. "He'll say—don't trouble yourself about hurrying home!"

"My lady," Mr. Sykes-Wycliff said, his voice all a-tremble, "the coachman has just put the horses away."

"Get that coachman back on his box or I will drive the team myself," Lady Marchfield said in grim determination.

Mr. Sykes-Wycliff fled the room to do as he was bid.

The next minutes were spent listening to Lady Marchfield lecture the duke, and then lecture Felicity and then give a dire warning to Mrs. Right—she had better watch her step or she would find herself thrown to the street with no reference.

Of course, nobody but Lady Marchfield thought there was the least danger of it.

Her final words to the duke were, "Grow up, Roland. For all of our sakes, grow up." She turned on her heel, practically ran over the butler, and left the house.

"What an evening, eh?" the duke said, pouring himself a

second glass of brandy. "Never been so amused in my life. By the by," he said, looking at a very shaken Mr. Sykes-Wycliff, "I will need nine pounds in ready money on the morrow to settle a bill. And I want it all in pence."

"In pence, my lord?"

"In pence, put it in a flour sack."

Naturally, their father was questioned quite closely by his daughters as to why he might need over two-thousand coins, but he would not say. All they could gather was that it amused him.

At the mention of the morrow, Felicity's thoughts drifted to the ball. Then they stayed there. As her father relived the amusement of the cyprian party over and over, her thoughts were filled with Mr. Percy Stratton.

She was beginning to even be a little fond of his given name, Percy, despite her earlier claim that it was a good name for a goldfish.

MRS. RIGHT COULD not be more pleased. Her plan to send Lady Marchfield to a cyprian's party had come off without a bump. After her girls had gone up to bed, she spent a comfortable hour with the duke as they sipped their brandy and he described the goings-on of the evening that he'd chosen not to advertise to his children. This, all under the wide-eyed gaze of Mr. Sykes-Wycliff.

How it had unfolded exceeded even her hopeful imagination. The carriage had arrived at a rather regular white stone house on Cork Street. There had been nothing going on out of doors that would have indicated anything amiss, which made perfect sense—any lady of that persuasion looking to ally her fortunes with a lord must be painstakingly discreet.

A liveried footman had opened their carriage door and helped Lady Marchfield to the pavement. Another older fellow in matching livery had opened the doors. Everything had an air of solid respectability.

They had proceeded in and found a lady greeting her guests.

That was when the duke's suspicions were first roused. The line was all gentlemen, and the lady greeting her guests went a bit wide-eyed at the sight of Lady Marchfield.

Lady Misery, it turned out, was a rather unobservant creature. They reached the head of the line and Lady Marchfield said, "Lady Cyprion, charmed. This is my brother, the Duke of Pelham," and then had proceeded right into the drawing room.

As for himself, he'd begun to guess at the lay of the land. He took one quick peek into the drawing room, saw ladies in various states of deshabille hanging on the arms of attending gentlemen. There was even a lady who had located herself on the lap of her preferred conversationalist. Lady Marchfield stood in the middle of the room, as motionless as a statue.

He hightailed it out the doors and laughed all the way home.

It was all very gratifying.

As for Mr. Sykes-Wycliff, he'd spent the better part of this morning collecting nine pounds in pence. Mrs. Right could not imagine what it was for, nor what he'd had to do to get it, but he was currently slumped at the servants' table. The sack of coins had been given over to one of the coachmen.

Charlie, the senior footman, came into the room and said, "His Grace needs a padlock."

"A padlock?" Mr. Sykes-Wycliff asked.

"That's what he says," Charlie said nodding. "He needs it for tonight."

Charlie sat down and helped himself to a biscuit.

Mrs. Right, always willing to grab at an unexpected opportunity passing by, shook her head sadly.

"What?" Mr. Sykes-Wycliff asked nervously. "Why do you shake your head? What do you know?"

"Well now, if you look at it rightly," the housekeeper said, "it is just good commonsense on the duke's part."

"What commonsense? Commonsense for what?" Mr. Sykes-

Wycliff asked nervously.

Charlie gave Mrs. Right a quick wink to let her know he was in on this game.

"I suspect the duke can feel it coming on," Mrs. Right said.

"Feel what coming on?" Mr. Sykes-Wycliff shrieked.

"I did mention," Mrs. Right said, "not to answer the door in the middle of the night if the duke knocks."

"That's right," Charlie said, "else he'll clobber you."

"But our duke is a very considerate sort," Mrs. Right said. "Never means to clobber anybody. So I reckon he's going to lock himself in his bedchamber tonight to avoid doing it. You see what I mean by the consideration?"

Mr. Sykes-Wycliff leapt up from his chair. "That is it. That is absolutely it! After what I witnessed last night, and the descriptions of all this, well, this, downright dangerous behavior, I will not spend another night in this house! I will not lock myself in my quarters so that I am not clobbered or run round the moors attempting not to be killed! It is all madness!"

As Mr. Sykes-Wycliff jogged from the room, Mrs. Right called after him. "Charlie here will get your valise out of the storeroom."

The housekeeper and footman smiled and nodded to one another.

This visit to Town was turning out to be very jolly, indeed.

CHAPTER THIRTEEN

"MY BEST COAT, Radcliff," Percy said. Lady Lewellyn's ball felt momentous in some manner. He planned to get there early and he was determined to take Lady Felicity into supper.

He'd spent the day at White's and he was growing concerned over the talk about Lady Felicity. It seemed just a moment ago that it had been *he* hailed as the hero of the hour for facing down a tiger. He'd been the tiger-slayer. Now it seemed all the credit was going to Lady Felicity.

The general consensus seemed to be that she'd held the fates of both him and her father the duke in her charming hands. Had she reacted as any lady might be expected to, she would have screamed or attempted to run away.

Sir Matthew, claiming to have a friend who was an expert on big cats, had written to him outlining the events of the night. He'd since received a letter back congratulating the lady involved for not provoking an attack by keeping her nerve. That had seemed to settle the matter.

He did not mind that Lady Felicity was now looked upon as a dashing heroine. At least, not very much. But he very well knew there would be a line of gentlemen trying to get on her card. They'd all want to go round on the morrow, casually mentioning their conversations with Lady Felicity regarding the tiger.

Idiots.

"May I inquire why it is to be your best coat for a rather run-of-the mill occasion?" Radcliff asked.

"Just a whimsy, that's all," Percy said.

"A whimsy? Now you're having whimsies, are you?"

"I can have a whimsy if I wish to," Percy said curtly.

"I suppose the tiger-tamer will be attending?"

"If you mean Lady Felicity, yes I believe so."

"Well here is something whimsical. It is whispered that the lady's aunt, Lady Marchfield, was seen attending a cyprian's party," Radcliff said.

"A cyprian's party? Lady Marchfield? That's completely ridiculous."

Radcliff shrugged. "It seems certain gentlemen of the *ton* were in attendance and the story is that the duke brought her and then left her there."

Percy mulled it over. That was slightly more believable, as who knew what the duke might do to amuse himself.

Or perhaps it was that housekeeper who had somehow arranged it. She had hinted at some mystery, some dinner that Felicity was meant to beg off at the last moment when he'd seen them all at Lackington & Allen.

Percy sat back. Of course. Lady Cyprion's dinner. That was why he'd never heard of the lady.

Having a housekeeper who would dare such a thing was… a lot more whimsical than wishing to wear one's best coat. It was also exactly the type of housekeeper the duke would choose.

"Apparently," Radcliff went on, "once Lady Marchfield caught on to the place, she ran out shrieking. First, she was yelling "Roland!" But then his carriage turned a corner and disappeared into the night. Then she began shouting for a hackney. The courtesan running the event managed the whole thing, flagged her one, and then paid the driver. I imagine she was glad to see the back of the lady."

Percy laughed in spite of himself. He did not know if all the details of this wild tale were true, but it was hilarious all the same.

"That duke sounds like he's not all there upstairs," Radcliff said.

"Oh, he's all there, I can assure you," Percy said. "He just doesn't give a toss for… anything really. He says and does what he wants and, from my view, confounding Lady Marchfield is one of his principal amusements. Though, confounding my father must be a close second. He calls him Sir Pineapple, for reasons I won't go into."

"That duke sounds like a rum sort," Radcliff said. "I only say, you might think carefully before connecting yourself to such a family."

"Who said anything about me connecting myself?"

"Your father. He's been raving about it all day."

"He doesn't know anything."

"So you don't have the interest, then? Might want to put the old soldier out of his misery."

"The whole point of the ruse with Lady Felicity is to convince my father I'm set on her, but that she prefers Wiles."

"Perhaps, but the viscount thinks the *duke* is set on a match, which means Lady Felicity may be too, all on account of the duke tricking you to dine at his house."

"I wish my father would just calm down, though I know it's not in his nature."

This caused Radcliff to laugh. "It certainly isn't in his nature this moment. Just now, he's in the front hall, making the footmen nervous and waiting for you to descend. He's a hound at a fox den, waiting for his quarry to show itself."

"Is he now," Percy said. "He's forgotten that any self-respecting fox den has more than one exit. I'll tell you what, I'll go down the servants' stairs and slip out the back of the house. I can saddle my horse and be off before the hound is any the wiser."

"And what am I to say about it when he asks where you are?"

"Just say you lost track of me—here one minute, disappeared the next, just like a fox. My best coat, Radcliff. There is not a moment to waste."

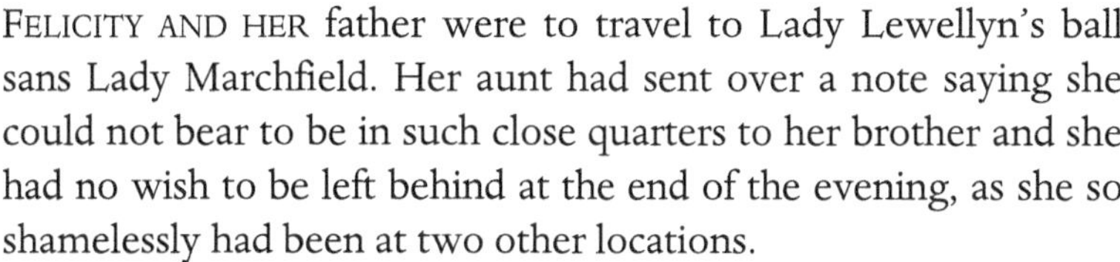

FELICITY AND HER father were to travel to Lady Lewellyn's ball sans Lady Marchfield. Her aunt had sent over a note saying she could not bear to be in such close quarters to her brother and she had no wish to be left behind at the end of the evening, as she so shamelessly had been at two other locations.

Felicity had the idea that the complaining note was meant to make her father feel terrible, though it seemed to have the opposite effect. He'd spent a half-hour outlining all the various locations he could leave Lady Marchfield, including a gaming hell, a pawn shop, and the dark walk in Covent Garden. He speculated that he was just getting started in thinking up places to leave the lady.

She met her father in the great hall. The duke was looking amused and the footmen were looking terrified. Felicity could not imagine what her father had been up to, though surely it was something.

"There you are, Felicity," the duke said. "Go ahead and ask one of these lads where Mr. Why is this moment. What is the reason our esteemed butler is not here at the ready to see us off, you wonder. Go ahead, ask them."

Felicity looked enquiringly at the footmen. Charlie said, "I believe, Lady Felicity, that Mr. Sykes-Wycliff is—"

Before Charlie could explain where Mr. Sykes-Wycliff was, the gentleman himself came storming into the hall. With a valise in hand.

"Get away from me! Don't come near!" he shouted, though nobody had made an attempt to approach him. "I don't need a reference and wouldn't take one if you offered it. You can clobber somebody else with your midnight door-knocking and if you ever believed I would run round the moors while you chased me with large knives, you've another thing coming. Furthermore, you can tell Lady Marchfield I said so!"

Mr. Sykes-Wycliff threw the front doors open and jogged down the street. From Felicity's viewpoint, he still was not very fast, despite all his jogging round the square of a morning. It was just as well that there was no such thing as a servants' hunt, else he'd have been done in attempting to scrabble round the moors.

"From that pack of nonsense, I detect Mrs. Right's hand in this," the duke said, all jollity.

The footmen looked in different directions, so Felicity suspected their hands had been in it too. As had her and her sister's hands. She supposed Mr. Sykes-Wycliff never stood a chance.

"Excellent," the duke said. "Wait until I inform Lady Misery that her latest project has failed spectacularly."

They proceeded out to the carriage and could just make out Mr. Sykes-Wycliff turning the corner and he was gone. Wherever that gentleman settled, he was bound to be happier. As they had all decided from the outset, Mr. Sykes-Wycliff's respect for himself would blossom when he was somewhere he was wanted. He might not see it yet, but they had done him a kindness in driving him mad.

Felicity was helped into the carriage and noticed a large sack on the seat. "Are those the pence you asked for, Papa?"

He nodded and seemed very pleased about it.

"Dare I ask why you are taking them to a ball?" She would not put it past the duke to hand them out to people he found tedious. Naturally, Lady Marchfield would be in receipt of most of them.

The duke had taken a folded sheet of paper from his coat. "Look at this—a bill from Lady Albright. She claims we owe her nine pounds on account of her very expensive sofa being ruined by bloodstains."

"That is outrageous!" Felicity exclaimed. "For one, she was the inattentive person who left the padlock off the tiger's cage. For another, she left us out there to be torn to pieces. And for another, it was Mr. Stratton's blood, not mine."

"Just as I thought too. But do not fret over it. I've brought the payment in pence and added in a padlock for good measure. We'll see how she likes it then!"

"Ah, so that's why we left so early," Felicity said, "we make a stop."

"No pulling the wool over your eyes, eh?"

"As that is the case, I suppose it is a good thing my aunt makes her own way to the ball."

"It is always a good thing when Lady Misery keeps her distance." The duke rubbed his hands together. "I can't wait to tell her I threw nine pounds worth of pence into Lady Albright's house. Then, just as she's staggering over it, I'll hit her with the news that Mr. Why lost his faculties and ran off into the night."

Felicity thought her aunt really would be staggered. She suspected Lady Marchfield had not quite regained her equanimity since the cyprian party. It was her understanding that it was talked about, and Lady Marchfield was advertising far and wide that it had been the duke's doing. Her father did not care at all about being blamed. He was happy to be known as the author of what he deemed a "hilarious turn of events."

The carriage proceeded to Lady Albright's house. The duke said, "Stay here, Felicity, I may have to wrestle the butler. Watch out the window if it amuses you."

Her father jumped down to the pavement with his sack of pence and jogged up to the front doors. Of course Felicity had every intention of watching from the window. She pulled back the curtain and peered out.

Her father gave the door a good pounding. Then another pounding. Lady Albright's butler answered, clearly out of breath. The poor fellow must have run all the way up from the servants' hall.

"Your Grace!" he said, "I am sorry, Lady Albright has gone out."

"Stand aside," the duke said in a commanding voice.

The poor butler did stand aside and there was no wrestling required. The duke took handfuls of pence out of his sack and proceeded to throw them into Lady Albright's great hall as the shocked fellow looked on.

The duke poured the last of them out and said, "Do not sweep these up or I'll come back with twice the amount in bricks! I want that confounded woman to see it just as I've left it. With any luck, she'll slip on them and break her neck. You can tell Lady Lunatic, she's been paid for her incompetence and disregard for her guests' lives. Oh, and here is an extra padlock, since she has so much trouble keeping track of them!"

The duke pulled his arm back and threw the padlock through Lady Albright's drawing room window. The glass shattered with a crash.

Gracious, her father was irascible. Felicity was not at all surprised that he'd showered Lady Albright's great hall with coins, and quite right he do so considering the bill for the sofa. However, she had not expected him to break a window. She wondered if Lady Albright would try to send a bill for *that*. She hoped not, as there was no telling what her father would do about it. He might really return with a farmer's cart of bricks if the lady were not careful.

The duke clambered back into the carriage very pleased with himself. Lady Albright's butler stood horror-struck at her front doors. The duke's coachman, being well used to his employer's interesting personality, remained stone-faced as if nothing at all untoward had occurred.

The duke rapped on the roof and they set off—the duke waving a genial goodbye to Lady Albright's butler.

"A job well done," the duke said. "Lady Albright will not dare trifle with me again, I've made it too much trouble to do so. That is the trick with people—make it deuced inconvenient to cross you and they won't do it, you see?"

"I do see," Felicity said, laughing. "But poor Grace—when it comes time for her season, or all my sisters that follow, I cannot imagine Lady Albright will send an invitation."

"I wouldn't allow your sisters to go to that blasted woman's house even if she did invite them," the duke said. "I've been clear as day on the matter—I want you all out of the house as fast as possible, but I don't fancy seeing any of you mauled by a wild animal. No self-respecting gentleman would condone it."

Felicity nodded, her father really could be sentimental on occasion.

"Speaking of getting you out of the house, what about Stratton? You could do worse, Almack's was filled with ungainly young men lurching all over the place. At least that fellow has two things going for him. If you ever face a tiger again, he's handy to have around. As well, I don't know how his valet is achieving that knot, but I'd like to know it."

"Oh, Papa, I do not know—"

"Nobody ever knows," the duke said. "You don't really know a person until they're in the same house with you. How could it be otherwise? That's why marriage is known as the great roll of the dice."

"Is it called so?"

"Well if it isn't, it should be. Do you like the look of him?"

"The look of him, well… he is handsome enough. People say. In the usual way of things."

"There you have it, then. He can get you away from a tiger, wears a very good knot, and you don't run screaming from him when you see his face. You've got as good a chance as any couple."

Felicity sat back. Did any of that make sense? She really did not dare take her father's opinions as gospel, as he was very free with the truth. On the other hand, what would she really know about the gentleman she chose to wed? Perhaps 'would save her from a tiger' was more than she would know about most gentlemen.

And then, while she knew so little about Lord Rustmont, she knew he would *not* save her from a tiger. Though, she was still interested to hear his side of things. There was still the slim chance he might have a reasonable explanation for his disappearance. Though she could not think what it would be.

Still, to consider Mr. Stratton? She had disdained him from the first. Though, she must admit, she had found him handsome from the first too. Then, his actions at Lady Albright's house had swayed her. And his attendance at dinner at her father's house had swayed her still. He seemed to take her father in stride, which so many people failed to do. There was no point in denying she found him more genial than she had initially done.

Perhaps she did like him particularly. She must do, she thought about him all the time.

"Papa, how was it with you and Mama?"

The duke laughed long and hard. He caught his breath and said, "Your sainted mother came near to engaged to a baron from Hertfordshire. Lord Randall, was his name. I saw which way the wind was blowing and laid out the facts. I said, Lady Mary, do you not see that Randall is a blowhard of the worst sort with an unbendable walnut walking stick for a spine? He will expect his lady to be staid in the extreme and will not allow her to put a foot out of place. If you wed *me*, you might do any ludicrous thing you like and I'll say nothing about it."

"Did she wish to do ludicrous things?"

"I suspected it, that's why I used that argument. How about this—one year, she decided she wished to know how to bake cakes. A duchess, in the kitchens, baking cakes? Who ever heard of it? Down to the kitchens she went. They were awful, by the by. Then, at another moment, she decided she'd rather be called Tulip, than Mary."

"And you did not say anything about it?"

"I ate the cakes and called her Tulip. The Tulip gambit only lasted a year, and I admit to being grateful for it. I think delivering the twins set her off in some manner. Set me off too, come to think of it. Daughters—they never stopped coming. Nevertheless, she wanted to be called Tulip, and so Tulip it was. Best advice I can give you on the marriage front—let people be as they are. People don't like to be constrained or bossed about."

Felicity thought that was probably wise advice. After all, she did not like to be constrained or bossed about, so why should anybody else like it?

The world thought her father was the sum total of what they could see. But he did have hidden depths he allowed to peek out from time to time.

"Here we are," the duke said, "let's track down Lady Misery and give her the good news about where nine pounds in pence ended up, and that her protégé of a butler has run screaming from the house."

And then there was the part the duke usually allowed people to see.

PERCY HAD CIRCLED the great hall of Lady Llewellyn's house like a shark cruising a fisherman's harbor. He was a rather awkward shark, actually. He supposed an actual shark would have the surrounding fish avoiding its eye and heading in opposite directions. As it was, it was turning out to be quite the trick to keep an eye out for Lady Felicity, without catching the eye of someone he'd rather not catch the eye of.

He'd studiously avoided Lady Marchfield's eye, though she'd glared at him as if her discomfort was somehow his fault. He had no wish to speak to the lady, as what was one to say about her attendance at a cyprian party?

He'd equally avoided catching the eye of several hopeful young ladies. He did not imagine any of them were particularly interested in him. Rather, it would be a feather in their bonnet to claim Mr. So-and-So had been determined to waylay them at the earliest possible moment.

He was not in the mood to be anybody's feather in a bonnet.

Finally, Lady Felicity was led in by her father. She was pretty as a picture. The duke was looking in exceedingly good spirits, which Percy assumed had left someone else encountering him in somewhat more depressed spirits.

Percy strode over and waited until they had made themselves known to Lady Llewellyn. After they had done so, he said, "Your Grace, Lady Felicity."

"Fast off the mark, eh, Stratton?" the duke said.

Percy only smiled, as he had no intention of confirming or denying that he'd been waiting particularly.

"My father means to say, how fortuitous that we should so speedily encounter someone we know," Lady Felicity said.

"By the by, Stratton, have you laid eyes on Lady Misery?"

"I presume you mean me to understand Lady Marchfield?" Percy said. He was not about to start referring to the lady by that name, though it was rather apt at the moment. "I have indeed, Your Grace, she is inside the ballroom I believe."

"Hah! Well do I have a few things to tell her! Our butler has run off, for one. Take Felicity to drop her cloak and pick up her card, if you will."

With that, the duke turned and hurried away, fast after his quarry.

"Oh dear," Lady Felicity said softly.

"Are you fearful, Lady Felicity?" Percy asked, thinking it was not very like her. "I assure you I can be trusted to escort you to the cloakroom."

"No, no, it is not that. I would hardly be fearful of a gentleman at a ball. It is just that my father is on the verge of sending my aunt into a right temper…when she hears all."

They began to walk down the corridor. Percy said, "Would it be too bold to inquire into what 'all' is?"

Lady Felicity nodded, which Percy was not sure meant he was too bold, or he was not.

She said, "We all drove Mr. Sykes-Wycliff from the house, I'm afraid. My father does not even know the extent of it."

Percy raised his brows. "How does one drive a butler from the house, exactly?"

"Oh, you know, the usual gambits," she said. "We mentioned my father knocks on people's doors in the middle of the night and then clobbers whoever answers. That sort of thing."

"*Does* he do that?"

"Goodness no, he is a very sound sleeper. Well, he snores and sometimes shouts, but he never gets up and walks around."

Percy was relieved to hear it, though he could well see how Mr. Sykes-Wycliff had believed the duke was cruising the corridors at night and tapping on doors. It sounded like just the sort of thing the Duke of Pelham would get up to.

"Well, I suppose Lady Marchfield cannot stay too distraught that you have lost your butler," he said. "She's still got her own butler, presumably."

"That is not all, though. After she hears of that she will be told of my father's visit to Lady Albright's house. We were just there."

"Returning to the scene of that debacle? I am determined never to set foot in that house again."

"Yes, well you see, Lady Albright sent my father a bill because I stained her sofa with blood. Your blood of course."

"Ah yes, mine. You were very good to risk your dress on my account."

"You were very good to throw my India shawl into the cage to lure the tiger back into it."

"It was nothing at all."

"You have healed, then?"

"Right as rain," Percy said, though that was not precisely the truth. "But I say, how very forward of Lady Albright to send a bill, considering her part in it."

"Yes, that is what I thought! My father did not take kindly to it at all."

Percy stopped in his tracks. "My god, he hasn't gone and let the tiger out as some sort of ill-advised retribution?"

"Heavens no, that would be rather dangerous. No, the lady demanded nine pounds in payment, and so my father delivered it in pence and threw it all over her front hall, much to her butler's distress."

Percy burst out laughing. It was marvelous. Only the duke could get away with such a maneuver.

"And then he threw a padlock through her drawing room window."

Now he was laughing harder. Really, if all the *ton* would go on as the duke did, London would be a highly amusing destination.

Lady Felicity began to laugh too. "Gracious, I hope Lady Albright is not here!"

"Because your father—"

"Yes, who knows what—"

"What he'd say to the lady," Percy said, tamping down his laughter. "Whatever it is, she will not like it."

"I am sure she will not."

"I will try to be nearby, I shan't like to miss it."

"Mr. Stratton, what a terrible thought."

"Is it?"

"No, not really."

They had reached the cloakroom and Percy helped her from her pelisse and handed it to the footman. The footman in turn handed over Lady Felicity's dance card.

"If I may, Lady Felicity?" Percy asked.

She nodded her acquiescence and he put himself down for the dance before Lady Llewellyn's supper.

Just then, Lord Rustmont approached. "Lady Felicity, I am pleased to see you looking well."

"Maybe you should be pleased to see the lady looking *alive*," Percy said drily.

Rustmont reddened, as well he should.

"If I might put my name down, Lady Felicity. I would be grateful for the opportunity to speak of the extenuating circumstances of that unfortunate evening," Lord Rustmont said.

"Very well," Lady Felicity said.

Percy could not read her tone, but it was not the tone of original enthusiasm she'd had for Rustmont. The fool ought to have known better—leave a lady to fight a tiger on her own and it was not likely to fan any flames of affection.

Rustmont penciled his name in for the first. He handed Lady Felicity's card back to her.

Percy leveled a stare at him. "Well? Was there anything else?"

"Careful, Stratton," Rustmont said, looking a combination of surprised and annoyed.

"Careful of my person, do you say? I ought to heed it, I suppose. You have become rather the expert of being careful of your person. By the by, you should probably avoid the duke—you know how a father can be about a daughter left to fend for herself when wild animals are involved. Downright devilish."

Percy was amused to see Rustmont clenching his jaw. He was certain the almighty Corinthian would like to give him a set down. But what was the fellow to say? He'd run from the tiger, just like everybody else.

Rustmont delivered a curt bow. "Lady Felicity," he said, and then turned and strode away.

"You were very naughty there," Lady Felicity said to Percy.

"Yes. Yes, I was."

Percy was beginning to wonder if the duke was rubbing off on him.

CHAPTER FOURTEEN

FELICITY WAS QUITE impressed with Mr. Stratton just now. He'd been waiting near the doors for her arrival, had handled her father with good humor, and when it came to Lord Rustmont… Well, she must think that Mr. Stratton had kept the upper hand in that exchange. It was beginning to seem as if there were more to Mr. Stratton than she'd originally thought.

Felicity paused. What did *he* think, though? He seemed to like her, but that had been their original agreement. He was to trail her about to make Lord Rustmont jealous, thereby driving that lord to her side.

It was just, she found herself not entirely certain she wished Lord Rustmont to be driven to her side. Did Mr. Stratton like her? Or was he a consummate actor, enjoying his part in the ruse?

Mr. Stratton had since brought her to her father. Lord Rustmont was down for her first and would collect her soon. Mr. Stratton said he would take his leave as he could not be trusted to be civil to that gentleman.

She'd quite liked that, actually. Mr. Stratton's incivility was very attractive. For that matter, her father rather approved of this new, more unbuttoned, Mr. Stratton.

Felicity had watched him stride away and noticed he did not approach another lady, but rather his friend, Mr. Wiles.

"Lady Misery blew her tiara off when I gave her the news of her butler," the duke said, enjoying looking back on that encounter. "Then I went right into the pence and broken window at Lady Albright's house—she was staggered!"

"Oh dear, where is my aunt now, Papa?" Felicity asked. "I do not wish to be scolded on your behalf."

"She's making the rounds; she wants to ensure everybody knows she was tricked into attending a cyprian's party and that her wretched brother left her there. She intends to drag my name through the mud, but we're from the Dales—what care we for a bit of mud?"

"Really, Papa, you ought not to have left her at that party."

"And ruin Mrs. Right's diabolical plan?" the duke asked. "I admire our housekeeper's diabolical plans—she saves me no end of trouble. I do not want a butler, and one, two, three, I don't have a butler."

Felicity could not argue that. Mrs. Right was the backbone of the house. She was housekeeper and mother and butler combined. Most of all, she understood the duke as well as his own daughters did.

"Young Stratton seems in spirits this evening," the duke said.

"Indeed he is," Felicity said. "He was very naughty in teasing Lord Rustmont for not staying behind to face the tiger."

"Hah!" the duke said, "as well he should. Those like Rustmont are all the same—they put on a good show but when it comes to it, they're good for nothing. On top of that, he seems a rather sour sort of fellow."

"Sour?"

"Oh you know what I mean—all wrapped up in his dignity with a damp blanket of seriousness. His household will be as dull as dirt."

Dull as dirt. That had not been at all what Felicity had imagined. She'd somehow conceived the idea that life with Lord Rustmont would be one of romance and daring. He would be adoring clay in her hands, but her hands only. As for the rest of the world, he'd be rushing off to one Corinthian thing after the next, all with that one sardonic brow raised.

"Whatever you do, Felicity, do not choose a humorless man. You are too prone to fun to tolerate it."

Humorless. Is that what Lord Rustmont was? She had taken his serious mien as manly maturity… or something like that.

"Here he comes, Lord Rusty."

Felicity turned and found Lord Rustmont, looking as grim as ever. Still, she could not entirely dismiss her earlier feelings. He was very handsome and he might prove to redeem himself. Perhaps.

"Your Grace. Lady Felicity," he said, holding out his arm for her hand.

"Cheer up, Rustmont," the duke said, laughing.

Lord Rustmont looked startled. He really did not understand her father's temperament.

She laid her hand on his arm and he led her to their places.

"Lady Felicity, I believe I must address at once the shocking events that occurred at Lady Albright's party."

Felicity stayed silent, as she very much agreed with him.

"It was a very chaotic moment, and when Lady Albright locked the door to the garden, I believed everyone had escaped. I then asked her how we were to go about securing the tiger. That was when she informed me that there was nothing to be done at that moment. She had sent a footman to retrieve meat from the kitchens, and he was to go round the back wall of the garden and throw it through the bars into its cage, hoping to lure it back in. He had a long hook he was to use to reach through the bars to shut the cage door."

"So," Felicity said slowly, "you did not know there was anyone trapped out there?"

"Not… initially. It did then come out that there were three persons still out there. I told the lady I would retrieve my pistols, but she said they would be useless against a tiger's hide and would simply enrage the beast. Lady Albright did assure me though that there was nothing to be done. The tiger would either attack or not, and an attack could not be stopped."

Felicity was not certain how she felt about that explanation. "I must point out, Lord Rustmont, that Mr. Stratton *did* stop an attack."

Lord Rustmont looked uncomfortable to have it mentioned. "Yes, well, I suppose none of us could have known a thrown shawl would lure the creature back into his cage."

Felicity did not point out that Mr. Stratton had known it. That was why he'd done it. She was not entirely satisfied with Lord Rustmont. He was less the conquering hero than she would expect a Corinthian to be. Nevertheless, it was one incident and not a situation that would be likely to ever occur again.

Perhaps she ought to take her father's advice and attempt to discover more about Lord Rustmont. Was he as humorless and staid as the duke imagined him to be? How he was in the day to day of life was bound to be more important than how he was when a tiger turned up.

The orchestra began to play and they stood waiting their turn as another couple danced their steps. She did not know the couple, but they seemed very admiring of one another. She wished she felt the same.

"Lord Rustmont," she said, "I recently heard of an interesting situation and would like to hear your opinion of it. It seems a lady decided she wished to learn how to bake cakes. I do not know how her lord viewed it."

"Deuced odd, is how he viewed it if he has any sense."

"So you would not tolerate such an interest?" Felicity asked. It was their turn and Lord Rustmont led her in the steps.

"I would wonder why a lady had taken such an idea into her head. What next? Are the couple to host a dinner and she will be in the kitchens, cooking the roasted beef? It all sounds very eccentric."

"And you do not approve of eccentricity?"

"I do not, Lady Felicity. Eccentricity is an indulgence. It may be acceptable for a dowager of high standing to trot it out on occasion, but that is the limit."

"I see, so I suppose if that same lady became dissatisfied with her name, if she preferred to be called another name, that would be eccentric too."

"In the extreme," Lord Rustmont said grimly.

"Well tell me then, what *could* a lady do to exercise some power over herself and her life?"

Lord Rustmont looked at her quizzically. "Lady Felicity, do you hint that you, yourself, have thought of venturing to the kitchens to attempt to bake a cake?"

"Not in the slightest, Lord Rustmont." She noticed he seemed very relieved to hear it. "But, you never know," she said. "If the idea ever came over me, I'd like to know I could do it without censure."

MRS. RIGHT HAD been having a very comfortable evening. Mr. Sykes-Wycliff was gone so she could put her feet up in the drawing room without that fellow fanning himself over it.

The duke and Felicity had gone out, and so she spent an entertaining evening with the rest of her girls, playing charades. It finally had to come to an end when Valor began guessing everything was a tiger—a sure sign the little mite was overtired.

Valor had been tucked in her bed with the company of Mrs. Wendover, though Mrs. Right had begun thinking of ways to slip that worn stuffed rabbit away and make further repairs to it. One of the ears was only hanging on by a few threads. It was always a tricky operation, as Valor was convinced that repairs were a comment on Mrs. Wendover's looks and hurt her feelings.

Just now, Mrs. Right and the older girls were lounging all over the drawing room while Grace read from one of her gothic novels. It seemed an innocent ingénue was hiding in her wardrobe on account of hearing far-off screams that sounded very ghostly.

There was a sudden pounding on the front doors, which startled them all. Grace dropped the book and it hit the floor. Charlie ran to answer it and they sat in some trepidation, waiting for him to return. It was all well and good to read a gothic novel, but rather frightening when it was followed by an unexpected pounding on the doors.

Charlie returned and said breathlessly, "It is somebody from Lady Albright's house, the butler I think, and he demands to return the nine pounds in pence that the duke delivered this evening."

"Oh he wishes to return it, does he?" Mrs. Right said. She did not know why the fellow would wish to return it, but as a rule she was against anybody crossing the duke's wishes. She must assume that if the duke dropped off the pence, he did not want it back again.

Charlie nodded. "He says he has packed it all in a sack, as Lady Albright was too dignified to engage in the duke's shenanigans by throwing it all over our great hall."

Mrs. Right chuckled over the idea that the duke had sprayed Lady Albright's great hall with nine pounds of pence. Then she sprang to her feet. "I will deal with this person. Stand aside, Charlie."

She marched out to the hall with her girls trailing behind to see what she would do. Mrs. Right found a very butlerish individual standing there, holding a sack with two hands.

"I'll take that," she said, grabbing the sack from his hands. It was indeed heavier than she'd expected, but she would not be put off.

"Thank you, madam," the butlerish fellow said.

"See if you'll thank me when I'm done with you," Mrs. Right said genially.

The butler staggered at this response.

"Charlie, follow me," Mrs. Right said, charging out of doors. She stormed toward the waiting carriage. "Open the door, Charlie."

Charlie rather happily did as he was bid. Mrs. Right over-turned the sack into the carriage, coins bouncing in every direction.

She shut the door against them and turned to the butler. "I imagine the duke will be very put out to hear about this," she said threateningly. "What I *can't* imagine is what he'll do about it."

The butler, who had hurried out to the pavement, went white as a sheet. "I did tell Lady Albright what he said about bringing bricks next time," he whispered to himself.

"Begone with you," Mrs. Right said, "and my advice is, don't come back or it'll be the worse for you."

The butler hurried to the carriage. Charlie opened the door for him and the fellow climbed in as a raining of pence fell to the road. Lady Albright's coachman appeared to be disgusted to be involved in the whole palaver and started his team. They were gone, with handfuls of coins scattered and gleaming in the moonlight.

"You might as well gather up what's been left behind, Charlie, and divide it up downstairs."

Charlie nodded with enthusiasm. Mrs. Right nodded back—sending unexpected money downstairs was just one of the many reasons she was, and would remain, the beloved ruler of the duke's household.

All in all, it had been a more entertaining evening than she'd been anticipating.

PERCY HAD NOT particularly planned on putting down his name on other ladies' cards, he'd hoped he might just fade into the background at the edges of the ballroom floor and watch Lady Felicity.

However, it became apparent, via Lady Llewellyn, that there were quite a few young ladies who did not have their cards filled.

It was a hostess's nightmare to see unattached young ladies sitting out a set. After all, it was embarrassing for the young lady and highly irritating to her parents.

Therefore, like any good hostess, she had commandeered both him and Wiles, along with other gentlemen, to get going in different directions, asking to be put on cards. No young lady was to be left behind.

Percy did not fault the hostess for it. Lady Llewellyn was doing her duty and so he must do his. He put a great amount of stock into the idea that manners greased the wheels of society and they required everyone to pull in the same direction.

Or at least most people pulled in the same direction. He did not suppose anybody in the wide world could direct the duke on which direction to pull.

Nevertheless, he did keep an eye on Lady Felicity when he could. Particularly when she'd danced with Rustmont. He'd been gratified to see that it did not appear that whatever excuse he'd made for himself had been joyfully received.

Lady Felicity was too clever to believe that fellow's excuses.

Now, he'd taken her through the set and she was as graceful as ever. He'd hinted around about what might have been her conversation with Rustmont. All she would say about it was she supposed it could be true. What the gentleman had actually said, though, remained a mystery.

Lady Llewellyn's dining room was far superior to Almack's, that lady having no notion of making her guests suffer. There was white soup, cold meats, pickled vegetables, warm rolls with herbed, compounded butter, scalloped potatoes, chops, potted meats, several types of broiled fish, beef tartlets, roasted fowls, and most importantly, plenty of good wines. That was where Almack's fell down the hardest in Percy's opinion. Though he'd been shocked that the duke had brought a flask of brandy into that institution, he also thought that serving lemonade at anything outside of a picnic was an abomination.

They had their wine glasses filled, Percy choosing the claret and Lady Felicity choosing the Canary.

"Mr. Stratton," Lady Felicity said, "I recently heard of an interesting situation and would hear your own thoughts on it. It seems a lady has suddenly become interested in baking cakes and has begun visiting her kitchens to do so. What do you suppose her lord makes of it?"

Percy could only imagine that Lady Felicity herself had developed a sudden interest in baking. After all, in what household could a lady march down to the kitchens and be up to her elbows in flour, but for the Duke of Pelham's?

"I do not suppose there is any harm in it," he said. "Except—"

"Except?"

"Except, the cook's feelings must be taken into consideration. Is he insulted because it is a hint that his own cakes are not up to snuff? Is he put out that his domain has been invaded without so much as a by your leave?"

"The cook, I hadn't thought…"

"Yes, well, they can be touchy and get hot at the drop of a hat, the good ones can anyway. And then, I really do feel that once you have given over some of the household's rooms to staff, you cannot just march into them at will. The kitchens, pantries, servants' quarters, the servants' hall, the valet's wardrobes, butler's closets, the cellars—all are forever off limits."

"Oh yes, I see, that is very true," Lady Felicity said thoughtfully.

Percy hoped that if she did plan on invading the kitchens, she'd smooth it over with the cook first.

"And then I heard another thing I could not really decide on," Lady Felicity said.

Gad, where was she going next? The stables? If she intended on imposing on the stablemaster, that would be another thing entirely.

"I heard of a lady who became dissatisfied with her given name. She wished to be called another name. In the privacy of her own house, of course."

Percy had rather strong feelings on that subject. "Lady Felicity, I have very decided opinions on that question."

"You do?"

"I do. It is one of the great injustices that a person is given a name before they have the faculties to rail against it. My own name was my grandfather's and so I do not like to disparage it, but I do not care for it."

"Percy. It is Percy."

Though he did not in fact like his given name much, it was very affecting to hear Lady Felicity speak it.

"So you *do* think that a person ought to be able to change their name at will?"

"I do think it," Percy said.

"And what would you have chosen if you could have picked for yourself?"

"Henry. Or Jonathan. Or Charles. Something very usual."

"Hmm. I will admit that I did not initially like the name Percy."

There, she'd said his name again, even though she did not like it.

"I thought, at first," she said, "that if I had a goldfish, I might name it Percy."

A goldfish. Was he to be relegated to a goldfish? He'd not thought the name as bad as that.

"But over time," Lady Felicity said, "it really has grown on me. I do not think I would like you to be a Henry or Jonathan or Charles. It would not suit."

"Well then, I will stay as I am."

"Yes, and if I ever decided I would wish to be named Tulip, you would not be against it?"

Percy laughed. "Tulip, Daisy, Marigold, Violet, whatever flower strikes your fancy."

He could not work out precisely why, but Lady Felicity seemed enormously pleased to hear it.

CHAPTER FIFTEEN

FELICITY'S SISTERS, AND Mrs. Right too, had been anxious to get her alone to hear about Lady Llewellyn's ball. She'd been out very late, and so by the time she rose and went downstairs, her father was in the breakfast room.

While she did not like to keep too many secrets from him, she wished to have a strictly womanly conversation regarding her thoughts about the previous evening.

In any case, the breakfast was taken up with her father's amusing descriptions of their aunt's outrage over Mr. Sykes-Wycliff's departure and then the report that the duke had showered Lady Albright's great hall with coins and then broken her window.

Lady Marchfield had claimed that if she had the power, she would commit him to the care of a doctor. A doctor, preferably, who endorsed the use of a locked room where the Duke of Pelham would only have the opportunity of harassing himself and not anybody else.

Felicity got the feeling that her aunt would not soon recover from so many close encounters with her father. For years, they had only communicated by letter—Lady Marchfield would write one and the duke would read it, scoff at it, and toss it into the fire. They had got on better when they'd not been in such close quarters.

The duke had ended with, "I think I've finally pushed that

harridan over the edge. Hopefully her lord will pack her off to the seaside to rest and recover whatever of her faculties she's got left."

The duke was further delighted to hear that Lady Albright's butler had made a weak attempt to return the coins that was handily foiled by his housekeeper. They left him in the breakfast room, musing over whether he ought to carry out his threat of delivering a cartload of bricks.

In the drawing room, they all picked up their sewing, including Mrs. Right, who made repairs to Mrs. Wendover's torn ear under Valor's concerned gaze.

"Spill it, Felicity," Patience said. "We are dying to know everything."

"What Patience says is true," Serenity said. "Usually, it is only she who is toe-tapping, but we all are eager to know."

"Shhh," Valor whispered. "Mrs. Wendover is having an operation."

Mrs. Right put in a last stitch and tied it off, cutting the thread. "Mrs. Wendover has come through it and is now resting. She shan't mind it if we talk."

Valor took her beloved rabbit and peered down at her. "It's true, she says yes."

"There is so much to think about, my mind is in rather a jumble," Felicity admitted.

"As one would expect," Verity said, nodding knowingly.

"What do you know about it?" Winsome asked her sister.

"More than you, apparently," Verity said with a sniff.

"Do tell us, Felicity," Grace said.

"All right, well, Mr. Stratton was rather forceful with Lord Rustmont when he approached me to put his name down on my card."

"Did he clobber him right in the face?" Valor asked, cradling her ragged rabbit.

"Heavens, no," Felicity said laughing. "Lord Rustmont said he was glad to see me looking well and Mr. Stratton said he must mean he was glad to see me looking alive."

Mrs. Right snorted. "There is a piece of wit for you. I always do like a good wit."

"Lord Rustmont did not have much to say to it, though he did claim he wished to explain his part in the events of that evening in Lady Albright's garden."

"Did he explain himself?" Winsome asked suspiciously. "I cannot imagine how he could."

"He might have, though," Verity said.

"He tried, but it was not very satisfactory," Felicity said.

"Have you gone off him?" Grace asked.

"I rather think I have," Felicity said. "It was not just that he was not very heroic about the tiger. Papa says he thinks Lord Rustmont's household will be deadly dull."

"Deadly dull!" Serenity cried, as if deadly dull was akin to the plague. Which Felicity supposed it was.

Really, that must be all her sisters' opinion. None of them would tolerate deadly dull.

"It sounds safe," Valor said to Mrs. Wendover. "We like safe, cozy places, don't we?"

Well, except for Valor. She was prone to nightmares and so safety was much on her mind. Deadly dull would not put her off.

"And then," Felicity went on, "I asked Lord Rustmont a few questions regarding how a wife might be treated and did not care for his answers."

"That's it for him, then," Mrs. Right said.

"Did Mr. Stratton take you into supper?" Grace asked.

Felicity nodded. "He did. I asked him the very same questions and I very much approved of his answers. As well, I really believe Mr. Stratton understands our papa."

"That is very encouraging," Grace said. "I have begun to think that not many people do."

"It's so true," Felicity said, "they cannot see past the… pence throwing. And the padlock throwing. And the insult throwing."

"But our papa does not mean any of it," Valor said. "When he says we cannot come home for Christmas, Patience always says we can and she'll break down the door if she has to."

"I'll do it, too," Patience said, nodding. "Papa knows the truth of it."

"You are not to worry about it, Valor," Felicity said. "It just amuses Papa to say such things. He would miss us terribly if we did not come for Christmastide."

"The duke does enjoy the holidays. As far as I'm concerned, if someone cannot understand your father's original way of thinking, then what can they understand?" Mrs. Right said, shaking her head.

"You did say, right from the start, Felicity," Winsome said, "that Mr. Stratton was handsome. We've seen the proof with our own eyes and he really is."

"He has very nice conversations about the weather," Valor said. "At least, that was my personal experience."

Of course, Felicity did remember how kind Mr. Stratton had been in taking Valor's attempts at conversation seriously.

Are you falling in hopeless love with Mr. Stratton?" Serenity asked breathlessly. "I should just cry if you were."

Felicity twisted her hands together. "I don't know if I would say *hopeless*," she mumbled.

"Your mother seems to think you are set on Lady Felicity," Percy's father said in a challenging tone.

"I am not surprised," Percy said. "I have said I was."

Percy did not elaborate on his earlier idea of preferring Lady Felicity though *she* preferred Wiles. As far as he was concerned, Wiles was out of it.

"You know my opinion of that family. How can you not see it? Do you know what was told to me at the club? It is said that the duke hurled coins into Lady Albright's front hall, for some deranged reason. Oh, and that was not enough—he then shattered one of her drawing room windows!"

"Indeed, Lady Felicity was there and saw it all," Percy said, suppressing his laughter.

"She was there and does not mind advertising it. Very typical of that family, I think."

"Lady Albright sent the duke a bill, on account of Lady Felicity dripping blood on her sofa. *My* blood, if you will remember."

"Why would she sit on somebody's furniture if she's got blood on her dress?" the viscount said, determinedly ignoring the cause of the blood.

"Why would Lady Albright put guests in the vicinity of a tiger that was not properly secured?"

"Well, as to that… why is that duke not dead on the moors like we all hoped? Or dead by way of Lady Albright's tiger? Or just gone?"

"You would probably like him if you got to know him," Percy said. "Or at least stop wishing he was dead."

"Do not tell me who I wish dead! What about this report that the duke took his own sister to a cyprian's party and left her there? I could hardly countenance it, but Lord Wainwright swears it is true!"

"I believe that it is true, though I am not entirely sure how either of them ended up there. I imagine it's a funny story."

"A funny story?" the viscount said, looking incredulous. "Somehow, you cannot see what they are." The viscount paused and a slow look of horror overcame his features. "My God, you are becoming like them, that's why you cannot perceive their derangement."

Percy shrugged. "The things that family get up to are all relatively harmless," he said. "What does it matter if they've driven off their butler or Lady Felicity wishes to bake cakes and be called Tulip? It hurts nobody."

Considering that his father staggered and collapsed into a chair, Percy thought he might have refrained from mentioning those oddities.

"I can just imagine the poor butler ran screaming from the premises," the viscount whispered. "Why wouldn't he? Lady Felicity imagines herself the cook and does not even remember her own name."

"No, she is perfectly aware of her own name and I do not know who she referred to as far as the cake-making goes."

"Who else could she refer to? Of course it was herself!"

Percy did not answer, as he did not have any strong feelings either for or against either one of Lady Felicity's ideas. "I must be off," he said to his father.

His father sputtered. Just at that moment, the viscountess entered the room. "Ah, here you two are. Oh, now what is this?" she asked, looking back and forth between them.

"What this is," the viscount said, "is me explaining, though it hardly needs explaining, that Lady Felicity must not be considered. And what does he say to it? She bakes cakes, thinks her name is Tulip, and he must be off. That is what you have walked in on!"

"Goodness, you are beginning to sound hysterical, dear. One of these days you are going to drive yourself to a nervous collapse."

"I warn you!" the viscount shouted.

As his father pointlessly warned his mother, Percy said, "I must retrieve my gloves." Said gloves were in his hand but it got him out of the room. Rather than jog up the stairs he bolted out the front doors. He was off to White's to clear up one little matter. It was essential to inform Magnon and Wiles regarding where the case stood between himself and Lady Felicity.

Fortunately, he'd called his horse before encountering his father and it was waiting for him. He leapt into the saddle and trotted down the street, leaving behind the shouts of "I warn you."

Someday, his father was bound to notice that the viscountess considered his warnings no more uncomfortable than shaking water off a duck's back—the viscount made himself hoarse for nothing. In the meantime, Percy could not imagine what the neighbors thought about all his warnings.

White's was rather full, as it was the late afternoon and a moment for gentlemen who were idling away the time before they must go home to prepare for whatever evening entertainments their wives had accepted on their behalf. Some would sensibly drink coffee or tea, and then some felt the need for something stronger before they faced their households. Lord Perry sometimes drank so much fortification that he never made it home at all. The joke about that gentleman was if one invited him to a dinner, one had better be prepared to remove an empty chair at the last possible moment.

Percy made his way into the coffee room and spotted Magnon. A number of gentlemen nodded approvingly at him as he crossed the room. He sat down and said, "It seems I am resurrected as the tiger slayer, at least it appears so considering the looks coming my way just now."

Magnon stretched out his legs under the table. "Perhaps," he said, "but the bigger news is it has gone about that you put down Rustmont. Everybody is tickled over the comment that he might be pleased to see Lady Felicity *alive*, rather than just looking well."

Percy laughed. "I did say that, though I did not realize it was overheard."

"Apparently, Rustmont has very suddenly realized he has an old aunt in Dorset who requires his attention. I believe you are being credited for driving him out of Town."

"He drove himself out of Town," Percy said. "The masterful Corinthian, running like a rabbit."

"Hmm, well, it seems a fellow like Rustmont has an Achilles heel—he cannot laugh at himself. Or worse, be laughed at. I suppose he'd rather die than look foolish."

"If that is the case, one wonders why he didn't face the tiger and die when he had the chance."

"I've also heard the Duke of Pelham took his own unique revenge on Lady Albright for nearly killing his daughter."

"The pence and the padlock," Percy said, laughing. "The cause, though, was a bill Lady Albright sent about a bloodied sofa."

Magnon shook his head. "You'd think she would know better than to tangle with the duke. I would not try it myself."

"Nor I, though he is perhaps a deeper character than he lets on. I am beginning to get the feeling that there is a point to the things he does."

"And how goes it with his daughter? Have you convinced your parents of your hopeless adoration that can go nowhere because Lady Felicity prefers Wiles?"

Percy hesitated. The entire point of tracking down his friends was to inform them that the ruse was off. Now that it came to it, though, he found it hard to say.

Nevertheless, it must be said.

"My father understands that I prefer Lady Felicity, and furthermore, it is the truth. I do prefer her. As truth."

"Truth? Since when do you go in for the truth when it comes to the marriage mart?"

"Since… lately."

"Really?"

"Yes."

"What happened to the oft sworn vow—*I will not be chained?*"

"I stand by that, obviously," Percy said. "It is just that I do not believe Lady Felicity is the type of lady to use chains. Don't ask me about it any further—that is my final opinion!"

"The forced proximity has done you in."

"Maybe."

"Does the lady know of your changed feelings?"

"I cannot be sure."

"Will you tell her?"

"Of course I'll tell her. What else am I to do? Not tell her? It would be rather eccentric to not tell her. A gentleman worth his salt does not go round not telling people things." Percy stopped himself before he rambled any further. If he could hear the ridiculousness of it, he was sure Magnon could too.

"All right, all right," Magnon said, his tone full of amusement.

"In any case," Percy said, "she can never know of my part of the ruse. As far as Lady Felicity is concerned, the ruse was to stir up some jealousy in Rustmont, who I now think she disdains. That's the end of it. I do not wish her to know that I may have had… my own reasons. Initially."

"Which are not reasons anymore."

"That's right. Now, where is Wiles?"

"I do not know. He is usually here at this time of day."

"Well, I cannot stay longer. It is the Marchioness of Glastonheld's dinner this evening. Lady Felicity and the duke will attend it, as will Lord and Lady Marchfield."

"Do you suppose the duke and Lady Marchfield will come to blows?"

Percy shrugged. "There's no telling, really. Do you not attend?"

"No, my mother committed me to Lady Jericho's musical evening. Think of me suffering through a dozen awkward performances while you have your dinner. Wiles will be with you, though."

"I'll speak to him there when I can get a private word. In the meantime, if you see him here be sure to tell him… what I've said… what the situation is."

"Ah yes, Mr. Percy Stratton is hopelessly in love with Lady Felicity Nicolet."

"I did not say *hopelessly*," Percy mumbled before leaping out of his chair and hurrying away.

MRS. RIGHT KNEW very well that the duke would once more be in close quarters with Lady Marchfield. That lady had accepted a dinner invitation on behalf of herself, her lord, the duke, and Felicity ages ago and it was marked in the calendar clear as day.

Perhaps any other person would wish things smoothed between the duke and Lady Marchfield. Mrs. Right was not any other person, though. She was determined to trip up Lady Marchfield at every step—it had been an effort to drive Mr. Sykes-Wycliff from the house and she had no wish to begin again with some new fellow that lady dug up.

Before Mr. Sykes-Wycliff had left the house, Mrs. Right had paid him a visit as he packed his belongings. She'd brought in tea to soothe him and sent the footman away.

As he *was* conveniently distraught, she'd suggested that he write Lady Marchfield a strongly worded letter in which he expressed all of his outrage. After all, she said, Lady Marchfield had all along known of the irregularities of the duke and his household. In truth, the lady took pleasure in sending unsuspecting butlers into the house and she laid bets with her lord regarding how long each of them would last. Mr. Sykes-Wycliff was the fifth.

The butler had been much struck by that piece of misinformation. He'd been told by Lady Marchfield that there had not been a butler on the scene for above five years. He'd been lied to! He'd been sent into a dragon's den for someone else's amusement! He'd been used in the worst possible way while Lady Marchfield laughed behind her fan! It was as if he were nothing at all. It was as if he had no feelings!

Mr. Sykes-Wycliff's outrage spilled out into a letter, and what a letter it was. As he wrote it, Mrs. Right told him ever more terrible things about how he had been badly used.

He had ended the missive with: "Your actions have been disgraceful, Madam. I do not leave a forwarding address because I never wish to encounter you or your extended relations again in my lifetime."

Mrs. Right was pleased as Punch with it and assured Mr.

Sykes-Wycliff that she would have it delivered for him. Then she'd taken it, *not* folded or sealed it, and arranged to have it delivered an hour before the lady would set off for dinner at the Marchioness of Glastonheld's house.

Leaving it unfolded and unsealed was really the stroke of genius in the whole thing. It would be received by a footman, or maybe the lady's butler, who would lay it on a silver salver. But what man or boy could resist reading it when it was there to be read? Delightfully, no man or boy could resist peeking, and Lady Marchfield would know that all those insults about her, coming from another household's butler, were known to her staff.

The icing on the whole scheme was that Lady Marchfield would detect Mrs. Right's hand in it. Lady Marchfield would see that it could become uncomfortable to cross the duke's housekeeper.

Mrs. Right had every hope that there would be steam coming out of that lady's ears.

CHAPTER SIXTEEN

FELICITY HAD DRESSED carefully this evening. The night was unusually cold, so she'd chosen a lightweight velvet in a bronze color with small red garnets edging the sleeves and bodice. It was modern, and yet its generous cap sleeves and discreetly gathered skirt gave off a somehow older air, as if she might be a lady-in-waiting in a Plantagenet court. The modiste claimed the color of the velvet did something well for her, as it was in the same range as her hair and eyes—it created a pleasing whole. She wore her mother's ruby necklace to compliment the garnets.

Mrs. Right had worked on her hair, quietly chuckling to herself. Felicity was certain the housekeeper had some plan in the works, but with Mr. Sykes-Wycliff gone from the house she could not imagine what it was. She did not trouble herself over it, their dear Mrs. Right always told them what they needed to know when it was time to know it. Felicity's sisters had piled on her bed as she got dressed, with only a minor scuffle between Verity and Winsome and gentle tipping over from Grace.

Valor had been carrying Mrs. Wendover around all day, as that rabbit was just now in recovery from her recent operation. She gazed down at her stuffed companion and said, "Felicity, Mrs. Wendover wants to know if you will tell Mr. Stratton that you are hopelessly in love with him."

"Excellent question," Grace said. "Brava, Mrs. Wendover."

Felicity did not need to look in the glass to see that her face would just now resemble the ruby round her neck. Mrs. Wendover could be uncomfortably inquiring.

"You can tell us, Felicity," Serenity said. "We can keep a secret."

"But you will end up weeping over it," Patience pointed out to Serenity.

"I will say it was the sunset that affected me," Serenity said. "Nobody shall know the real cause."

"That's believable," Verity said.

"Stop arguing and let Felicity speak," Grace said.

Felicity had been hoping they'd keep arguing and entirely forget the point of why they began arguing. Grace was too clever for it, though.

"I will not be saying anything of the sort to Mr. Stratton. I do not even know what my true feelings are, and I will not know until a gentleman declares himself. That is how it is done, I've been told."

"Ah, I detect the ideas of that governess you all had," Mrs. Right said. "She was an over-romantic soul—forever talking about knights and courtly love. I expect that's where you got the idea."

"Miss Pynchon," Verity said laughing. "The note she left behind—"

Patience snorted. "One word—Goodbye!"

"But Mrs. Right," Felicity said, concern creeping into her voice, "Miss Pynchon was correct? I am not to entirely know my feelings until something is said?"

"Nonsense," Mrs. Right said. "Your feelings are your feelings, not some strange flock of birds that come flying in when a gentleman has declared himself. They are there all along. No, I suppose Miss Pynchon meant to say that you keep them under wraps until something is said. To avoid advertising disappointed hopes, which makes a girl look silly."

Felicity imagined Mrs. Right must be correct. It did sound

more realistic to know oneself ahead of time, rather than having feelings suddenly wash over one because a gentleman spoke.

What she did know of her feelings was that they had grown for Mr. Stratton. Mr. *Percy* Stratton. She'd even grown to like his name and would lay down her life before she allowed any of her sisters to name a goldfish Percy, though she'd threatened to do so herself.

And then, when she thought of the idea that he would *not* speak it was very discomfiting. Though she had at first viewed Lord Rustmont as the height of romance, Mr. Stratton had risked his life to save her from a terrible tiger-related death. He'd gravely injured himself to do it. What was more romantic than that?

Perhaps not blinking an eye if she decided to bake a cake or insist on being called Tulip was even more romantic. She found she very much liked his easygoing manner. Of course his looks, well, everybody could see he was handsome.

One of the housemaids poked her head in the door. "Mrs. Right, I thought you'd wish to know—His Grace has just poured a third brandy."

"Gracious, thank you, Letty!" Felicity said, hopping up from her dressing table.

"Yes, good heavens," Mrs. Right said, "it is well that your father has greased the pig, as it were, but he can go too far."

With that, they all hurried downstairs.

PERCY HAD QUIETLY walked his horse down the mews and handed him over to a groom. Then he'd slipped through the servants' door in the back garden and up to his bedchamber without detection.

Without detection from his father at any rate. He'd given a kitchen maid a scare, but once she realized what he was doing the saucy girl had winked and pressed a forefinger over her lips.

Radcliff had been waiting for him.

"He's been looking out for you all afternoon," his valet said. "He questioned me about where you went and where you were going this evening. He even proposed driving by the duke's house to see if you had called there."

Percy laughed. "I do not suppose he had a particular plan for what to do when he would have arrived to that house."

"No, I think that's what held him back from doing it. That, along with the viscountess pointing out that the duke would make some sort of joke about it and tell people Lord Denderby had been haunting his house, wishing to be invited inside."

Percy nodded. "I suppose my mother was then promptly warned to no purpose."

"Precisely."

"Does he know where I am engaged this evening?"

"No, I hid the invitation and blacked it out on your calendar in case he looked."

"Good man. I'll go back out the way I came in and he'll be none the wiser."

"So this is it? You will defy your father, and your own plans I might add, and secure Lady Felicity?"

"Do not be so nosy. I will do what I will do when I decide to do it and that is all."

Radcliff smirked. "I see. Have you sent flowers? That way, when you do what you will do when you decide to do it, you do not take her unawares?

"Flowers? Are you mad? They make her sneeze. What sort of gentleman would I be if I set out to make her sneeze, I wonder?"

"Ah yes, the sneezing. Well, I suppose you'll want one of your best coats."

"Naturally."

"And a spectacular Radcliff knot."

"Of course."

Radcliff seemed much cheered by even the mention of his knot. "They see it, they want it for themselves, and they cannot have it!" he whispered to himself. "They'll never figure out how it's done."

His valet had since crept down and back up the servants' stairs with a pitcher of hot water, Percy was cleaned up and dressed, capping off his attire with the wondrous Radcliff knot.

Getting out of the house should have been as straightforward as getting into it, but that was not the case. He was once more waylaid by his father.

It seemed the saucy kitchen maid could not help telling the cook of Percy's slipping in, who in turn told the butler, who in turn told the viscount.

The crafty old soldier had the door to the servants' stairs locked and Percy was forced to use the main staircase. The viscount had been waiting for him in the great hall.

"That's it!" the viscount shouted. "You are not to set foot out of this house until you've taken in some sense!"

The viscountess, hearing the shouting, came out from the drawing room. "Stratton, I did not even know you were at home," she said.

"Neither of us would know," the viscount said, "as he crept in through the servants' entrance like a housebreaker."

"Father," Percy said, "I am going to be late for the Marchioness of Glastonheld's dinner."

"I don't care whose dinner! I don't care if it is the queen's dinner."

"Do not be ridiculous, of course you would care if it were the queen's dinner," the viscountess said laughing.

"I warn you!"

"Of what, pray?" the viscountess asked.

Percy pressed his lips together to stop himself from laughing. He suspected his mother had been saving up that question for twenty years.

Naturally, his father did not answer her. He'd been vaguely warning her throughout their marriage and was not about to start explaining himself now.

"Do not set foot out of this house, Stratton," the viscount said. "Consider that an order."

Percy had no intention of remaining in the house. "I am afraid that is not possible. And really, Father, what will you do when I leave?"

"What will I do? You wish to know what I will do?"

"That's what he said, darling. What will you do?" the viscountess said, clearly enjoying the viscount's discomfiture.

"I will cut you off. You can live penniless until I am dead and I will not be dead for a very long time!"

"So you keep threatening…" the viscountess said quietly.

Before his father could shout another warning at his mother, Percy said, "With any luck, Lady Felicity will agree to wed. You know how eccentric the duke is—I doubt he will mind having a son-in-law join his household."

The viscount seemed dumbstruck to hear it. As well he might. Percy had no idea if that was even close to the truth. The duke advertised far and wide that he was looking to unload all of his daughters. Though Percy did not take that too seriously, it was unlikely that leaving Town at the end of the season with more young people than he'd arrived with would fit in with his plans.

"You see what you are doing, my dear?" the viscountess asked. "You are driving him into the lady's arms. You are creating a Romeo and Juliet situation. Really very amateurish, if you ask me."

The viscount spun around to his wife. "Oh really? Amateurish? And what would you do about this?"

The viscountess shrugged. "I haven't any idea."

"I really must be off," Percy said. "I am already going to have to apologize for my lateness, I do not wish to insult the marchioness any more than I have to."

He strode toward the front doors, making two silent bets. One, his father would not attempt to physically stop him. Two, the stables would have brought his horse round on Radcliff's direction.

The viscount did not attempt to stop him and that was a relief. As determined as Percy was, he could not envision wrestling his own father. His horse was saddled and ready to go.

Now, he must hurry. He really was going to be late.

He was halfway to the Marchioness' house when his horse threw a shoe. It was as if the fates conspired against him to keep him away from this dinner.

Percy dismounted and took the reins, fast-walking his horse to her square.

FELICITY COULD NOT imagine why Mr. Stratton had not turned up, nor sent a note of explanation to the marchioness.

Her father was in grand spirits—one, because he was certain Mrs. Right was up to something, and two, because her aunt's expression was one of fury. They were all just now milling round the drawing room waiting to go through and the duke kept attempting to catch his sister's eye while waving at her.

The Marchioness of Glastonheld approached. Felicity had already been introduced to her and found her a very genial lady. "My dear duke," she said, "I did receive your note earlier in the day requesting a certain arrangement? But it seems the arrangement in question has not arrived."

Felicity stared at her father. Certainly, it must be something to do with Mr. Stratton, as he had not yet arrived.

"Where is that devilish colt?" the duke asked. "I had hoped, Felicity, that Stratton would take you in."

"Oh, I see," Felicity said quietly. Her father was such a dear to think of it, and also had no notion of how embarrassing it was to hear it mentioned.

"I do not know what has happened," the marchioness said, "but Mr. Stratton's manners tend toward the perfect so I expect it will all be explained. For now, though, Lady Felicity, I will put you in the capable hands of Mr. Wiles. He is a friend of Mr. Stratton's and that is the best we can do just this minute."

Felicity nodded her gratitude, though she was not particularly grateful. Mr. Wiles was a perfectly fine fellow, she supposed, but he did not have much to recommend him.

"Now Marchioness," the duke said, "I do not suppose you will want me to take my sister, Lady Marchfield, into dinner?"

The marchioness tapped the duke's arm with her fan. "I am not such a lunatic as that, duke. I will see to it that you two are as far apart as possible. You will take the dowager duchess."

The duke laughed heartily. "I see you are on to my game!"

"All too well, I'm afraid," the marchioness said, smiling. She drifted away and Felicity noted her talking to Mr. Wiles.

It was very nice of her to go to the effort, but Felicity held out hope that Mr. Stratton would appear before they went in.

Shortly after, the marchioness made the announcement. It was time to go through. Mr. Stratton was still nowhere to be seen.

"Well, let me go dig up the dowager duchess," the duke said. "I hope she's either amusing, or deaf so I can amuse myself. Cheer up, Felicity, the chances of Stratton being dead on the road are exceedingly slim."

Dead? She had not even considered that there might have been an accident!

Mr. Wiles appeared by her side. "Lady Felicity?" he asked, holding his arm out.

She laid her hand on his arm and worked to regain her spirits. Certainly, nothing grave had happened. And then, Mr. Stratton was likely to turn up at some point. Even if they did not sit by one another at dinner, there was after dinner to think about.

Felicity was determined not to be imprisoned at the pianoforte after dinner. She had already decided she would claim a sore finger. She was not particularly good on the instrument, and she wished to be available if Mr. Stratton had anything to say in particular. Further, a sore finger could even be used to excuse oneself from a dreary game of whist. A sore finger could set one free in an after-dinner drawing room. Perhaps she would wish to read, and Mr. Stratton could hold the book and turn the pages, on account of her sore finger.

As the dinner was a large one and many of the guests came with elevated titles, Felicity found herself almost in the middle of the table. Her father was to the marchioness' right at the head with the dowager on his other side. Her aunt was further down on the same side. Felicity suspected the marchioness had thought that through carefully. Unless her father leaned very forward to peer down the table, they would be out of sight of one another. It was not out of the question that he would do so, but the marchioness had done her best.

Just across from Felicity and two chairs down, a chair sat empty. Clearly it was being held for Mr. Stratton. It did leave Miss Feldstone in a rather awful situation. If Lord Stranger on her left turned to his other partner, what was she to do? Talk to the empty chair? If Miss Feldstone was left with an empty chair next to her, why had not the marchioness left it to Felicity instead? She would have been perfectly happy to vaguely stare at the paintings on the far wall as if she did not notice the awkwardness of the situation.

Felicity supposed Miss Feldstone was singled out for the discomfiture because her father was only a baronet. Just now, she would have happily taken Miss Feldstone's place.

The wine was poured and the courses began arriving. Mr. Wiles said, "I can't think what's held up Stratton. He is very particular about arriving on time to a dinner, he finds it a ghastly thing to put a hostess in an uncomfortable position."

"I hope there has not been an accident of some sort," Felicity said. She kept telling herself that it was impossible. But in fact, it was possible.

"He'll turn up and then he'll tell everybody what happened, I'm sure of it," Mr. Wiles said. "One time, I was late to a dinner because none of my neckcloths came back from the laundry. I had to borrow one from Sir Henry—he is a neighbor, you see. Deuced inconvenient."

Felicity smiled through that ridiculous story she hardly wished to know the details of Mr. Wiles' clothing mishaps! Though, at the same time she also reminded herself not to be a goose regarding Mr. Stratton's absence. If she could not speak with Mr. Stratton, then perhaps hearing about him from his friend would be the next best thing.

"Have you known Mr. Stratton long, Mr. Wiles?"

"Most of my life. Our estates border one another. His father is the local viscount and mine is the local baron. Our first meeting was along the fence line. He pointed out he would someday hold rank over me, I pointed out his family was new-minted and mine has been around since the Tudors. Then we rolled around punching each other for a while and then became fast friends."

"That seems an odd beginning for a friendship."

"Well, we were both seven and it did eventually occur to us that there were not so many other boys to carouse round the wood with or go fishing or shoot arrows with."

"Oh I see," Felicity said. "Is that what young boys do? I only have sisters, so I do not have any experience with brothers. We never had bows and arrows, only fowling pieces."

Mr. Wiles dropped his fork and hurriedly picked it up again. "I see," he said, though Felicity was not certain he did see. Perhaps his own sisters had not owned their own guns? Perhaps it was not usual outside of Yorkshire? Lady Marchfield had warned her not to advertise that idea but she'd not taken her seriously.

"I suppose you went away to school?" Felicity said. "I understand that is the tradition with boys."

Mr. Wiles nodded. "Stratton and I went to Eton the same year and it became very advantageous to have a friend there. That's where we met Lord Magnon and a few others. We were a very jolly group, though just three of us are what's left of our set now."

"What's left? Did they all die?" Felicity asked, not too sure she understood what went on at Eton.

"Die? No, they got married," Mr. Wiles said.

"Married?"

"Well, you know what happens," Mr. Wiles said. "Chained down with obligations."

"Chained?"

Mr. Wiles laughed. "Stratton always says, I will not be chained!"

"Does he?" Felicity asked.

"But now, you cannot hold that against him," Mr. Wiles said. "He's been very helpful to you regarding Rustmont." Mr. Wiles paused, then said, "Are you very put out that Rustmont has left Town? I should have thought…"

"I was not aware that Lord Rustmont had departed the town," Felicity said. "Though I cannot claim to be put out about it."

"Excellent. Stratton said you were a good sport. You'll still help him with his own little ruse, though?"

What little ruse? What on earth had gone on that she did not know about?

Felicity smiled. "Naturally, Mr. Wiles."

"He'll be glad to hear it. Deuced funny too—his father thinking he's set on you, but you are set on me. He won't be chained!"

Mr. Wiles laughed heartily at this joke, though Felicity herself did not find it at all amusing. It seemed that the real reason Mr. Stratton had put himself at her service regarding Lord Rustmont was to trick his father into thinking he had developed a doomed affection.

What an idiot she'd been. He'd claimed he wished to do it because he enjoyed a ruse. Even her sisters had seemed skeptical of that idea.

He would not be chained, indeed. To think, she had almost given him her heart! Or maybe she had already and must take that secret to the grave.

She clenched her fork and felt her temper bubbling inside her like a volcano in the southern seas that she'd once seen in a drawing. Mr. Wiles would be lucky if she did not stab him for being the nearest person to her.

"Lady Felicity?" Mr. Wiles asked in a hesitating tone.

She did not answer him, as her feelings were such that she would like to overturn the table. Felicity turned to stare at him, wondering what on earth he could possibly say next.

His expressions were rapidly changing from jollity to confusion to a sort of panic. "Forget everything I just said," he whispered. "I talk nonsense, everybody knows it!"

Partners all round the table were turning to their other seatmate. Felicity turned without answering Mr. Wiles.

She was stunned and furious. It had all been a game.

CHAPTER SEVENTEEN

Felicity seethed with fury. Mr. Percy Stratton had been playing a game. A game at her expense. A game with her heart.

Lord Leland was making pleasantries and Felicity was doing her best to hold up her end of the conversation even though she wished to throw a gravy boat at him. None of it was Lord Leland's fault though. The fault lay in the empty chair at the other side of the table. She wanted to smash it to bits.

Her terrible temper, the temper she'd worked hard to master, had made a raging reappearance.

As if to add salt to an already blistering wound, she heard Mr. Stratton's voice suddenly ring out. "Marchioness, everyone," he said, "my deepest apologies for my tardiness, I met with some trouble on the road. Marchioness, you have every right to throw me out on my ear."

"Do not be ridiculous, Stratton," the marchioness said good-humoredly. "I was quite sure you would turn up. As you can see, I've left your place open."

"You are everything gracious, Marchioness."

Though Mr. Stratton's arrival had taken everyone's attention, including Lord Leland's, Felicity kept herself turned toward the lord and tried to ignore how much she wished to throw the nearest salt cellar at Mr. Stratton's head. Or maybe set his hair on fire with a candle and call it a ruse.

Lord Leland turned his attention back to her. "Well now, I suppose Stratton was bound to be forgiven for his late arrival. He's known for his particular manners."

"Is he?" Felicity asked. What she would really like to ask was how mannerly it was to trick a lady into thinking he was interested, all in an effort to avoid being "chained."

"Yes, I do think so," Lord Leland said, looking at her quizzically. "It is unlikely to happen again."

"So many things will not happen again," Felicity said quietly.

"Lady Felicity, are you quite well?" Lord Leland asked.

"Very well, Lord Leland," she said, forcing a smile. "I am just taking in an education about Town—it is my first season, after all."

"Oh, I see," Lord Leland said, looking confused.

Felicity realized she should have taken in that education before she'd set foot in London. Mrs. Right, who could be so counted on for truth and wisdom, had straight out told her that the gentlemen of the town were all feckless. Why had she not taken that in, so that she would not have herself been taken in?

She realized that she'd been very naïve, and that understanding made her even more furious.

When it was time to turn back to Mr. Wiles, she could not help but notice Mr. Stratton attempting to catch her eye and smiling as he did so. He would go on with it, as if she knew nothing! As if she were just a convenient rube to be used for his own purposes.

"Um, so," Mr. Wiles said, "Stratton has turned up after all. That's jolly, is it not?"

"Is it?" Felicity said, her voice full of ice.

Mr. Wiles looked as if he would faint, and she was glad of it.

PERCY HAD FINALLY arrived to the marchioness' house and had a consultation with the lady's stablemaster. That good fellow had sent off for a farrier to reshoe his horse. Then Percy had gone in and made his apologies, which the lady graciously accepted.

He thought one of the benefits of doing his level best to never inconvenience a hostess was that on the odd occasion that he did so, his crime was readily forgiven. All those dinners where he'd entertained somebody's drab miss, all those balls he'd made sure no lady sat out, all those house parties where he'd played right hand to the hostess, had added to his credit to be excused.

While the marchioness seemed cheerful to see him, he could not work out if Lady Felicity was cheered to see him. It seemed she was positively refusing to meet his eye. As he talked to his dinner partners, he very regularly glanced over but she would not look at him.

Perhaps she was annoyed that he'd not been in time to take her in?

No, that did not sound like Lady Felicity. She was not some tightlipped miss who was affronted so easily.

What was more concerning, was that Wiles *was* meeting his eye every time he glanced over. What was the fellow attempting to communicate with all those wide eyes, raised brows, and head shakes in Lady Felicity's direction?

He would not untangle any of it at table, but the dinner would not go on forever. Afterward, there would be that tedious period of time over port with the men and then they would enter the drawing room. Then, he would be able to take the lady's temperature. If she was put out about something, he must find it out and smooth it over.

In the meantime, both his dinner partners carried on the very usual sort of conversation to be had. Percy usually did not mind, but he discovered that just now it bored him a bit.

That was, until Miss Feldstone glanced toward the head of the table and said, "One hears the most alarming things about the Duke of Pelham."

"Does one?" Percy asked.

"Indeed. As a usual thing, one hears something and thinks perhaps it has been exaggerated. The tales that go round regarding the duke, though, are so outrageous that one thinks they must be true. One of the tales has been told by his own sister!"

"Ah, the cyprian party," Percy said.

Miss Feldstone made a great show of becoming flustered at the mention of a cyprian's gathering, as if she did not know such things existed. Percy was near certain she did know. He could not fathom why young ladies pretended they did not know a thing.

"Naturally," Miss Feldstone said, "I cannot know what those parties are, but I understand they are of low moral character."

"That is one way to describe it."

"A father of seven daughters, willing to leave his own sister among such debased women—well, one wonders what sort of standards he has instilled in them, if any at all."

Percy was beginning to feel some animosity toward Miss Feldstone, which was not a usual thing for him. He was very much in the habit of ignoring what did not suit him with all good humor. Unlike his father, he never saw the point in arguing with all the world. He would like to argue now, though.

"Do you imply that Lady Felicity has some deficiencies in that area?" he asked, attempting to keep his tone pleasant.

"Well, one does hear things. I understand there was some sort of attack while she danced at Almack's? And that she let Lady Albright's tiger from its cage."

"She simply had a sneezing attack at Almack's, which was entirely justified. Lady Felicity is sensitive to strong scents, particularly of flowers. Apparently, some other lady had unnecessarily doused herself in rose water. As for the tiger, again, it was a sneeze and she fell onto the latch, which ought to have had a padlock on it, but did not."

Miss Feldstone sniffed. "It seems sneezing does cause the lady much trouble, and cause trouble for you too. As it was you that ended injured from that tiger."

"It was no trouble at all," Percy lied. Of course, it had been a pile of trouble. His back still stung from it and he'd been sleeping on his stomach ever since it occurred. He found the end of the day particularly problematic, as his shirt had been rubbing against the scabbed-over wounds all day.

"I see," Miss Feldstone said. "I suppose the Nicolets will grow on us all. They had better, I suppose, as there are six more of them behind Lady Felicity."

Percy did not answer. Though, it was perhaps the only true thing Miss Feldstone had said. The Nicolets *did* grow on a person.

The duke, for all his eccentricities, had raised some very fine daughters. Unusual daughters, to be sure. But then, Percy had come to the conclusion that usual daughters could be too usual for his taste. He'd railed against becoming chained to somebody's *usual* daughter.

After the dessert course had been served for a suitable amount of time, the Marchioness of Glastonheld rose and said, "Gentlemen, Lord Jeffries will see to your port." The ladies rose and the marchioness led them to the drawing room.

Percy did his best to catch Lady Felicity's eye, but she was intent on catching her father's eye. The Duke of Pelham, odd though he was, appeared very attuned to his daughter. He rose and said, "I will return in a moment, gentlemen—pour me a very large glass!"

He followed his daughter out of the room and Percy could just make out Lady Felicity and the duke talking in the hall before the dining room's doors were closed again.

As the port went round, Wiles continued making his faces, Lord Jeffries went on his usual tirade about poachers, and Percy waited for the duke to return.

He never did return, though.

FELICITY KNEW SHE could count on her father. As much as he claimed he wished them all out of the house, he was very astute in conjecturing over his daughters' moods and tempers.

When she'd been younger and had far less control over her temper, he would note that she was reaching a boiling point and say, "Hold on, everyone, Lady Ferocity is set to make an appearance."

Just now, she'd given him a very decided look when the marchioness rose to lead the ladies out. He'd not needed more than that—he would follow her out to discover what it was for. Another father might have noticed their daughter's distress but feel constrained not to follow her out when he was meant to stay seated. Her father had no such compunction about breaking a rule when it seemed expedient.

In the hall, he looked at her quizzically. "I can see very well that Lady Ferocity is on the verge of turning up," he said.

Felicity nodded but did not answer, as she was working very hard not to weep. The idea of weeping made her in even more of a temper. She should go mad if anyone were to see her eyes leaking.

"Right," the duke said. "Wait here."

The duke had a word with a footman nearby, who hurried off. Then her father went into the drawing room and came out again in under a minute.

"I've given the marchioness the bad news that you have a terrible headache. Then I gave her the good news that I will not be in the drawing room to harass my sister. I sent a footman to fetch our coachman. We will be off in a thrice. In the meantime, say nothing—I know you will end up throwing something if one tear falls from your eye."

Her father really was so very good. If only people understood him as she and her sisters did. All they saw was the outrageousness of him, but he really did understand his daughters.

Soon enough, the front doors were opened and their carriage was ready for them. Another footman brought Felicity's pelisse.

They hurried out to the chill night and the duke helped her inside.

The doors were shut, the carriage rolled forward, and the duke said, "Well? What's set you off?"

"Papa, you will not believe what I have discovered by way of Mr. Wiles. Mr. Stratton has all along just been playing a game. He claimed he wished to help me make Lord Rustmont wild with envy simply because he enjoyed a ruse. You know, when I wished to make Lord Rustmont jealous, which I do not at the present time."

"What is the game that young rogue is playing, exactly?"

"He wished his parents to believe that he was set on me, and that I was set on Mr. Wiles. He wished them to view it as a hopeless case. And guess why?"

"Because young men are idiots?"

"Because, as it seems he says quite often, he will not be chained!"

"Is that so?"

"Indeed, Mr. Wiles let it all out at dinner, thinking I already knew it. Mr. Wiles did not know that perhaps my opinions of Mr. Stratton had changed. Significantly. Do you see what's happened to me, Papa? I am the victim of disappointed hopes."

"I'll wring his neck like a chicken," the duke said.

Felicity was a bit startled by that idea, as it could only lead the duke into a prison. A person of her father's rank could get away with quite a lot, but murder was not one of those things. As well, as much as she would like to hurl all manner of things at Mr. Stratton's head just now, she did not wish for his neck to be wrung. It was rather too permanent.

"Please do not do anything so foolhardy," she counseled.

The duke shrugged. "Perhaps you are right. The law is never set up the way one needs it to be! If there were any justice, I might wring his neck with impunity!"

"Now, Papa, I know you have been so set on getting us all out of the house, but I think I cannot wed just now. It is not possible for me, at least not this season."

"Well, my girl, I've put up with you for eighteen years, I suppose nineteen won't do me in. For now, we will go home and you will have the comfort of that horde of hooligans you call sisters."

"And Mrs. Right, too," Felicity said.

"Ah yes, is there anything Mrs. Right cannot fix? I suppose a broken heart will be no different."

Felicity did not answer. She did not wish to own that she was just now in possession of a broken heart. Though, she was just now in possession of a broken heart.

It really did make her wish to throw something.

PERCY HAD KEPT an eye on the doors, all the while toe-tapping under the table, but the duke had never returned to the dining room.

Lady Felicity had met the duke in the hall and then he'd not come back.

Was the lady ill? Or was it just Wiles who was ill? That fellow kept staring and staring at him with wide eyes like Percy was a specter suddenly spotted on a dark and forested lane.

Finally, Lord Jeffries came to the thrilling conclusion of his tale of an old reprobate in his neighborhood who was forever poaching on his land but could never be caught red-handed. Joe Candle was his name, and Joe Candle still was not caught.

Every gentleman at table refused a second glass of port, as they all knew it would just lead to a second poaching story from Lord Jeffries. Joe Candle would probably be surprised to know how boring he could make a meeting over port.

This was the sort of moment when the Duke of Pelham's attendance would come in very handy. The duke would not have allowed Jeffries to get two minutes into that story without interrupting him with a joke.

Jeffries rose. "I suppose we'd best go in, then," he said.

Percy leapt from his chair and it clattered and nearly fell over. Was Lady Felicity in the drawing room or not? Had she been taken ill and gone home? Had she been perfectly well and the duke just decided he preferred the company in the drawing room?

It was not out of the realm of possibilities to think it—if the duke preferred to break with convention and be elsewhere, he would not think twice about it.

It was something to hope for anyway.

As he made his way out, Wiles hurried behind him and said, "Make your way to the back of the drawing room. There is an alcove back there with a bookcase. We will pull out books and pretend to be engrossed."

Percy stared at his friend. Why had Wiles transformed himself into a spy intent on scheduling clandestine meetings in the back of the drawing room?

He began to get a very troubling feeling. Lady Felicity had dined with Wiles. Had he said something about the ruse? Percy had been sure Magnon would have encountered him this afternoon and informed him of the new lay of the land.

But even if Magnon had not seen Wiles, surely Wiles would not have approached the subject and given the game away? Not even if he did not know there was no longer a game to give away.

Nevertheless, he did as he was bid, searching for Lady Felicity or the duke as he made his way to the back of the room. Both were absent.

She had gone.

He avoided the marchioness' eye, as he was all but certain she would pull him into a game of whist. He did not care for it very much, but he was rather good and so was sought after more than he would like.

Percy reached the alcove of the drawing room, took a book and opened it. "Here I am, pretending to be engrossed by a book I do not even know the title of. What is wrong with you? What has gone on?" he asked Wiles.

Wiles flipped pages of a book and he did very much look as if he were reading. Reading intently, as a matter of fact.

"Whatever it is," Percy said, "you will not find your words in there, but only in your mind. Out with it."

Wiles let out a plaintive sigh. "The unfortunate thing is, Lady Felicity tricked me into believing that you'd told her all about the ruse."

Percy could feel the blood draining from his face, as if it did not wish to be in the vicinity of what his ears had just heard. "How, pray, did the lady trick you?" he asked.

"She pretended. She pretended she knew all about it. I guess it started with her asking me how long we'd known each other, and then I mentioned our old set at Eton, but now it was only me, you, and Magnon."

Wiles paused and laughed a little, though Percy failed to see the amusement in anything that had been said so far.

"She thought the others died, you see," Wiles said. "So then I told her no, they did not die, they just got married... and that somehow leapt to chains and how you would not be chained down. Hard to say how it happened, really."

Percy had a great urge to hit Wiles over the head with the book in his hand.

"Now," Wiles continued, "when you reflect on it, I think you'll see that my slip was actually a good thing. I've saved you some trouble, my friend."

"You've saved me trouble? How have you worked that out?" Percy asked, incredulous.

"Because it seemed to me that Lady Felicity was not as pretending about you as she had been in the beginning. I think she'd started to get ideas, you see?"

"Yes, I do see," Percy said tightly. "And here's the problem—I've started to get ideas too."

"Ideas? You? But you said you would not be chained... Many times and very firmly, actually."

"I know what I said many times and very firmly," Percy said. "I merely changed my mind. Firmly."

Wiles tapped his chin. "I did not know, you should have told me. Well, how about you tell her I was lying? I made the whole thing up because I was jealous. Or I made the whole thing up because I am unreliable and a terrible fibber. Just say I made it up. Yes, that would do very well, I think."

"It would not do very well at all because Lady Felicity is not an idiot. My god, what will she tell her father?"

Wiles did pale at that idea. "Oh no, what will he *do* about it is the better question? You might want to take yourself off somewhere. Rustmont went to Dorset to look in on an old aunt—you could go there too and see how she gets on."

Percy ignored that rather ridiculous suggestion. He was going nowhere. He had to fix this unfortunate turn of events.

He had no idea how, just this moment, but he would fix it. Lady Felicity would attend the Jameson's rout on the morrow, he would fix it then. If only he could send flowers in the meantime, but he could not. She was put out enough without being thrown into a sneezing fit.

Percy had begun to wonder if there were types of flowers that did not make one sneeze. Roses were out, but perhaps there were other choices? He would have to look into it.

"Mr. Stratton," the marchioness called, "I insist you put that book down and pair at whist with Miss Feldstone."

Percy slapped a smile on his face and nodded. Though, it was the very last thing he'd like to do.

CHAPTER EIGHTEEN

F ELICITY HAD BEEN grateful that her sisters had gone to bed early. Most of them, anyway. Grace and Patience had still been awake and reading in the drawing room, but she'd claimed she came home because of a headache and could not bear to speak. They sensibly let her be, though it would have tortured Patience to do so.

Mrs. Right had not looked particularly fooled, especially not with the glance her father had given the housekeeper, but that good lady always knew when one of them wished to talk or preferred to be left alone.

She awoke to an early dawn that promised a sunny day, which seemed a rebuke to her mood. Felicity had not slept much, her stinging feelings, which only served to fuel her temper, did not like rest and repose. They only wished to rage and shake the windows.

It did not help that she considered herself a first-rate idiot for falling for Mr. Stratton's charms. Really, when she thought about it, he was charming to everybody. He'd even been charming to Valor.

It was the tiger that had pushed her over the edge of commonsense. He'd saved her from a tiger. She supposed she might have been anybody at all and Mr. Stratton would have done just the same.

Felicity gripped the bed sheets in a fist. She had been taken down a notch. She had been shown she was not all that alluring. Perhaps all along, Mr. Stratton had his eyes on Lady Mary—that lady of the frothy blond curls who was supposed to be the season's diamond of the first water.

It was infuriating.

There was a quiet tap on the door, though it was still very early. Mrs. Right came in with a cup of tea in hand. "Extra milk, just as you like it," the lady said. "I thought I might pop my head in before your sisters are up."

"You can tell something has happened before even being told it," Felicity said.

"It was as clear as day that *something* happened, though not at all clear what it was."

Felicity poured out the story.

Mrs. Right sighed. "I did not take that gentleman to be a bounder, though I should have known."

"Yes, you did say before we even left Yorkshire that they were all feckless."

"So I did, and yet I thought…"

"It is no matter, Mrs. Right, I was just as fooled as everybody, and I spent far more time with that gentleman than you did. I suppose even Papa was fooled."

Mrs. Right's expression took a sudden turn. "Your father," she whispered. "Heaven help Mr. Stratton with whatever the duke will send his way."

Wishing to relieve Mrs. Right's mind on that front, she said, "Oh, you are not to worry about anything of that sort. Papa did consider wringing Mr. Stratton's neck, but I dissuaded him from it."

Mrs. Right did not look as comforted as she imagined the lady would. "Well, let us hope he does not have any other ideas come to him," Mrs. Right said.

Before Felicity could answer, her door was flung open and Grace, Patience, Serenity, Verity, Winsome, and Valor streamed into the room.

Piling on Felicity's bed, Patience said, "I hope your headache is gone, we could not wait for you to come down. Valor was helping Charlie practice answering the door again and he told her something… well, it was surprising."

Valor sat up straight, pleased to be the bearer of news. "Charlie said that our coachman has been sent to buy up as many chains of all descriptions as he can find and then he is to drop them at Mr. Stratton's doorstep."

Felicity leaned back on her pillows. She ought to have known that her father would not sit back and do nothing. She had convinced him not to wring Mr. Stratton's neck, but she had not extracted a promise not to do anything else.

"What does it mean, Felicity?" Grace asked. "Why is Mr. Stratton to be in receipt of chains?"

"Because according to Mr. Wiles," Felicity said, "Mr. Stratton has said many times that he will not be chained by marriage."

"Not chained by marriage?" Patience asked. "What is he planning if he is not to be chained in marriage? Is he to live alone for the rest of his life?"

"That I do not know," Felicity said. "He means to avoid matrimony for now and has tricked his father into believing that he prefers me, but that I prefer Mr. Wiles. I suppose that at some point, he will be bowled over by some lady, but that time is not now and that lady is not me."

A tear rolled down Serenity's cheek. "I am so sad I could cry, Felicity."

"You *are* crying," Winsome pointed out.

Felicity did not point out that she was so sad she could cry too, as she did not like to cry in front of people, not even her sisters.

"So Papa has heard of this idea that Mr. Stratton will not be chained and has sent chains to aggravate him," Winsome said.

"A well-known insult in a case such as this," Verity said.

"How would you know?" Winsome asked, narrowing her eyes.

"Everybody in the world knows it but you," Verity said. "Why else would Papa have thought to do it?"

"I think Papa has been wonderful to do it," Patience said. "Mr. Stratton deserved a good scolding and think how heavy all those chains will be to move. And move them to where, I wonder? It will be very inconvenient."

"Mr. Stratton deserves more than an inconvenience, to my mind," Mrs. Right said in a grim tone.

"Oh, do you think our father will do something else?" Grace asked.

"I've no idea," Mrs. Right said.

"I wish I could send Mr. Stratton something terrible," Valor said. "He tricked me into thinking he was a good person by talking about the weather so nicely."

"We would all like to send him something terrible," Winsome said.

"I think Mrs. Wendover might like to write him a very terrible letter," Valor said.

Felicity was not certain what a letter from Valor's stuffed rabbit would say, but she gave it little thought as she was certain Valor would never get around to doing it.

"What shall you do when you see him, Felicity?" Grace asked.

"I shan't see him. I do not wish to go anywhere he might be. I will only go to small affairs where he is not likely to appear."

"You do not go to the rout this evening, then?" Patience asked.

"Certainly not. I intend to have an evening in with my very genial sisters and shall be happy to do it."

"And have an evening in with Mrs. Wendover," Valor added.

Felicity nodded. "Of course, Mrs. Wendover."

She supposed that would be her life now—having a night in with Mrs. Wendover.

★

PERCY HAD NOT yet descended the stairs, as he'd been up very late thinking about Lady Felicity. It was after eleven o'clock in the morning and Radcliff was just now putting the finishing touches on his neckcloth when they heard a terrible shriek from down stairs.

"That sounded like your father," Radcliff whispered.

"What now?" Percy asked.

The next half-minute was taken up with the viscount shouting a string of oaths.

"I'd best go and see, I suppose," Percy said. "Perhaps his warnings to my mother have finally come to something and he's very predictably ended on the wrong side of the stick. I've told him before, the viscountess will push back if pushed too far."

"I'll wait here," Radcliff said.

"Coward," Percy said, hurrying from the room.

What he found below stairs was an interesting scene. His father was holding one hand in the other and hopping, the front doors were flung open, and the front steps were covered in iron chains of various sizes.

Before he could inquire into what had happened, the viscount shouted, "I fell! I wished to step out for some fresh air and fell over on top of that heap of metal. My finger is broken, and my toe might be too!"

"Why is it there, though?" Percy asked. "Did you order it?"

"Why would I order all that? Do I look like I'm deranged?"

Percy did not answer, as the old soldier *did* look rather deranged at the moment.

"Of course I did not order it!"

"Then what is it doing there?" Percy asked.

"How should I know!" the viscount shrieked.

Just then, his mother came out of the drawing room. She looked about and said, "Gracious, why have you had that pile delivered to the doorstep? How are we to come and go with that in the way? Are we meant to jump over it?"

As his father began the predictable shouting, peppered with "I warn you," Percy stepped outside.

It really was a significant amount of chains, in all sizes, some looking new and some well-used, all piled atop one another. He supposed that somebody had ordered such a conglomeration and it had been delivered to the wrong house. How odd that it would have been dumped at the front doors though. One might have thought the driver would have knocked and inquired or put it in the mews out of sight, at the very least.

As he stared at it, he noted a small paper folded up among the chains. He reached down for it, certain it would reveal the address this mess was supposed to go to.

He unfolded it.

You will not be chained, eh?

Percy fumbled and nearly dropped the note. It was obviously from the duke, as nobody but that gentleman used the term "eh" as much as he did.

Lady Felicity had told her father all about the ruse before he even had a chance to explain!

He would not be chained; he'd said so many times. And now, just as he'd changed his mind about chains, his words had come back to haunt him by way of a pile of chains.

Percy slipped the note into a pocket, turned round, and went back into the house. His father had calmed somewhat, or at least as calm as he ever was. The viscountess had made arrangements for someone to climb over the pile of chains to fetch a doctor and she'd poured the viscount a glass of brandy.

"I'll get to the bottom of whose idea of a joke this was," the viscount said.

"What is the joke, though?" the viscountess asked.

The viscount did not answer, as he was too worn out to even warn his lady.

"I'm sure it was simply delivered to the wrong address," Percy said. "While we wait to be informed of the rightful owner, we can have the grooms move it to the mews."

The viscount nodded his consent to the idea, the brandy going a good way to soothing him.

Before Percy could make that arrangement, a young man appeared on the other side of the pile of chains. A young man in the duke's livery. A young man who Percy recognized as the duke's footman.

"A message for Mr. Stratton, sirs," the lad called, holding out folded paper.

Percy hurried out. It seemed the duke was not satisfied to leave a note in the pile of chains but had written him a letter too.

He reached over the pile of chains, took the letter, and tipped the boy a coin. Percy slipped it into a pocket along with the other note.

"What is it? Who is it from?" the viscount asked querulously.

"Oh, from Magnon," Percy said casually. "He said he would write about... a matter. Well! Everything seems to be in good order here, I'll just go above stairs—Radcliff is not finished fussing with my knot."

Percy took the stairs two at a time, leaving the viscountess to manage her viscount. He hurried into his room and shut the door behind him. Radcliff stood staring expectantly.

"The condensed version of events downstairs is that the Duke of Pelham has had chains of all sorts piled high on our doorstep, my father fell over them and broke his finger and probably his toe, there was a note tucked into the pile that said, 'You will not be chained, eh?' and then the duke's footman arrived with a letter addressed to me. My father does not know about the note or the letter, did not recognize the duke's livery, nor yet guessed where the chains came from."

Radcliff looked as bowled over by the report as was to be expected. It was not everyday that one's doorstep was piled with chains and one's father broke appendages falling over them.

Percy pulled the letter out of his pocket, dreading what it would say. He hoped the duke did not plan to call him to a green for insulting his daughter, even though he was well aware that the gentleman had a habit of not turning up at the appointed hour for such meetings.

He broke the seal and slowly unfolded it, not failing to notice that Radcliff had casually moved next to him to read over his shoulder.

Mr. Stratton,

We are very ~~dispointed~~ ~~disappointted~~ disappointed in you. We thought you were nice but you are mean! Everybody knows being mean is very bad. You are a terrible person. We hope my Papa wraps you in chains and throws you in a lake.

Lady Valor Nicolet and Mrs. Persephone Wendover

"Valor," Radcliff said, "she is the youngest."

"Yes."

"Who is Mrs. Wendover?"

"Her stuffed rabbit," Percy said.

"Well now, that's a rather murderous stuffed bunny," Radcliff said with a snort. "I suppose you ought to be grateful the duke left the chains on your doorstep, rather than take Lady Valor's advice to wrap you in them to drop you in a lake."

"Now the whole family is against me, even the youngest of them and the inanimate among them."

"What will you do?" Radcliff asked.

Up until this moment, Percy had not been sure what he would do. He had a vague plan of finding Lady Felicity at the rout this evening and explaining himself.

However, Valor had done him a service. She had left him an opening. She had written to him, so he could write her back. Whatever he wrote, he was certain Lady Valor would show it to Lady Felicity.

"Get me my writing things. Lady Valor deserves a timely response to her heartfelt letter."

MRS. RIGHT DID not often find herself ready to explode with anger. Mostly, she was amused by the things in her view. Even a butler needing to be driven out of the house had its amusing moments.

What did not amuse her, though, was any attack or insult to one of her girls. That, she had discovered long ago, really set her off.

She remembered as if it were yesterday the grim denouement with a farmer down the road in Yorkshire. That fellow claimed her girls were disturbing his sheep by firing off their fowling pieces at all hours. Helder, that was his name, had gone so far as to name them heathens and claim they ought to have more feminine dignity if they were to go round announcing themselves as ladies.

Very naturally, Mrs. Right had been forced to put an end to it. What frightened sheep more than gunfire? Wolves. Though there were no wolves left in England, it had been built into their instincts to fear them, handed down from one generation to the next. Anybody could see a sheep's reaction when faced with a large, rangy, dark dog with pointed ears. If that dog happened to show its teeth, expect a stampede.

Mrs. Right had got to work with needle, thread, stuffing, two black buttons for eyes, and some masterful strokes of paint. She fashioned a wolf's head and attached it to a tree by the gate the farmer used to move his sheep into his far field to graze. She positioned it as if the wolf was cagily peering round the tree, hiding in wait. The coloring of it was very similar to the tree bark it was attached to. It could easily be overlooked. Except overlooked by a herd of sheep—they were attuned to danger, always on the lookout for it, and it only took one of them to notice and send out the alarm to the rest of them.

The farmer could not reason out why the sheep had to be

forced through that gate, and neither could the herd dogs. For some weeks, he spent vast amounts of time wrangling them through it, the bleats of panicked sheep carrying a half mile.

Even after he got them into the field, they huddled together far away from the gate and did not eat as much as they should have. Then he had the further trouble of bringing the herd through it again.

Then one day, the farmer discovered her fashioned wolf's head, ripped it from the tree, and came marching over to speak to the duke.

Mrs. Right had answered the door, gave him a severe dressing down, took the wolf's head from his hands, beat him over the head with it, and slammed the door in his face.

When that devil went to the vicar to complain, Mrs. Right simply asked for the evidence, which could not be produced because she'd taken it from him and promptly thrown it into the kitchen fire. She'd slipped on her best affronted matron demeanor and asked the vicar how it was to be believed that she would have sewn a wolf's head and attached it to a tree. Perhaps Mr. Helder was losing his wits.

Not a word of complaint was ever again spoken about the girls' fowling pieces.

Now, though, what could she do? Managing a farmer was easy work. Punishing Mr. Stratton for toying with Felicity's heart was a bit trickier.

She would think of something, though. Mr. Stratton would pay dearly for hurting her girl. Mrs. Right would see to it.

THE DAY HAD passed slowly and Felicity began to wonder if time would always go so slow, now that she was in possession of disappointed hopes.

Her sisters had rallied round her and did their very best to cheer her. Her father had been surprised that she did not wish to go to the rout that evening, but he had not pressed her over it. Rather, he had ordered her favorite dinner, which everybody knew was a baked chicken with potatoes quartered and roasted until they were just shy of burned, a simple greens salad, rolls with ample butter, and berry tarts for dessert. He further attempted to cheer her by ordering up one of the good Canary wines from the cellars.

Over dinner, Patience had posited that Mr. Stratton was not worth worrying over. Felicity would meet some gentleman far superior and find herself glad to forget all about a gentleman who proved himself so unsteady.

Serenity counseled rising early to view the sunrise, as it would teach her heart that a new day had dawned.

Grace hoped that Felicity would recover her spirits in time, and that time was hoped to be a short time.

Verity announced that the time that was very usual to recover from such things was six days.

It was not a surprise to anyone that Winsome challenged that idea. For all Verity knew of it, she said, it might be five days.

Valor had brought Mrs. Wendover to dinner and told Felicity that her friend was very disappointed in Mr. Stratton, and had taken steps.

As Felicity did not know what steps could be taken by a stuffed rabbit, she chose to simply appreciate the sentiment.

Her father poured her an extra glass of the Canary and said he'd answered Mr. Stratton's insult and hoped that young idiot fell over his answer.

"Fall over the chains, Papa?" Valor asked.

"That's right," he said nodding.

"Maybe he broke his neck," Valor said in a gruesomely hopeful tone.

The rest of her sisters agreed with that sentiment and nodded. Sisterly loyalty could really be very touching.

The family eventually made their way into the drawing room

and Mrs. Right joined them after supervising below stairs. They played lottery tickets for a while and then lapsed into desultory conversation.

They were all mightily surprised when they heard the door knocker smartly rapped.

CHAPTER NINETEEN

FELICITY, AND EVERYBODY really, stared toward the drawing room doors. Charlie, having grown relaxed leaning on the doorframe, almost fell over from the surprise knocks coming from outside. He regained his balance and ran for the door.

"If it's my sister come to complain about something, don't let her in," the duke shouted after Charlie.

In a moment, Charlie was back and looking exceedingly perplexed. "It is a letter delivered. For Lady Valor," he said.

"What, ho?" the duke said, laughing. "Has my youngest been keeping secret liaisons I know nothing about?"

Valor looked very concerned to hear of the letter, and then more concerned over her father's joking. "What is a liaison, Papa?"

"Never mind it," the duke said jovially. "Let us see who this letter is from and what it says."

Valor, having received the first letter of her life, looked at it, marveling. She broke the seal and unfolded the paper.

The paper was written in a close hand and entirely filled.

"Why is there so much writing?" Valor asked. "It's like a whole book!"

"Who is it from, though?" Grace asked.

Of course, Felicity wished desperately to know too. Who else could it be from but Mr. Stratton? She did not say so, though, as she was in the midst of pretending he meant nothing to her.

Valor peered down at the paper and ran her finger down to the end. "It is from Mr. Stratton. I am afraid he is not as ashamed as he should be, or he would not have written us back."

"Written us back?" Felicity blurted out.

"I told you that me and Mrs. Wendover would write him a scolding letter," Valor said.

"I know you said…" Felicity trailed off.

"But none of us thought you would do it," Winsome said.

The duke filled the room with laughter. "You didn't think she'd do it, but she did do it. Eh, Valor, you went and gave Mr. Stratton the what-for!"

"Mrs. Wendover and I were very stern and told him he was mean."

The duke guffawed, though Felicity felt her cheeks burn. It was giving something away for Valor to tell Mr. Stratton he was mean. It gave away that she'd been injured, which she did not wish for.

"Give me the letter, Valor," Felicity said. "It is too long for you to read and if there is anything in it that anybody needs to know I will tell you."

Though Valor had been honored to receive her first letter, she was equally willing to give over the task of reading such a long missive.

Felicity took that opportunity to flee to her room with it. She would trust Mrs. Right to stop any sisters who had a notion of following her.

PERCY WAS BEGINNING to think his father's house in Town was somehow beset by bad luck. The doctor had been to see the viscount and confirmed that both a forefinger and a big toe were broken. There was not much to be done about it other than wrap them and allow them to heal. After the doctor left, the viscount had added brandy into the prescription. He'd been sipping it all day.

Naturally, no person arrived to claim the chains. Percy was not certain what to do with them. Eventually, he had the grooms straighten them out and run them along the side of the house so the horses going in and out of the mews could get by them.

Just when that problem was solved, the cook had some sort of breakdown in the kitchens. A large order was delivered, but nothing he'd ordered was in it. Instead of the variety of staples he usually ordered, all he got were sacks of cabbages.

Percy could hear him shouting about it from the library.

That turned out to be only the beginning of it. Later, it was discovered that the wine delivery the viscount had so painstakingly composed had been cancelled. The final discovery was that the laundry where they sent out their clothes had been told to donate them to the poor.

By the time Percy heard a good number of his shirts had become charitable donations, he began to suspect the duke's hand in it. There was no possibility that so many disasters could befall one house, all on the same day.

The oncoming problems one after the next did not mix well with the viscount's self-prescribed brandy and sore finger and toe. The viscountess finally ordered the carriage and left to nobody knew where. Percy, himself, left by the servants' stairs, pretending not to hear his father's shouts for him to get to the bottom of this trickery.

He'd already got to the bottom of it, he was certain, and the last thing he'd do was tell his father of his suspicions.

In any case, he was in a hurry to get to Lady Jameson's rout. He must find Lady Felicity and somehow put an end to this misunderstanding. Well, not misunderstanding, exactly. It really was more like a transformation, where she had heard about where it started, but not where it was now.

With any luck, Lady Felicity had read his letter and would already know all about it. He'd arranged for it to be delivered just before they would leave their house for the rout. Then, some-how, he'd have to soothe the duke and make him stop sending disasters to his house.

By the time he arrived, he found the rooms crowded. He edged his way past the crowd, looking over their heads for any sign of her. She was nowhere to be seen.

He eventually found Magnon, who had not seen her either.

"Do you suppose she was too put out to come?" Magnon asked. "Knowing you'd probably be here?"

"Perhaps," Percy said thoughtfully. "Though I did write a letter explaining everything."

"You wrote her a letter? Hm, I wonder if the duke would have confiscated it. Not the thing, you know, to send letters to unmarried ladies."

"Yes, well, the youngest of them, Lady Valor, wrote me a letter first. She wished to inform me that I was a terrible person and she hoped the duke would wrap me in chains and throw me into a lake."

Magnon guffawed. "She is not wrong," he said.

Percy ignored that comment. "In any case, I wrote her back, certain she would show it to Lady Felicity."

"And yet, the lady does not appear."

"No, and the duke is wreaking vengeance on my house. My father is slipping into madness over it."

"Over what?" Magnon asked.

"Well, let's see, first there was a pile of chains on the door-step, which the viscount promptly fell over and broke a finger and a toe. Then, his wine order was canceled, the cook received sacks of cabbages instead of his regular order, and a significant part of our wardrobes were donated to charity unbeknownst to us."

Magnon snorted. "Everybody knows not to tangle with that duke. You only sent a letter, and he has answered it a thousand-fold."

Percy paused. There was something in that. It was true—the duke kept sending disasters. He'd only sent a letter. Perhaps he ought to be sending other things. Not disasters, but nice things. Perhaps he had only to wear them all down with gifts.

"I know what I will do," he said.

"What?"

"Never mind," Percy said. "But the first thing I will do is get out of here. If Lady Felicity were coming, she would be here already. I have been iced out and I need to start some fires to melt their wall against me. I have much to plan."

FELICITY HAD SHUT her door, lit a candle, and sat in the over-stuffed chair by the window. Mr. Stratton had written Valor and certainly it was meant for her eyes.

She smoothed out the paper.

Esteemed Lady Valor—

I received the recent communication from yourself and Mrs. Wendover accusing me of being mean, as well as a terrible person, and the wish that the duke would tie me up in chains and throw me in a lake.

Gracious, that was what Valor wrote? She'd not mentioned anything about a drowning.

If I consider the matter based only on what you may know of my history, I would have to agree with those sentiments.

However, if you would indulge me in reading this letter, I would like to lay out the case of the thing.

I did come into this season announcing to my friends that I would not be chained. In part, this was because I came under terrible pressure from my viscount to speedily choose a wife. I suspect that, at your age, you can sympathize with my contra-riness. It is a hard thing to be told what to do and one's instinct is to announce that one will not do it.

Then, and this is where I really am at a terrible fault, I thought it would be clever to join forces with Lady Felicity. She wished to make Lord Rustmont jealous, and I wished to convince my father that my feelings were engaged where they could not succeed.

My fault is in not informing Lady Felicity of this at the outset.

As it happens, I have found my dedication to refusing to be chained on the wane. In fact, it seems to be gone altogether.

Alas, my crime of secrecy and the stupidity of announcing something to my friends that could not hold over time have both come back to haunt me.

My apologies, and I did enjoy our conversation about the weather. As well, give my regards to Mrs. Wendover—I hope that enchanting lady-rabbit does not hold a grudge.

Stratton.

Felicity did not know what to think. It was a fine letter, if she could believe it. Or even know what to make of it. It hinted that she might be preferred, but it did not come out and say so. All it really said was that his announcing he would not be chained was an idea he now recognized as foolish.

But who was the cause of this change of heart? Was it her? Was it someone else? Why did he not make himself more clear?

She tucked it into her pillowcase as she had no intention of allowing anybody else to read it. At least, not yet. She did not wish to hear anybody else's opinion about it until she had formed her own.

Felicity would be happy to inform Valor of Mr. Stratton's regard for her good opinion, and for Mrs. Wendover's too, but that was all.

She had much to decide. She had been determined not to encounter Mr. Stratton again, but would that hold? Could she dare to trust him? He had lied once, perhaps this entire letter was a lie.

Felicity did not know what to do or how she felt, or whether she was cast down or buoyed up. All she could decide right this very moment, was to ring for her maid, get into her nightclothes, drink her half glass of Canary, brush her teeth, braid her hair, and go to bed.

Perhaps sleep might bring clarity.

MRS. RIGHT KNEW very well that she would have an excellent night of repose. It was always so when she had accomplished her aim.

Her aim at this moment in her history was to enact retribution against Mr. Stratton and she had done a fine job of it. She'd discovered his butler's name and she already knew where they lived, the rest was an easy walk down a shady lane. She set out to impersonate the household via letters to various places.

First to the grocer everybody in that neighborhood used, indicating that the regular order must be put aside. They had a great need for cabbages, as Lady Wentworth, whoever she might be, had decided to hold a cabbage festival for charity. Mrs. Right had even included the following: "As you might imagine, good sir, the race to locate a suitable number of cabbages will be furious. Please do secure three large sacks before there are none to be had."

A person wishing for sacks of cabbages was the most absurd thing in the world, but the *ton* were so known for their absurdities that the grocer would not blink over it. It would be just another amusing story he would relate to his family regarding the vagaries of the high and mighty.

For the wine merchant, she decided to go in a different direction. That letter she made appear as if it came from the viscount himself, accusing the merchant of overcharging and taking him for a rube. Viscount Denderby was not such a country turnip to be had in such a manner. He demanded the order be canceled, as he had secured a merchant who charged fair prices.

And then, the coup de grâce. Mrs. Right informed the laundress that serviced the house that the pile of clothes sent to her had been a mistake. That particular pile was meant for the poor. If she would be so kind as to forward them on to some reputable charity, the viscountess would be most obliged. Lord Denderby would, of course, honor the bill, as it had been their own mistake. The laundress would be delighted—she would sell the clothes for as much as she could get and then be paid the bill too. She'd never wish to question such a happy circumstance.

Mrs. Right suspected Mr. Stratton's house to be in turmoil just now—full of cabbages, empty of wine, and short of clothes. That was exactly what she wished for. Let no person hurting one of her girls ever have a moment's rest or peace.

If there were one thing niggling at her mind just now, one loose thread that had not been tied up, it was that letter from Mr. Stratton that Felicity had taken to her room.

Mrs. Right had the experience and good sense not to follow her up the stairs and pry into it, and she held the rest of the girls back from doing the same, but she did wish to know what it said.

She reminded herself that all things come in their own time. Sooner or later, Felicity would wish to discuss it, and then Mrs. Right would discover what Mr. Stratton had to say for himself.

FELICITY HAD WOKEN just as hazy-feeling as she had when she'd retired the night before. That was, her feelings were not clear, but rather hidden somewhere in a fog. Or perhaps it was not that. Perhaps her feelings wished to go one way, and her logic and sense wished to go the other way.

Her sisters had attempted to question her about the letter from Mr. Stratton, but she had been firm in her refusal to hand it over. Valor, though, was most gratified to know that Mr. Stratton had taken her thoughts seriously and had enjoyed their conversation about the weather. Mrs. Wendover had also been sent regards, which Valor promptly informed the rabbit of, as Mrs. Wendover could not understand anybody's words but Valor's.

They had decided that they would take both carriages out for a trot round the park. It was early, and they would not encounter crowds. Everybody was in agreement that Felicity must have some fresh air to put the pink back in her cheeks.

Felicity was glad of it on several fronts. It was highly unlikely that they would encounter Mr. Stratton or anybody else at that time of day. Further, they had all agreed that if Mr. Stratton *were* somehow spotted, the curtains to the carriage windows were to be closed immediately. The other benefit to going out when it was not likely they would encounter anyone was that that the duke would not encounter anybody he'd like to have a set-to with. He had, perhaps, had enough confrontations for one season, though it was unlikely he viewed it that way.

Felicity wished to see Mr. Stratton, and also not see him, therefore it seemed at this moment that not seeing him was the best choice. It was as if she wished to play for time, though she could not see what benefit extra time would bring.

Before they set off, a further circumstance occurred to fluster her. Tulips arrived, addressed to her. They were not signed, but she knew instantly that tulips were sent in reference to their conversation about a lady suddenly deciding she wished to be called Tulip. All the note said was: *I consulted with a florist and tulips are not likely to make you sneeze.*

Even if she had not guessed they were from Mr. Stratton, she recognized his hand from the letter to Valor. Furthermore, they were red tulips. Did he send a message of love? He did not say! He only said they would not make her sneeze.

Her father found great amusement in it. "We are to be buffeted by flowers now, eh? Perhaps not very original, but tried and true all the same."

Her father was less amused by what followed. Just as the tulips were being put in a vase, Lady Marchfield was led into the room by a rather downcast Thomas.

Felicity was certain the junior footman feared he would be blamed for letting Lady Marchfield in, though everybody knew she was very hard to keep out.

"What do you do here?" the duke asked his sister. "I thought I'd done enough to drive you off."

Lady Marchfield sniffed. "It seems you have done enough to drive Lord Rustmont off. He's left Town, in case you did not know it—all hope of that match has gone up in a puff of smoke."

The duke laughed and said, "You are behind the times as usual, Madam. We were on to another match but that's gone up in a puff of smoke too!"

Lady Marchfield turned to Felicity. "Another match? A match with who, pray?"

"Do not you interrogate my daughter, you old harridan," the duke said. "She's got no interest in informing you of it."

Lady Marchfield's eyes drifted toward the flowers. "Who sent those?" she asked, walking over to them.

Nobody answered, and Valor went so far as to slap one hand over her mouth and the other over Mrs. Wendover's mouth to signal her refusal to comment.

Unfortunately, Thomas had left the note next to the vase.

Lady Marchfield picked it up and read it. She made a sighing sound and laid it down. "Tulips will not make her sneeze. I see we have not managed to get past the Almack's sneezing display. It is not at all promising that it is still being bandied about like a joke and now some gentleman has been so bold as to send this."

"You never mind what is well and what is not," the duke said. "Now why are you here? Has Marchfield finally given you the heave-ho over the side of his ship? I told him a hundred times, when you throw her out, do not throw her toward me!"

"I have come because despite my intense disgust over my brother's behavior, I still have a care for my niece. You are woefully unprepared to shepherd your daughter into her married life. I am holding a dinner on Thursday and have invited two unmarried gentlemen who would be appropriate in station and breeding. Felicity is invited, and you certainly are not."

"What say you, Felicity?" the duke said laughing. "Care to enter the dragon's lair alone?"

Felicity hardly knew what to say. While her father's teasing of her aunt was endlessly amusing, and she really did find Lady Marchfield too stern for anybody's good, she did also have a certain respect for the lady as a senior relation.

Lady Marchfield crossed the room and held her hands. "Felicity, while I am not so freewheeling as my brother, I have a deal more sense. Furthermore, I have your interests at heart and one cannot be certain your father even has a heart. It is one dinner, and I am asking you to attend."

Felicity glanced at her Papa. He good-naturedly nodded. "Go on, girl, see what delights Lady Misery has in store for you. We will all be vastly entertained to hear of it."

Felicity nodded her acquiescence, and it was settled. She would go to her aunt's house for dinner on Thursday. She supposed it would be tedious, but she also supposed Mr. Stratton was not one of the gentlemen her aunt had invited.

It was hard to say if that was a welcome idea or not.

Just then, Mrs. Right bustled in, tying her bonnet. "The carriages are outside," she said. The housekeeper noticed Lady Marchfield and frowned.

"Very good, Mrs. Right," the duke said. "Well, Lady Misery, I would invite you to come along on our sojourn to the park, but sadly there is no more room—goodbye!"

Lady Marchfield glanced at Mrs. Right, and then an idea began to dawn. "Roland, you cannot be serious."

"I try not to be, though it's a heavy slog up a steep hill with you hanging about the place," the duke said with a snort.

Valor covered her face with Mrs. Wendover's floppy worn-out body and giggled uncontrollably.

"You know of what I speak. You cannot possibly bring your housekeeper to an outing in the park," Lady Marchfield said.

"Of course I can," the duke said. "I have two carriages, that's eight seats comfortably—nine with a little bit of a squeeze and Valor is still small enough to make it feasible. My god, woman, it's as if you cannot work out the simplest thing anymore."

"People will see you! It will be noted!"

"And then?" the duke asked.

"It will be talked about."

"And then?" the duke asked again.

Quite predictably, Lady Marchfield did not have a particular answer for that. Felicity supposed most people would not like to be talked about as having done something that was not exactly right, but the duke did not give a toss about it.

Felicity was glad of it. It would have been terrible to have to leave Mrs. Right behind just because it was not the done thing to take one's housekeeper to the park.

Lady Marchfield said, "Felicity, I will see you on Thursday. Roland, I am beginning to hope I will never see you again."

"Finally! We are agreed!" the duke said, laughing heartily at his own joke.

Felicity's aunt turned and marched out of the drawing room, nearly running over poor Thomas.

Goodness, what a morning.

CHAPTER TWENTY

PERCY SPENT A deal of time at Lackington & Allen attempting to discover another book on stoats. When he had last met Lady Felicity at that location, that was her interest. She was considering having a stoat of her own and wished to know what might be the joys and challenges of keeping a stoat in the house. Percy suspected a stoat would land more on the challenge side of things, but who was he to say?

Mr. Lackington had been perplexed that he had a second person interested in stoats, and that it could not be a copy of the first book he'd sold to Lady Felicity.

The poor fellow had searched high and low and finally found a book on mustelids, of which the stoat was one.

Mr. Lackington had been further perplexed when Percy put a bookmark on the chapter about stoats and then ordered it delivered to Lady Felicity Nicolet, daughter of the Duke of Pelham. The shopkeeper even went so far to say, "Mr. Stratton, in the usual way of things, I regularly have gentlemen buy books for ladies on flowers, or sketching techniques, or some such. A book on mustelids seems a rather unusual choice."

Percy had nodded. "Lady Felicity is an unusual lady from an unusual family."

"Oh yes, that is true, it seems," Mr. Lackington said.

Percy had arranged for the delivery and then set off to the park to clear his head. He'd decided he would pepper the duke's house with gifts of every sort and must think up more ideas. He had already thought of the book on stoats.

He'd had the further inspiration of visiting a dress shop and spending quite a while convincing the shopkeeper that he wished for an India shawl, but it must be cut down to a very small size. He would send Mrs. Wendover her own fine shawl in a bid to win over Lady Valor.

He needed to think of at least one other thing that would be meaningful.

As he trotted down the paths, it came to him. He would buy Lady Felicity a set of cake pans. She had inquired what he thought about a lady deciding she would like to bake cakes. He'd had no idea if she inquired because she planned on doing it, or was already doing it, or if it was just a passing idea. It did not matter, though. She would understand the message.

Just as he was wondering where one went to buy a set of cake pans and toying with the idea of asking the viscount's cook about it, he spotted the duke's carriages. They could not be missed—the park was near empty, both carriages were very fine and sporting the duke's crest, and they rode one in front of the other.

Now was a moment handed to him by the fates.

He trotted over, his thoughts racing as to what he would say—what would be his opening gambit?

Before he had time to say anything at all, he saw the duke's face peer out and the curtains close with a swish. He dropped his horse back and rode to the other side of the carriage.

Mrs. Right, the housekeeper, who was inexplicably riding with the duke, glared at him and inched the curtain closed, all the while attempting to burn a hole through his face with her expression.

He trotted up to the carriage ahead, but it was no better a reception. Lady Valor looked at him wide-eyed and wrestled with the curtain to close it. Then, when he tried to get ahead of the carriage to make a last attempt on the other side, the coachman would not let him pass.

Percy was being frozen out. The whole family was ranged against him. It was such a coordinated effort that they must have talked about the eventuality of encountering him and to close the curtains against him.

He dropped his horse back and allowed them to proceed unhindered. He had better send those cake pans before the sun set today.

FELICITY HAD BEEN certain they would not encounter Mr. Stratton in the park. They had gone early for just that reason. It was well before the usual promenade of seeing and being seen.

And yet, there he was. He was so handsome on his large bay and from what she could briefly see, had full control of his animal.

Her father had closed the curtains next to him with alacrity, but then Mr. Stratton had ridden to the other side. Felicity had leaned back to be out of view while Mrs. Right gave him the what-for with her eyes as she slowly closed her own curtain.

They'd then all peeked out to see that he'd attempted the same with the carriage carrying Grace, Valor, Patience, Verity, and Winsome.

He'd finally given it up, so Felicity assumed her sisters had remembered what they were to do.

"Hah!" the duke said, "he may be an idiot, but he's got a certain stick to it in him that I can admire."

"I suppose he was driven to get out of his house just now," Mrs. Right said grimly. "It's bound to be chaos."

"From the chains Papa sent over?" Serenity asked.

"That, and perhaps other things," Mrs. Right said, folding her hands in her lap.

"What now, Mrs. Right?" the duke asked. "Have you been stirring up some trouble with us none the wiser?"

"Me?" Mrs. Right said with a smile. "How extraordinary you would think it."

Felicity took that to mean that their dear housekeeper certainly had done something. She also knew the lady would give over the details when she was ready to and not a moment before. But what in heavens name could she have done?

"Did you feel sad when you saw Mr. Stratton?" Serenity asked Felicity.

The fact was, she did feel sad. However, while Serenity wore her heart on her sleeve, her eldest sister wore her heart very private and out of view.

"Not particularly," Felicity said.

"That is the difference between us, I suppose," Serenity said. "I should have cried and cried."

"Just wait until Serenity's season comes round," the duke said. "It'll be weeping from here to America over sadness, joy, sunsets, sunrises and who knows what else. I'll have to ask the doctor for something to settle my nerves. And her nerves too, if I've got any sense."

"Oh Papa!" Serenity scolded. "You know I only cry for very good reasons."

"I know no such thing, my girl," the duke said, laughing. "You've been crying since the day you came into this world. I always speculated that it was because you looked over in your bassinet and saw Patience—you realized you were not alone."

Felicity was rather relieved that the rest of the carriage ride was taken up by joking and not inquiring whether Felicity Nicolet felt like crying.

Later that day, after Felicity had regained some of her equanimity, two further gifts arrived to the house. Mr. Stratton had anonymously sent a set of cake pans and a very small India shawl addressed to Mrs. Wendover.

Valor was nearly overcome by the compliment to Mrs. Wendover. As she told everyone repeatedly, never in her life did she imagine that Mrs. Wendover would receive the anonymous gift of a very fine shawl. Felicity supposed never in *any* of their lives had they anticipated such a circumstance.

Mr. Stratton was showing himself to be persistent, but to what aim? Was he merely uncomfortable that he'd made a person angry? Did he only regret his actions? Or was it something more?

The only thing Felicity could be sure of was that she was determined to protect her heart. She would not allow herself to be fooled again. She had been silly and naïve, and she was determined to become a savvy and experienced woman of the world.

They did not go out that evening, as it was a Wednesday and neither she nor the duke particularly cared to revisit Almack's— she because of sneezing and he because of weak tea and sour lemonade.

She did wonder, though, if Mr. Stratton was there. And if he looked for her.

The following night was Lady Marchfield's dinner and whatever unmarried gentlemen might be thrown to her notice. Her aunt was likely to have rounded up the most staid gentlemen alive and Felicity suspected it would be a tiresome evening. Still, her aunt was due respect because of her age and connection to the family, so Felicity would go with all good humor.

The daytime, though, leading up to the dinner, was anything but boring. Things were delivered to the house at all hours. A paint box, stationery and a crystal inkstand, a fine parasol, sheet music, a garnet encrusted quizzing glass of all things, and a sketch pad and watercolors. And then finally, a book on wild creatures with a bookmark on the chapter about stoats. All sent anonymously and all surely sent by Mr. Stratton.

Nobody was more amused by it than her father.

Mrs. Right helped Felicity dress for dinner and would accompany her in the carriage to Lady Marchfield's house. The various gifts that had been sent were piled on a chair nearby.

"I suppose he's determined enough," Mrs. Right said, staring suspiciously at the pile.

"Determined in what, though?" Felicity asked.

"Hard to say," Mrs. Right said. "For all these presents, he hasn't used any words."

"That is just what I think! He sent flowers and all he said was they won't make me sneeze."

"I find myself with mixed feelings over that fellow," Mrs. Right said. "I don't know what to make of him at this point."

"Nor I," Felicity said. "Now I wonder, Mrs. Right, what you might have done to inconvenience Mr. Stratton's household? You did hint at something and it might lift my spirits to hear of it."

"Oh that? I just canceled the wine order, changed the grocery order to nothing but cabbages, and had the clothes that were sent out to the laundress donated to charity."

Felicity giggled despite herself. "You are very resourceful, Mrs. Right."

"Well now, everybody knows I get a bit touchy when one of my girls has been affronted. Revenge soothes my feelings."

"I imagine you are very soothed at the moment, then."

"Exceedingly. I'll casually mention it to the duke when he needs a bit of cheering."

"I think I am ready," Felicity said.

"Yes, we better go. Nobody needs Lady Marching Orders throwing a fit on top of everything else. Don't tell her about all these things Mr. Stratton keeps sending unless you want an hour-long lecture about it."

Felicity nodded, as she hardly need be told it. Lady Marchfield would go mad if she knew that all of these things had been accepted. They should have been stopped at the door, but as much as Thomas practiced all the possibilities of answering a door, when the door knocker actually sounded, it all seemed to go too fast for him to think.

PERCY HAD RUN all over Town, sending one thing after the next to Lady Felicity. He'd finally come up with a firm plan—he would go to her house this evening and demand an audience. He would go and bring something so significant that if she accepted it, then she accepted him.

What else could he do? She was taking steps to avoid him. She had not appeared at Almack's the night before, certainly she had kept away on his account.

In the late afternoon, he stopped at White's for a coffee and to rest his horse. He found Wiles and Magnon at a table and sat down.

"Well?" Magnon asked. "Have you managed to smooth over Wiles' gaffe with Lady Felicity?"

"No," Percy answered.

"She pretended she knew all about it!" Wiles said. "I keep telling you that."

"What have you done, though?" Magnon asked. "Have you at least talked to her?"

"I have not, I believe she is studiously avoiding me. The entire family shut their carriage curtains when I approached them in the park."

"So you've done nothing," Magnon said.

"No, I have done some things," Percy said. "I've sent some things. A lot of things, actually."

"Like what?" Wiles asked.

"Never mind what. I have a plan for tonight. I will bring a big thing and if she accepts it, well…"

"What big thing?" Magnon asked.

"Jewelry, obviously," Wiles said.

"What sort of jewelry?" Magnon asked.

"It's not jewelry, though maybe I should have thought of that," Percy said.

"What is it then?" Wiles asked.

"A horse."

His two friends were silent for some time over that idea.

Then Wiles laughed and said, "Oh I see, a porcelain horse or some such. Because she likes horses."

"Everybody likes horses," Magnon said. "Horses are man's best friend."

"I thought that was dogs," Wiles said.

"Dogs? That's ridiculous. Can you ride a dog to a neighbor's house in the countryside? Could you even ride a dog to a house in Town, though the houses are so close together?" Magnon asked.

"No, but the phrase…"

It was incredible how quickly his friends could wander off a subject.

"It's a real horse," Percy said. "I found a lovely filly at Tattersall's. My father will go mad when he gets the bill, but he's nearly there at the moment, so I suppose it is little matter."

"You bought her a real horse?" Magnon said incredulously. "That is absurd. Is there a reason for it? What is the significance of such a gift? What does it mean?"

Percy shrugged. "I ran out of ideas and I was passing by Tattersall's…"

"So you will just go to the duke's house? With an extra horse?" Wiles asked.

Percy nodded and drained his coffee. "I'd best get going then. I do not know what I might face in my own house or how long it might take to manage it before I can get away. The duke has been creating havoc."

"The duke? What's he done now?"

Percy rose. "Well, after the delivery of a pile of chains, sacks of cabbages arrived. Then our wine dealer canceled our order and will not reply to inquiries. Oh and half my shirts have been donated to charity. That sort of thing."

"Are you certain you wish to connect yourself to such a family?" Magnon asked.

"Very certain."

When Percy arrived home, he was relieved that the duke had seemed to run out of ideas on how to harass him. The grocer had been ordered to pick up the cabbages and bring the food that was ordered, so at least his parents would get dinner. They would not have new wine to choose from when they dined, nor would Percy ever recover his shirts, but at least no more surprises had rained down upon the house.

His father was snoring in a chair in the library, having soothed his broken finger and toe into oblivion with brandy. The viscountess was nowhere to be seen, likely keeping herself away in her sitting room.

Percy was dressed and out of the house in good time. Even more fortunate, it had not come to his father's notice that there had been an extra horse in the stables all afternoon.

He mounted his own horse, while a groom rode the filly through the streets to Grosvenor Square. This was the moment—everything hung on this. Would she accept the horse, and him, or would he be sent packing?

The house was lit up, the lights showing through the curtains of the drawing room windows. They were at home. He dismounted his horse and handed his groom the reins. Percy jogged up the steps and gave the knocker a good rap.

The young footman he'd seen the night he'd been to dinner opened the door and then stood slack jawed, staring at him.

"I must see Lady Felicity immediately," he said. "It is a matter of great urgency."

"She ain't here, though," the young man said. "I mean, isn't. She isn't here."

Calling out from the drawing room, he heard the duke's voice. "Is that Stratton out there? Send him in, this should be amusing."

Amusing? Things that amused the duke were usually far less amusing to the other people involved. Nevertheless, he must speak to Lady Felicity.

"Go in, I guess," the footman said.

With that rousing encouragement, Percy did go in.

FELICITY COULD NOT imagine what her aunt had been thinking. When she arrived to the house, she was introduced to a certain Mr. Reginald Armstrong, son of Viscount Something-or-Other, who was the least prepossessing gentleman she'd ever encountered. He was gangly and it seemed his arms were too long for him to have full control of them, as they swung in all directions in an odd fashion. Mr. Armstrong turned red as a beet, sweat sprung up in rivulets on his forehead, and he mumbled, "Hello."

His mother, a towering lady with a stern demeanor, poked him in the ribs. He added, "Honored."

The second offering was a baron from Cornwall, Lord Haraby, who looked all of sixteen and positively giggled over making her acquaintance. Lady Marchfield was quick to point out that he was the eldest son of an earl, as if that could somehow overcome his childish demeanor.

So that was it—one gentleman near fainting from the stress of meeting a lady and one giggling over it.

They went into dinner and Lady Marchfield did most of the talking. She expounded on the estates of the two gentlemen in attendance, while Mr. Armstrong's mother added in such encouragements as she saw fit. Apparently, she was well-prepared to guide a daughter-in-law in proper directions. Lady Marchfield nodded, approving of the idea, while Mr. Armstrong sweated profusely over the mere mention of a daughter-in-law.

The only saving grace to the whole thing was Lord Marchfield. She did not see her uncle very often, but he was a very genial gentleman. He had the good sense to turn the conversation when he could.

"I was saying to Felicity, just the other day," Lady Marchfield said, overriding her husband's game attempts, "there is nothing a lady must be more careful of than selecting the right husband. These modern ideas of romance fly in the face of sense."

Felicity's eyes drifted toward her uncle.

Lady Marchfield paused, as if just remembering that her lord was in hearing of this opinion. "That is not to say, of course, that I am not exceedingly fond of Lord Marchfield."

Mr. Armstrong's forehead once more began leaking at the mention of romance and he mopped his brow with his dinner napkin. Lord Haraby giggled like a schoolboy's first encounter with an off-color jest.

"Tell me, Lady Felicity," Mr. Armstrong's mother said, "how have you found your first season in Town?"

How could she possibly answer that question? If she were to be honest about it, she would say it had been a time of staggering highs and devastating lows, ending at the very lowest point.

Instead, she said, "Oh, very well, I suppose."

"I always counsel young people," the lady went on, "do not be bowled over by suave manners or good looks or smooth dancing. These things do not last."

"Manners do not last?" Felicity said, keeping her expression innocent, though knowing perfectly well that Lord Marchfield would be laughing into his napkin.

"It pains me to admit it, but they do not," the lady said. "Once a man becomes comfortable with his bride, the real manners, or lack thereof, will be revealed."

Felicity did not know how to respond to that original opinion.

Mr. Armstrong said, "It's on account of my father." He snorted and said, "He's gassy and she never knew it until it was too late."

His mother frowned at him and shook her head warningly. Felicity did not dare glance at her uncle lest they both collapse in laughter.

Felicity managed to mumble, "Oh, I see. I hadn't known." She was in the middle of a perfectly ghastly evening. The only thing that could be said for it was how hard the duke would laugh when she told him about the gassy viscount. She must cling to that idea.

What else was there to cling to? If Mr. Armstrong and Lord Haraby had affected her in any way, it was to highlight just how superior Mr. Stratton was in every possible sense.

How she longed for Mr. Stratton. Mr. Percy Stratton. She should not, she should put him out of her thoughts, but these two fellows seemed to drive him right into her thoughts.

CHAPTER TWENTY-ONE

A S PERCY ENTERED the duke's drawing room, he felt rather like a Roman preparing to face the lions. Still, it was of the utmost importance that he speak directly to Lady Felicity, else she avoided him forever.

He walked in and scanned the faces, this way and that. Where was she? She was not there.

The rest of them were there, including the youngest who hoped he would be drowned by the duke's hand. They looked at him in curiosity. Except for the duke, who seemed exceedingly amused to see him.

"Well, Stratton, have you brought more pots and pans for our girl?" the duke asked.

"Why did you send the pans, Mr. Stratton?" Lady Patience asked.

"Lady Felicity mentioned that she might, at some point, wish to learn how to bake cakes."

"Oh, she never said…" Lady Serenity said.

"Do you suppose that would be fun?" Lady Winsome asked. "I hadn't thought…"

The duke was shaking with laughter. "Never mind the cake pans. What are you doing here, Stratton?"

"Yes, Mr. Stratton," Lady Valor said. "After the stern scolding from me and Mrs. Wendover, I am surprised to see you here." Lady Valor paused. "Though, Mrs. Wendover's feelings might have gone a little soft over the India shawl."

Percy could see for himself that Mrs. Wendover found favor with the shawl as she was just now wrapped in it. And really, considering the dilapidated shape that stuffed rabbit was in, the shawl did something well for its appearance.

"Yes, Lady Valor," Percy said, "that was quite the rousing letter from you and your friend. I sent the shawl as I thought Mrs. Wendover might need some soothing after expressing her feelings so violently. I suppose you received the letter I sent back, too?"

Lady Valor nodded. "Yes, but Felicity took it and none of us have seen it. She's hidden it very well; I looked all over her room." The little girl paused, and then as if she remembered something, she said, "Snooping was very wrong, I won't do it again, I feel terrible about it."

"Don't make promises you cannot keep," the duke advised his youngest daughter.

"That's true, Papa," Lady Valor said. "I *will* do it again, but I really will try to feel terrible over it next time, if that helps."

"What did the letter say?" Lady Grace asked. "Felicity has not breathed a word of it, except for your approbation of Valor's conversation about the weather."

Percy had no intention of advertising the details beyond what was known. "That conversation had to be mentioned, it was one of the finest about the weather I have ever taken part in."

Lady Valor was evidently much struck by this compliment. She blushed, then she whispered furiously to Mrs. Wendover, as if alerting her to this news. Percy hoped she and Mrs. Wendover had finally given up wishing him chained and thrown in a lake.

"Your Grace, I am here to see Lady Felicity. And to ask an important question."

"I see, so no more gifts, then?"

"Actually, I brought a horse," Percy said. Now that he'd just said it out loud to the duke, it did not sound as rational as it had initially seemed.

The duke doubled over in laughter. The five sisters raced to the windows and pulled the curtains.

"He *has* brought a horse," Lady Grace exclaimed.

"She is no Dales pony, but she looks to be very fine all the same," Lady Patience said.

"There's really a horse out there?" the duke said, heaving with laughter. "Oh this is too good."

"I happened to be nearby Tattersall's," Percy said, by way of a ridiculous explanation.

Just then, Percy heard the front doors open. He turned, very much in the hopes that it was Lady Felicity making an appearance.

From the hall, Mrs. Right called, "I know I am late in returning, but the housekeeper was keen to hear about the cyprian party. We laughed and laughed."

Mrs. Right came into the room, handing her bonnet to a footman. She stopped dead in her tracks when she saw Percy.

"Mrs. Right, you'll never guess," the duke said, "Stratton here has brought a horse for Felicity!"

"Why should she need a horse?" Mrs. Right asked. "I took her in one of the carriages."

"No, no," the duke said, "it's not to ride now. He's brought her a horse to keep for her own."

"Has he now?" Mrs. Right asked suspiciously.

"That's right—cake pans and now a horse," the duke said. "What do young men get up to these days?"

"Took her to where?" Percy asked. "Took Lady Felicity where?"

"Now this is even better, wait until he hears where she's gone," the duke said.

"Our Felicity has gone to our aunt's house for dinner," Lady Serenity said. "She is to meet eligible gentlemen there."

"Gentlemen who don't need to be chained up and thrown in a lake," Lady Valor said, ominously slipping back into her original opinion.

"Eligible gentlemen?" Percy asked. "Who? What eligible gentlemen?"

"Who knows?" the duke said. "My sister picked them out so all I know is that they will be humorless and grim. She'd get Rustmont if she could, but I heard he left Town."

"I do not like the sound of this," Percy muttered.

"I am afraid it is your own fault, Mr. Stratton," Lady Winsome pointed out.

Percy thought Lady Winsome was not being very winsome at the moment.

"Nobody to blame but himself," Lady Verity said, shaking her head. "It is an all-too-common tale."

"Is it?" Lady Winsome asked Lady Verity.

"What will you do now, Mr. Stratton?" Lady Grace asked.

"What will he do?" the duke asked. "He'll go straight over there, taking that horse with him. I don't suppose anybody else will have arrived to Lady Misery's house with an extra horse in tow—it's bound to give him a leg up on things."

"Lady Marchfield will not like it at all," Lady Grace pointed out.

"Yes, I know," the duke said. "That's the other half of the fun."

"Oh I see," Lady Valor said, "Papa, that *is* very funny. Our aunt makes me laugh when she's mad. Now that I'm used to it. Because you've made her mad so many times that I got used to it."

"It's one of the primary purposes of my life, my girl. Well, I suppose we all ought to go," the duke said. "Mrs. Right, call the carriages if you will."

Mrs. Right nodded and hurried from the room.

Things were moving a bit too fast for Percy to keep up. First it was proposed that he ought to go charging over to Lady Marchfield's house to interrupt her dinner party. Which really, he was not opposed to. What was the lady thinking, inviting eligible gentlemen to a dinner for her niece?

But now they were all going with him? This family was an absolute circus. He was not so certain bringing a circus with him would be at all helpful.

"Charlie, fetch the girls' coats, we are going out on a nighttime adventure!" the duke said jovially.

The six sisters were all too willing to join in on the idea and leapt up from their seats.

Lady Grace inexplicably seemed to get her feet in a tangle, fell to the ground, rolled, and then hopped upright without anyone taking the smallest notice of it.

Lady Valor clutched Mrs. Wendover and exclaimed that she'd never gone anywhere so late in the nighttime, and it was all very exciting and scary.

The ladies Winsome and Verity took that moment to have a dispute. Lady Verity claimed horses traveled faster at night because of the cool air, Lady Winsome said they probably went slower because they were tired.

Lady Patience pushed past them and grabbed the pile of cloaks and pelisses from the footman's arms and began throwing them to their owners.

Lady Serenity brushed a tear away on account of, she said, this touching display of family unity.

Percy girded his loins—they were all going. Even Mrs. Wendover.

FELICITY WAS RELIEVED to see the dessert course come round. The stages of the dinner marked the time passing by. With any luck, they would soon be in the drawing room. Lord Marchfield was to take her home and she was toying with the idea of claiming a cold coming on to end the evening before she was trapped into a card game with the two awkward boys who were attempting to pass themselves off as men. She might even deliberately sniff at some flowers to frighten them off with sneezing.

The conversation had never got more interesting than discovering that Mr. Armstrong's father was gassy. Though really, every time Felicity thought of that moment in the conversation, she had to bite her lip not to laugh.

Just now, Mr. Armstrong's mother was expounding on the charms of the wilds of Cornwall, which apparently involved a lot of opportunities to break one's neck by way of falling off a cliff. Lord Haraby was attempting to make eyes at her from across the table.

"I always say," Mr. Armstrong's mother said, "that there is nothing more steady than a Cornwall man."

It was an interesting thought that was in direct contradiction to what was in front of them—her son had seemed to perspire out all the liquid in his body and looked anything but steady.

Quite unexpectedly, there was the sound of the door being pounded on. Felicity craned her neck to see the butler dashing through the hall to answer it.

In a moment, the duke appeared, along with all her sisters and Mrs. Right. Goodness, why had they all come? Was somebody taken ill? Had the house caught fire?

Lady Marchfield leapt from her chair. "Roland! What is the meaning—"

"Don't bother going on a tirade," the duke said. "Stratton is here to say his piece and he's brought Felicity a horse."

Felicity felt as if she could not move. She was bereft of speech. He was here. Was he really here? Or was this some strange joke her father had thought up to drive Lady Marchfield mad?

The duke stepped aside. There he was. He was here. Gloriously here.

Had he really brought a horse? Why? What did bringing a horse say? Was there some meaning in bringing a lady a horse?

"My apologies, Lady Marchfield," Mr. Stratton said, glaring at Mr. Armstrong and Lord Haraby. "The interruption could not be helped."

"I dispute that strongly, Mr. Stratton, this is outrageous," Lady Marchfield said. "Bursting into a private dinner? Bringing one's housekeeper through the front doors? It is everything inappropriate. You ought not to allow yourself to be influenced by my deranged brother."

"Don't worry about her," the duke said to Mr. Stratton, "she's a regular polecat, sticking her nose into henhouses that don't belong to her."

"You see what he is. I strongly counsel you to avoid his influence," Lady Marchfield said.

Mr. Stratton nodded. "Yes, well, perhaps too late for that, I'm afraid. Now, Lady Felicity, I've come to tell you, with your whole family who it was not my idea to bring, that I *did* say I would not be chained. But that was only until I realized I wanted to be chained. To you. You see, that was the whole problem—I could not envision marriage because I'd not met the lady I would wish to marry. Now I have. I have acted a disgraceful idiot—"

"He really has," Valor said.

"But that is the truth. If you do not harbor any feelings for me, you may tell me to be on my way. I will keep sending things to the house in case you change your mind, including the horse I brought with me tonight. I swear I will never marry anyone else. If I cannot wed Lady Felicity, then it's all up for me. I am undone."

"Say nothing to this outrage, Felicity," Lady Marchfield said, rising. "I will shortly have Mr. Stratton, and my brother and his diabolical housekeeper, removed from this house."

Felicity stared at her aunt as if she spoke in a foreign tongue. Did she say remove him? Was the lady mad? She leapt up and pushed past her aunt.

Felicity grabbed Mr. Stratton by the hand and pulled him into the drawing room, slamming the doors behind her. "You've brought me a horse?" she asked.

"Well, yes, I ran out of other ideas, and I was passing by Tattersall's…"

She threw herself at him and his strong arms caught her effortlessly. Somehow, somewhere very deep in her heart, she'd always known they would.

"I am forgiven, then," he said quietly.

"I am not sure," Felicity said. "You'd better kiss me first, and then I will be convinced."

Mr. Stratton turned out to be very obliging. As Felicity had never been kissed before but had been imagining kissing Mr. Stratton for quite some time, it was marvelous. His lips were soft, but delightfully firm.

He played with her hair, which it turned out he found stupendous, and kissed her eyelids, as it turned out she had the prettiest eyes of any lady living.

Outside the doors, she could hear her father gamely guarding it as Lady Marchfield made attempts to get in. "Step back, Lady Misery, lest you injure yourself! Or I injure you! Doesn't much matter to me!"

Her poor dear uncle was gamely attempting to calm the situation, but pleas for his wife to stop beating the duke about the head with a napkin seemed to be going nowhere.

"I will always save you from a tiger, that I swear to you."

"And you won't mind if I decide to bake cakes or change my name to Tulip?"

"Not a bit."

"And then, there is one other thing."

"I am prepared to hear you plan on driving your own team of horses or taking up a sword."

"It is far worse, I'm afraid," Felicity said, firm in her mind that there could be no more secrets between them. "I have a bit of a temper. More than a bit, on occasion. My nickname is Ferocity."

Mr. Stratton laughed surprisingly hard at that revelation. "I am not surprised."

"You are not put off by it?"

"No. I do not have much of a temper at all, but I am so inured to my father threatening to burn down the world that I suspect I will hardly notice."

Though Felicity was vastly relieved to hear that Mr. Percy Stratton was not at all put off by the idea that she might have a temper from time to time, she did pause at the mention of his father.

"Gracious, your father," she said. "How will your father take the news of an engagement? He does not seem too very fond of me. I do not suppose he is at all fond of my father."

"Do not you worry about my father, and I'll do my best not to worry about *your* father."

"Papa is a darling really, once you get to know him. And I will counsel him sternly about calling your father Sir Pineapple."

Percy laughed into her hair. "The duke may be a darling to *you*, but perhaps less of a darling to other people. Though, he has grown on me, I will not deny it."

They walked, hand in hand, to the very back of the drawing room where Felicity noticed it was delightfully dim. There, very conveniently, Lady Marchfield had what was meant to be a small reading nook. There was just a large and overstuffed chair meant for one person, but they squeezed in together.

Now that her face was so near his it was no trouble at all to kiss it all over, and end on her lips.

Nobody had ever said anything about kissing to her. Of course, nobody had said anything at all about anything of the sort to her. For all that, she was not unaware of how human relations proceeded, she lived on a working estate after all. One could not miss how the animals got on with it.

But the animals did not kiss.

She felt very sorry for them, it was marvelous. Her hair was becoming terribly disheveled, as was her dress. Felicity did not give a toss about it—Mr. Percy Stratton could muss her all he liked.

He kissed the tip of her nose. She said, "Tell me of our future—what will it be like? Where will we live?"

Percy leaned back and Felicity settled comfortably in the crook of his arm. "I will leave it up to you. There are two choices, really. There is the main house, the dower house which is just now occupied by my grandmother, and a hunting lodge about a mile off from the main houses. The main house is plenty large, but it also contains my father. He shouts a lot. The lodge is smaller, but still commodious for a lodge and far enough away that my father's shouts cannot be heard."

"We'd best go to the lodge," Felicity said. "And then of course we will wish to visit Yorkshire for extended periods."

"Of course," he said. "I must suppose your father's various harassments will not extend to a son-in-law?"

"Well, as to that…"

"I see," Percy said, laughing.

"You will get used to it, though, and then you will find it amusing."

"My god, I did not even ask him for permission to ask for your hand."

"Goodness, yes, you ought to have done. I thought you must have before they all set off with you to come here."

"He understood my intentions," Percy said. "Though I never came right out and asked."

They were silent for a moment, the only sounds that of the duke telling Lady Misery she might as well calm down.

"Wait here," Percy said, disentangling himself.

Felicity was loath to let him go, but confident that he would come back in all haste.

Percy made his way to the door and called, "Your Grace, might I ask permission for Lady Felicity's hand?"

"That's rather shutting the stable door after the horse is out! I suppose you'd better get on with it," the duke called back.

"Mr. Stratton," Lady Marchfield shouted, "open this door at once!"

Percy did not answer Lady Marchfield. Rather, he said, "Your Grace, if you could guard the door for, let's say, a half hour?"

"Go on, then," the duke said.

"Go on, then?" Lady Marchfield cried. "Go on with what?"

Percy Stratton was back by Felicity's side in a flash. They did stay a further half hour, and then longer. Felicity began to wonder if it were at all ladylike to wish to tear a person's shirt off. Then she satisfied herself with the only advice Mrs. Right had ever given her—things of this nature naturally take their course.

She supposed they would do, and then there was the further unladylike thought of wishing to hurry things along. Felicity had somehow got the impression, possibly from hints from the vicar, that a lady ought not be interested in such things. If it *had* been the vicar, then either she was not a proper lady, or the vicar had told a very egregious fib.

By the time they emerged from the room, Felicity was very disheveled and engaged to be married. Mr. Armstrong, his mother, and Lord Haraby had departed, and Mrs. Right was seated on the floor with Valor dead asleep in her arms. Her other sisters had made their way into the dining room to demolish what was left on the table.

Lady Marchfield, like any wise general, had left the field when it became apparent she would lose the battle. Lord Marchfield had fetched a brandy for both himself and the duke and sat bemusedly on the staircase.

What a lovely evening.

CHAPTER TWENTY-TWO

A S PERCY HAD not had plans to wed, he'd never bothered to envision what a proposal of marriage would entail. If he *had* envisioned it, he supposed he would have imagined some sort of suave speech on a dark balcony at a ball.

Nothing so regular could have ever been hoped for when it involved the duke's family. He was not sorry for it, though.

Lady Felicity had accepted him, and they'd had a rather delightful interlude in Lady Marchfield's dark drawing room. So delightful that he really wondered why he'd been so eager to avoid a wedding to begin.

They'd finally emerged to find the duke still guarding the door, Lady Marchfield retired, her guests gone, the ladies Grace, Winsome, Patience, Serenity, and Verity all helping themselves to Lady Marchfield's desserts, and Lady Valor asleep on the housekeeper's lap. Lord Marchfield sat on the stairs with a brandy bottle at his side. He rose and kissed his niece on the cheek in congratulations, which Percy did not imagine would endear him to his wife very much.

Before they retreated from Lady Marchfield's house, there had been some debate as to whether Lady Felicity could ride her newly-acquired horse back to Grosvenor Square. The duke did not take issue with it, but the housekeeper wisely pointed out that as Lady Felicity was not in a riding habit, perhaps too much leg would be shown. Then, of course, Percy recalled that the horse was not properly saddled for a lady.

They compromised by the groom taking her horse and Percy riding his own next to Lady Felicity's carriage window. It had not been the easiest thing to keep pace with the carriage while controlling his horse with one hand and holding Lady Felicity's hand with the other. There were moments when it seemed he might pull her out the window or she might pull him through it. They'd managed it, though.

After a long goodbye, in which the rest of the family gave up and went inside, Percy finally took himself off when both of the duke's coachmen started yawning, loudly. He made his way back to his own house in the best of spirits.

It would perhaps be tedious to recount the various shoutings and ravings that were heard in Mr. Stratton's house when the news of the engagement was announced the following morning. Everybody in the house was warned loudly and repeatedly. And yet, the wedding would go forward.

In the end, the viscount found his son resolute. Confoundingly resolute. Percy claimed he would collect Lady Felicity and ride off to Gretna Green with her if his father attempted an impediment. The viscount, having been exposed to the duke and his lack of rationality, very much feared the couple would not even need to slip away under cover of darkness. That mad duke would probably pack them a basket from the kitchens and wave them off.

A scandal of that sort weighed heavy on the viscount's mind. He could not escape his constant uneasiness over how new their title really was. One misstep could spell the end of all their progress. He could not escape the idea that if a viscount's son were to elope with a duke's daughter, it would be assumed that son was a grasping climber of the worst sort.

As well, he could not ignore that a proper wedding between his son and a duke's daughter would more firmly cement his family as respected members of the *ton*. Even if that particular duke was known to be mad as a spring hare.

Those ideas caused him to put up with quite a lot and quell his querulous nature. That was well. With the duke involved in the negotiations, the haggling over the marriage contract had been as no other. The Duke of Pelham amused himself with various outrages and impossibilities, while the duke's solicitor spent most of his time sighing. By their third meeting, though, a new and more rational duke turned up. It was discovered that Lady Felicity had banned her father from calling the viscount Sir Pineapple even one more time, and had scolded him over dragging his feet for his own amusement.

The contracts were signed and the wedding was on.

Seeing as events moved forward without the least consultation as to her opinion of them, Lady Marchfield did as matrons of the *ton* have done for time immemorial. She put it about that she had long hoped for the match and had been instrumental to its success.

The service was very well done—held at St. George's and overseen by family and friends. The only flowers allowed anywhere near Felicity were tulips, and all the wedding party carried extra handkerchiefs just in case she was to get a whiff from an errant posy. The duke and the viscount were kept on opposite sides of the aisles so that all that could go on between them was glares on one side and laughter on the other.

Felicity wore a lavender silk dress and her mother's diamonds. She had debated on the choice of a dress endlessly, but then was pleased with her decision when she noted Percy slightly stagger when he first saw her in it.

The breakfast that followed the ceremony, while suitably elaborate, was perhaps more eccentric than the *ton* was used to seeing.

The duke had employed the services of a certain Sergeant Major Philip Astley to provide the entertainments. As the guests dined, they were entertained by jugglers and acrobats. One of the jugglers even employed lit torches.

It might have been anticipated that a duke's dining room was not particularly set up for such performances and there were moments that did give the diners pause.

Lady Marchfield was unceremoniously knocked off her chair by a stray acrobat and there was much debate for months over whether the duke had paid the fellow to be so clumsy.

The juggler of the lit torches was very skilled indeed, but for the moment when he set a pair of curtains ablaze. The duke promptly threw a jug of water at the fire, which also managed to douse Lady Marchfield.

Then there was the fellow whose skill was walking on his hands. He was so accustomed to it that he found moments to grab at various lady's ankles. Very naturally, Lady Marchfield's ankles were among the grabbed.

The breakfast was capped off by a horse-riding display round the park of Grosvenor Square that served as a sendoff to the young couple setting out on their wedding trip. If certain individuals who were out for a stroll at that moment found themselves inexplicably knocked to the pavement, well, did they not know that the duke's eldest daughter had been married that morning?

Before that blessed day had arrived, Percy and Felicity had debated at length on where they would go for the wedding trip. By happenstance, Percy's friend Mr. Wiles had come up with a cracking idea. His family were connected to the O'Neils, that family having their roots in Ireland but long-established in Scotland. They had a lovely old castle in the Outer Hebrides.

Naturally, this struck the couple as quite the interesting adventure. As the negotiations between the duke and the viscount had dragged on, Mr. Wiles wrote to his relations. Word was received back that the family was not currently in residence there. The newly married couple were welcome to its use if they thought they could get by with a rather bare-bones staff to serve them.

They were entirely enthusiastic over the idea and neither of them gave a toss for how bare-bones the staff was. Felicity even speculated that she might be encouraged to learn how to bake a cake after all.

Percy was not so foolish as to spend the first night of his wedding trip at some inn arrived at through exhaustion and lack of choice. He promptly relocated his bride to a lovely place just ten miles out of London. It was small but well run and set in the prettiest little valley with green all round.

It was fortuitous that he did think to stop so early that first day, as it was not likely the couple would have made it another ten miles before doing something shocking in the carriage.

Felicity had never given too much thought to marital relations before she had fallen for Percy. Very naturally, once she *had* fallen, it had occupied her mind day and night. She'd even had some whispered conversations with Grace and a heart to heart with Mrs. Right. Grace had nothing much to offer, other than pressing Felicity to come back and tell her all she'd found out. Mrs. Right stuck to her original and only advice—things would naturally take their course.

As Mrs. Right was a long-time widow and the most experienced person she could speak to regarding such personal matters, Felicity took that advice.

It turned out that counsel was very apt. If one were to think of the whole thing at once, it was almost off-putting. But minute by minute, it was rather lovely.

This was also the moment when Felicity first saw Percy's scars. She had of course been there when the attack occurred, she had seen the blood, it had soaked her dress. For all that, she had not imagined the severity of the scars left behind. Those scars would be there for the rest of their lives to remind her of what had happened. Each time she looked at them, she fell in love with Percy all over again. In truth, when Percy occasionally strayed into her bad books, he made a point of walking round without his shirt on, turning his back to her at every opportunity.

In these early days, Felicity discovered that marital relations became even more lovely as one became accustomed to it. By the time the couple came near their destination a fortnight later, Percy Stratton was rather exhausted.

They reached the coast and arranged transport to Barra by way of a fishing vessel. It was not glamourous by any means, and perhaps made less glamorous by Felicity's heaving over the side for most of it, but they managed to dock without a worse disaster than seasickness.

That was when they discovered that Castle Kisimul was not actually located on the island of Barra. One must cross another body of water, albeit so narrow one could likely swim it if currents did not sweep one away.

This discovery led to a series of negotiations with the local fleet of fishermen. These negotiations were not friendly, as the local people did not seem very charmed to have newlyweds from London in their midst. One finally whispered to Percy that he would take them over under cover of darkness, albeit for an exorbitant price.

As Percy had begun to believe that their choices were narrowing down to a frantic swim while being dragged down to the bottom of the sea by their sinking luggage, he agreed. For the next hours until the sun set, they sat on the pier with their luggage, attempting to ignore the glares from passersby. It had been a long day, they were tired, hungry, and thirsty, Felicity was weakened from being sick, and the day was growing longer still.

These difficulties inevitably led to Percy's first glimpse of his beloved wife's renowned temper. First, she listed all the terrible things to be done to Mr. Wiles when they returned to Town. Some of them found Percy rather shaken, as he really did not see the need to burn Wiles' house to the ground, especially since it was rented.

As the hours wore on, Felicity turned her ire toward the local people who glared at them as they passed by. If a local Hebridean had come under the notion that she was to put up with such nonsense when she was thirsty and tired and had been sick over the side of a boat, they were quickly informed of their mistake.

One after another of the glares was met with his delicate wife's shouting that if they wished to say something, they ought to have the courage to step up to her and say it and they should be very glad she did not have her fowling piece on hand.

The shoreline slowly emptied, though Percy could see the white curtains of nearby houses being pulled back on occasion. He presumed they'd all been warned off regarding the mad Englishwoman on the pier who may or may not have brought along a gun.

Finally, the sun sank below the horizon. The fisherman who had agreed to take them over crept on his boat and cautioned them to be quiet.

This was, apparently, the last straw. Felicity picked up the nearest piece of luggage and threw it at him. They were ferried over to the castle in the bay in all haste.

Percy had rather serious doubts that the fellow would ever come back for them.

After the housekeeper, an old and wizened woman, took one look at Felicity, she said, "Ya poor thing, this ain't no place for the likes of you. I'll fetch you a whisky, that'll help you forget whatever day you've gone and had for yourself."

The old woman hurried off. Felicity burst into tears. "Now you've seen it," she said. "My terrible temper. You've married an awful shrew."

Percy took her in his arms and kissed her head. "You were hard-pressed."

"Yes, I really was!"

"You were sick, then we had nothing to eat or drink and we were left in the sun all day and those people were giving us terrible looks."

"Yes, all of that happened!"

"I suppose anybody would have reacted just the same."

"Really?" Felicity asked.

"Well, perhaps not exactly the same," Percy said with a snort of laughter. "But you *were* hard-pressed."

The housekeeper, Mrs. MacLeod, returned with the whisky. Felicity recovered quite a bit of her spirits after downing that strong drink. The good lady set her up with a hot bath and then made them a simple but very good dinner accompanied by more whiskey.

Mrs. MacLeod explained that there was one other servant in the place, a young man named Angus MacCray who acted as man of all work.

Mrs. MacLeod wondered how they planned to occupy themselves on this little patch of rock as there was not much to do other than look out the windows. Even the little fishing boat the family used for outings on shore was gone for repairs.

Naturally, they had not considered that. They had both imagined a lovely castle on a remote beach where they might take long walks. They might even stop in at a friendly publican's house of an evening. If there were a publican nearby, they did not suppose he would be friendly, nor could they walk there.

"Now," she said, "what arrangements did you make with Finley MacDonald to come and collect you?"

"Finley MacDonald?" Felicity asked.

"The fellow who ran you over here."

Felicity and Percy looked at one another. Felicity said, "I expect Mr. MacDonald will not have an interest in returning."

"Finlay? Not get paid for a return trip?" Mrs. MacLeod said, her brow wrinkling. "That man would sell his wife for a shilling."

"My wife was hard-pressed," Percy said by way of vague explanation.

"I threw my luggage at him," Felicity admitted.

"Oh aye," Mrs. MacLeod said. "He won't be back."

Percy and Felicity retired that evening, their heads rather too full of whisky and dire ideas of never getting off the pile of rocks that had now become their home. They both stared into the darkness for some time before sleep overtook them.

The morning brought a better outlook. They had both been far too tired the evening before to be any good at rational thought.

The day was bright, Mrs. MacLeod made a fine hearty breakfast, and they discovered a sun drenched balcony to sip their second pot of tea. The second pot restored them quite a bit and Percy speculated that lack of tea the day before had been responsible for... what happened.

They further investigated the castle and found a well-stocked library. One might not have imagined that reading would end up being a primary activity on one's wedding trip, but they took to it. Lazy mornings on the balcony unless it rained, walks round the ramparts of an afternoon, simple but hearty dinners smoothed out with whisky, and cozying up in the library's overstuffed settee of an evening before retiring early. On the nights they did not choose to read, they played cards and butchered the rules of piquet with abandon.

Perhaps the nights, with the heavy blackness enveloping them and only the sounds of the waves lapping outside the windows were their favorite. Neither had ever experienced the sort of silence that was to be had at Kisimul Castle. At home, one of Felicity's sisters was always talking and Percy's father was always shouting.

It was as if they were the only two people left in the world. They did not mind being the only two people left in the world, as they were well able to occupy themselves through those dark hours.

Eventually, these halcyon days began to wane. It began with noticing the breakfasts had started to get a little sparse. Then the dinners were served on smaller plates. The dinner the evening before had been entirely devoid of meat and the housekeeper had called it a traditional Scottish Pinch in honor of Saint Monroe Day.

Then Mrs. MacLeod gave them the bad news.

There was no such thing as a Scottish Pinch, or Saint Monroe, or a Saint Monroe Day. They were running out of food. A grocer was meant to come every fortnight by boat, but he'd been due eight days before and had not turned up. As the grocer was long known to her and as reliable as the rain, Mrs. MacLeod guessed that they were being ostracized. She speculated that the local people had found too much time to discuss Lady Felicity's issuing challenges to various people to approach her and speak, and possibly having a gun, and her throwing her luggage, and then the fact that they were English and not particularly wanted in the first place.

As the food stores dwindled, they took to rationing their supplies and attempting to send smoke signals from the ramparts. Day after day, they watched fishermen with weathered faces hoist their sails and tack by the castle, refusing to even look in their direction.

They were down to their last few pieces of stale bread when a distant relation of the O'Neils turned up. Somebody had sent him word that an English couple was being held captive in his cousin's castle and he'd arrived prepared to do battle with criminals. He was rather surprised to find that the enemy to be thwarted was only a handful of offended fishermen.

Nevertheless, he got them off safely and saw them all the way to Glasgow. The adventure was to stay with Felicity always. Whenever she felt her temper beginning to bubble, she reminded herself that it had once led to her being starved in the Outer Hebrides. It also reminded her to send a Christmas gift to Mrs. MacLeod each year, for as long as that lady lived.

The couple sped their way out of Scotland as quickly as possible. Percy's viscount had remained in London, and so they made their way to the estate. Along the way, Felicity wrote long letters to her sisters, her father, and Mrs. Right, detailing their experiences. She was well aware that the duke would laugh all his life long over their wedding trip to the Hebrides.

Felicity and Percy made a short stop at the viscount's main house, which was really very fine. They did not even stay the night, though, as they had only come to collect Blueberry and take him to the lodge.

That cat would not prove to be much of a mouser, though the lodge urgently needed a mouser. It was a commodious sort of place reached by a narrow track of road and set in a pine forest. Blueberry was more of a lounging sort of cat. An impudent mouse, of which it seemed they were well supplied, might march up and tap him on the nose and not get much of a reaction.

Still, Felicity, Percy, and Blueberry settled in with a small staff. The viscount and his viscountess eventually returned to their house and the couple fell into the habit of dining with them once a week. As was inevitable, the viscount one night lost his temper over something or other.

His shout of "I warn you!" was met by Felicity shouting back, "I warn you more!"

The viscountess became hysterical with laughter and she and Felicity became firm friends after that. As for the viscount, he had never in his life been warned back and he gained a wary respect for his daughter-in-law. He became leery of crossing her and satisfied himself with crossing the duke, though he was nowhere in the vicinity. If one listened closely to his mutterings, one would likely hear: "For all I know, he's dead on the moors by now. It's pleasant to think about."

When children made their appearance, those children found themselves the owners of two entirely strange grandfathers. One they saw a few times a year and he was always threatening to throw them out the doors, and they would not even be allowed back for Christmas. This was at least more specific than the shouted warnings from their more local grandfather, as it was never explained what they were warned of. In both cases, the children were highly amused and bet with one another over who could set off one of the old gentlemen first.

Daisy was usually the most successful, as she had inherited Felicity's quick, off the mark temper. Felicity spent long hours in consultation with her daughter regarding it, and the mishap in the Hebrides was often discussed.

As for Felicity's own temper, that was mellowed over time by two things. One, her children. And two, her husband.

Her children were dear little persons, but even dear little persons were known to accidentally set a fire, or drag in somebody else's dog, or break only the most expensive items in the house. She could not bear to be cross with them.

And then her husband's more easygoing temperament began to influence her. She could not help but notice that a temper rarely affected the outcome of anything, other than to make everybody in the vicinity uncomfortable.

Of course, most of those things were still to come. For now, the newlyweds feathered their private little nest and made plans for the next season. They were determined to be on hand for Grace's debut season. Felicity was looking forward to helping her sister and Percy was interested in viewing what went on.

He was not at all certain what would go on, but as it was the Nicolet family he was sure *something* would go on.

Mr. Stratton was very perceptive.

The End

About the Author

By the time I was eleven, my Irish Nana and I had formed a book club of sorts. On a timetable only known to herself, Nana would grab her blackthorn walking stick and steam down to the local Woolworth's. There, she would buy the latest Barbara Cartland romance, hurry home to read it accompanied by viciously strong wine, (Wild Irish Rose, if you're wondering) and then pass the book on to me. Though I was not particularly interested in real boys yet, I was *very* interested in the gentlemen in those stories— daring, bold, and often enraging and unaccountable. After my Barbara Cartland phase, I went on to Georgette Heyer, Jane Austen and so many other gifted authors blessed with the ability to bring the Georgian and Regency eras to life.

I would like nothing more than to time travel back to the Regency (and time travel back to my twenties as long as we're going somewhere) to take my chances at a ball. Who would take the first? Who would escort me into supper? What sort of meaningful looks would be exchanged? I would hope, having made the trip, to encounter a gentleman who would give me a very hard time. He ought to be vexatious in the extreme, and *worth* every vexation, to make the journey worthwhile.

I most likely won't be able to work out the time travel gambit, so I will content myself with writing stories of adventure and romance in my beloved time period. There are lives to be created, marvelous gowns to wear, jewels to don, instant attractions that inevitably come with a difficulty, and hearts to break before putting them back together again. In traditional Regency fashion, my stories are clean—the action happens in a drawing room, rather than a bedroom.

As I muse over what will happen next to my H and h, and

wish I were there with them, I will occasionally remind myself that it's also nice to have a microwave, Netflix, cheese popcorn, and steaming hot showers.

Come see me on Facebook! @KateArcherAuthor